James W. Taylor

Historical Antiquities of Fife

chiefly ecclesiastical, connected with some of its districts - Vol. 1

James W. Taylor

Historical Antiquities of Fife
chiefly ecclesiastical, connected with some of its districts - Vol. 1

ISBN/EAN: 9783337423803

Printed in Europe, USA, Canada, Australia, Japan

Cover: Foto ©Andreas Hilbeck / pixelio.de

More available books at **www.hansebooks.com**

HISTORICAL ANTIQUITIES

OF FIFE.

I.

THE NORTHERN, THE EASTERN,

AND THE

CENTRAL PORTIONS.

the side of perpetuating these feelings. People
seldom flitted. They very rarely travelled from
home. Now, removals are very frequent; there
is much more travelling, and very many leave
their country to settle in foreign lands. It was
to preserve local facts and traditions that this
work was first undertaken, and published in
parts. Now, the parts are collected into a volume, that in these days of railway trains and
emigration ships, the " folk lore " and local feelings of the past may not be altogether lost.

The reader may be curious to see what we
subjoin, a description of the district which this
volume traverses, taken from " Hardyng's Chronicle of the Tounes and Myles of Scotland."
This Chronicle is said to have been written by
Hardyng, an Englishman, in the reign of Edward
III., somewhere about A.D. 1360, to facilitate the
march of the English armies through Scotland. It is
entitled " How the maker of this booke reporteth
the distance and myles of the tounes in Scotland,

and the way how to conveigh an armie as well
by lande as water into the chifest parts thereof."

*   *   *   *   *   *   *   *

Then from the Doune, a waie ye have right faire
Throughout Monteith and eke Clakmannanshire,
And so through Fiffe to Falk land to repair,
Therty long miles without mosse or myre,
For so it is compted, with horse and carte to hyre,
From Sterling eastward, to the high Oyghills,
Which some menne call montaigns and some fells.

From Falk land then to Disert toune, south east,
Twelf myles it is, of fair ready waye,
And from Falk land to Saynte Andrews east
But other xii myles, withouten onye waye,
Wher the byshoppe's See is, and Castell as thei say,
And at Kyngorne and Disert may ye meete
You for to vytayle all your English fleete.

Then ryde northwest from S. Andrews toune
Alongest the south syde of the water of Taye,
Up to the burgh of Saint Jhons Towne
Ryte north from Fiffe, a countrie fresh and gay,
And from Saynt Andrews xxiiii myles thei say,
A pleasant grounde and fruitful countrey
Of corn and cattell with prosperitie.

Which countrey of Fiffe along the Scottish sea,
And from S. Andrews to Oyghylls thei say

Is xliii myles long of good countrey,
And sometyme in bredth vi myles of fayr way,
But from Logh Leven eastward without way
Of right good way, briefly to conclude,
xii miles conteyne it doth in latitude.

At Ennerkeithen and Saynt Margarites Hope
Your navy may receav vytale in that countrie
Alongest the water of Forth as I can grope
With hulke and barge, of no smal quantite
You to supporte in your necessytie,
So that you maye not in those countrys fayle
To have for your army redye vytale."

CONTENTS.

PART II.

Cupar and its Neighbourhood.

<div style="text-align:center">~~~~~~~~~~</div>

PART III.

Falkland, Kettle, and Leslie.

CONTENTS. xiii

PART IV.

St Andrews.

Historical Antiquities

CONNECTED WITH THE

North of Fife.

PART I.

By no object is the imagination more sensibly affected than by the sight of an old castle or tower. The mind is immediately roused into activity, as the scenes which these decaying ruins may have witnessed rise before it. Though nothing certain may be known, yet fancy stops not in her busy work. Brave knights, noble lords, and ladies fair, may have walked through these deserted courts. These silent and mouldering halls may have seen much of human sorrow and of human joy. Domestic peace and horrid war, revelry and lamentation, may have reigned here in turn. Yet does the mind feel relief, and curiosity is made glad, when we can fix upon some

A

particular incident connected with the place we see, which history or tradition has made sure.

The object of the present Essay is to clothe with the interest of truth the old and decaying ruins with which our neighbourhood abounds, and to make them suggest to the peasant as he goes to his work—to their favoured proprietor as he surveys them—and to the curious stranger as he passes by—or to the

> " Citizens, who take the air
> Close packed and smiling in a chaise and one"—

the scene which history sanctions.

There is a preference given to ecclesiastical antiquities.   And if we are asked the reason of this, we would answer in the words of the following beautiful and truthful quotation :—" The Church is the dwelling-place of history ; the churchyard is her symbolical flower-garden." Of Scotland can this be said more truly than of any land.   It is her Church that has made Scotland great.   It is her Church that has made Scotland interesting.   Foreigners contemplating the contendings unto imprisonment, exile, and death, endured alike by her peers and her peasants, on behalf of the principles of her Church,. have regarded Scotland with veneration.

The notices introduced in this little sketch connect themselves with the three most important and prominent periods in our history. The *first* of these is the glorious Reformation from Popery, when Protestantism was established in 1560. The *second* was the important era of 1638, commonly known as the Second Reformation, when Presbyterianism was vindicated and fully developed. The *third* has reference to the twenty-eight years of suffering, commonly known as the Killing Times, which preceded the memorable Revolution of 1688. Speaking of this period, an eminent statesman (Mr Fox) says, " That Scotland was in a state of more absolute slavery than, at that time, existed in any part of Christendom."

Were an ecclesiastical statistical account of Scotland prepared, there would not be a spot of our land but would have its strange story to tell of one or other of these eventful times. And it would be curious to observe, how that, in different parts of the country there have been different struggles, and different principles that have taken root, and prolonged their stay.

A summer's day might enable one to see all the places which are here noticed. The leisurely survey of two days would be better. And let him who goes carry with him the words of Johnson, which in spirit are most appropriate—"Far from me, and from my friends, be such frigid philosophy as may conduct us indifferent and unmoved over any ground which has been dignified by wisdom, bravery, or virtue."

Abdie.

The Parish of Abdie supplies many spots of interest to the student of the past.

LINDORES LOCH AND CASTLE.

This beautiful Loch is the eye of the landscape. It imparts animation to the scenery, and is itself ever varying in its expression. On a quiet summer day it reposes placidly in the sunshine, the water-hen gently rustling the reeds on the margin, and the strong-billed duck circling the waters in the centre, as with a sharp plunge it dives for its prey. At other times, when the sea-fowl frequent its shores and the north-west winds blow, its waters are stirred, and the mimic waves form into foam, and imitate a storm. It was from its stormy appearance that it received its name. The Picts were the inhabitants of Fife when places got their present names. These Picts spoke Gaelic, and they called this loch Lindores—the Rough Loch. Linne in Gaelic signifying a lake ; and dorr, rough.

Six hundred years ago there stood on the northern bank of this Loch a strong castle, which was called the Castle of Lindores. Until lately some ruins on the high ground, immediately to the south and east of the village of Lindores, where the policy wall of Inchrye now stretches, indicated the site of that Castle. It figured in the wars of Scottish Independence. These wars extended for the space of thirty years, betwixt 1286 and 1315, when the battle of Bannockburn was won. Edward I. was determined to annex Scotland to England; and had not Wallace fought and Bruce conquered, Scotland, from being an independent kingdom, would have been converted into an English province. In 1300 Edward sent a great army into Fife. The Castle of Lindores was occupied by them as an important military position, for it stood at the entrance of one of the principal passes through Fife. In June of 1300 there was a battle fought betwixt the English, who held the Castle of Lindores, and Sir William Wallace. The English were overcome, and Sir John Pseworth, their General, was killed. " This battele," says Sir James Balfour in his Annals, " is called Dillecarrens Field, quherin 3000 English wer killed, and 500 takin prisoners : the Scots lost not above 300, in respect the woods and passages of the montans and quagmyres were weill knowen to them, only Sir John Synton, Sir Thomas Lochore, and Sir Johne Balfour, Shriffe of Fyffe, wer woundit and hurt."

If the reader would wish to visit the scene of this battle, he will find a rough hill road turning off at Inchrye Lodge, which will conduct him to the spot.   As he toils up the rough ascent let him relieve his panting breath, and while he stands and looks back he will see through the opening of Clatchard Pass, the rocky grandeurs of Kinnoull Hill, displaying on its side the castled Tower of Kinfauns, lighted up with a gleam of the Tay, and shut in by the distant background of the Logiealmond Hills. When he reaches the top, he will see betwixt the hills a rocky cairn, dark with the bonnet fir tree. It is this cairn which gives name to the place. Dal-a-cairn means the

Field of the Cairn, from dail or dal, a field ; and carn, a heap of stones—a cairn.

The whitened villa of Lindores was the property and residence of Sir Frederick Maitland, who, in 1815, intercepted with his ship the Bellerophon, Napoleon Bonaparte. Sir Frederick published, at the time, a modest, well-written, and most interesting account of the capture.

THE OLD CHURCH OF ABDIE

fringes the Loch. Its unroofed walls, belfried gable, and reclining tombstones, throw back the mind on bye-gone times. And yet we can find little to relate in connection with it. Of the eight ministers of Abdie from the Reformation to the Revolution, there is only one of whom anything is known—this is Mr Andrew Murray. His ministry extended from 1622 to 1638. It is rather as a courtier than as a clergyman that he is distinguished. Mr Andrew lived at the time of the crisis of the great national struggle, which involved the double question, shall the King of Scotland be an absolute or a constitutional King, and shall the Scottish Church be Presbyterian or Episcopalian ? In this great contest, the Kirk contended for those great principles of civil and religious liberty which were afterwards ratified in the glorious Revolution of 1688, and which form at this day the foundation of the British Constitution. Mr Murray sided with Charles I. against the Church and country, when Charles attempted despotically to subvert the liberties of both. For this, he was first knighted by the King, and afterwards created Lord Balvaird. By inheritance, Mr Murray acquired the barouies of Arngask and Balvaird, and subsequently succeeded to the title and estate of Stormont. He is thus the ancestor of the Mansfield family. Lord Mansfield is the present patron of the Church of Abdie, in which his ancestor served as minister.

There is an old low stone in the churchyard which records a loyalty of a different type from Mr Murray's. The stone is placed to the east of the Church. It has an open Bible sculptured on one side, and on the other there is the following inscription:—" Here lies the body of Mr John Adamson, Minister of the Gospel, who died May 3, 1723 ; that faithful contender for the Church's intrinsic power, and witness against the encroachments made upon his Lord and Master, Jesus Christ's royal prerogatives."

INCHRYE.

Let us now retrace our steps to Inchrye. Within the policy there are two water-worn hollows, known as the Big Ship and the Little, which, in days of persecution, were hiding-places where the Presbyterians assembled for worship. Pleasant places they are to visit on a summer day. And yet, even amid the smiles of summer, when the sunshine lies cheerily on hill and hollow, on dreamy wood and gleaming lake, there is an undertone of feeling, grave and solemn, which affects the thoughtful mind, as it reflects that here the men and women of Scotland met to worship God, and to maintain a believing testimony for Him at the risk of liberty and life.

Inchrye means the Island of the King, or the Large Island. The observant eye can readily trace the evidence of a morass and bog all round Inchrye.

KINNAIRD AND DENMILNE.

The property which adjoins Inchrye, a little to the north, is Kinnaird. It is celebrated as the property of Sir James Balfour of Denmilne and Kinnaird, Knight and Baronet, Lord Lyon King at Arms to Charles I. and Charles II. Here Sir James chiefly resided, although there is now no trace remaining of his mansion-house. An imposing pigeon-house, a park-line of elderly trees on either side of the public road, and two handsome chesnut trees, indicate the whereabouts of the house in the time of Sir James. No modern poet has thrown a lasting interest over the Knight of Kinnaird, as Sir Walter Scott, in Marmion, has done to his predecessor in office, Sir David Lindsay of the Mount. But although,

> " All unnamed in
> Hero-scroll or verse,"

Sir James Balfour is worthy of being remembered as one who devoted himself to the study of his country's history. Many manuscripts he collected; many works he wrote in illustration of Scottish history. We have seen a list of twelve separate works of which he was the author. As Sir David Lindsay took part with the Reformers, Sir James shows, in different parts of his Annals, that although by office connected with the Court, all his sympathies were with the Presbyterians.

Sir James died in 1657, and lies buried in the ivy-covered aisle of the old Church of Abdie.

A strange mystery overhangs the last Knight-

Baronet of Denmilne. Upwards of 100 years ago he rode off from Denmilne attended by his groom. No after trace of him was ever found.

We have been told that every year a letter comes from France, addressed to the Balfours of Denmilne. This, the tenant who receives it, transmits to the proprietor.

What connection these two things have with each other, or whether any at all, we have no means of knowing.

We now reach the ruined

ABBEY OF LINDORES.

It is from this Abbey that the Parish derives its name of Abdie. Some think that *Abdie* is just an abbreviation of the words *Abbey on the Tay*. But it is more likely that, like most other old names in the locality, it is of Celtic origin. Abaid in Gaelic means an Abbey. By a transposition, not uncommon both in names of persons and places, Abaid has been popularly changed into Abdie. Sir James Balfour, in his Annals under the year 1178, thus writes :—" This same yeire King William foundit the Monastery of Aberbroth in Angus ; and his brother, Earle David, after his returne from the Holy Land, foundit the Monastery of Lindores, in the woodes in Fyffe." Episodes of interest have taken place within the walls of this Abbey, and connect themselves with great names and important eras. Here is one which occurred in 1306, the year in which Robert the Bruce was crowned at Scone:— " This zeire ther was a mutuall endenture made betwix Sir Gilbert Hay of Erole, Sir Neill Campbell of Lochaw, and Sir Alexander Setton, Knights, at the Abbey of Lindors, to defend King Robert and his Crown to the last of their bloodes and fortunes; upon the sealing of the said endenture, they solemnly toke the Sacrament at St Marie's Altar in the said Abbey Church."

About the year 1488 there might be seen, on sunny days, an old man sauntering within the enclosures of the Abbey. He is tall of stature; he is a shorn monk; but his tall form, and the tones of his voice, and the glance of his eye, tell of one accustomed to command, though he is now broken with age and weary of the world. This is the Earl of Douglas, warded for life by James III. as a shorn monk within this Abbey. Here he died and was buried.

A low and irregular square of ruins, which the ivy is fast covering to hide the ravages of time and of men's hands, and high garden walls which stand entire, readily mark out the site of this once renowned Abbey. The situation is right sweet, says Sibbald; and so famed was it in times of Popery, as a place of sanctity, that Christopher Irvin, who wrote a small Topographical Dictionary two hundred years ago, says of it—" it is thought nothing venomous liveth there." The vastly big old pear * trees, which Sibbald notes, still stand around it, as an evidence of the richness of its soil.

This Abbey, when in the zenith of its prosperity, could name two men of note, as holding close connection with it.

The first was Lawrence of Lindores. In the early part of the 15th century (1406), he held the appointment of Inquisitor General of Heresy. He is spoken of as † a priest most sound, and a celebrated theologian. By his sentence was James Resby burnt at Perth in 1407—the first who suffered for the Protestant faith. His

* The pear-tree seems to have been a favourite in the grounds of monasteries and nunneries. Near to Elcho Nunnery there is an old pear-tree. Its name is " Carl Hemp." Its circumference is 16 feet around the trunk. It is 400 years old, and still brings forth fruit. Probably it is the largest pear-tree in Scotland.

† Clericus solidissimus et theologus famosus.

name is also mentioned as Inquisitor in 1433, when Paul Craw was burnt at St Andrews. This Lawrence of Lindores had the spirit of his office always alive within him. Old historians say that he gave no rest to the heretics, or Lollards (another name for Protestants), within the kingdom, and he is accounted author of a book entitled "The Swarm of Heretical Lollards which he Drove out of the Whole Kingdom." Lawrence held the situation of rector of Criech.

The name which sheds most lustre on this Abbey, however, is that of John Leslie, Bishop of Ross. He held the Abbacy of Lindores *in commendam*. The history of the Bishop of Ross is closely interwoven with that of his royal mistress, Mary Queen of Scots. He was commissioned to France to invite Queen Mary over to her Scottish dominions. He accompanied her. Amid her varying fortunes he was her counsellor, and, as herself testified, the most pious and devoted of her servants. For her sake he suffered imprisonment and banishment, dying at Rome in the 69th year of his age, somewhere about 1580.

A portrait of the Bishop hangs in the hall of King's College, Aberdeen. The sharp features and the compressed lip give indication of the shrewdness and firmness by which through life he was distinguished.

~~~~~~~~~

Newburgh.

Newburgh was disjoined from Abdie, and erected ecclesiastically into a parish in 1622. This ecclesiastical disjunction was ratified by a deed of Parliamentary Commissioners at Holyrood House, 3d February 1632, "whereby the said Kirk of Newburgh is separat from the Kirk of Ebdie, and declares the same to be an separat Kirk be itself in all time coming."

PITCAIRLIE

is in the parish. *Pit* is a Celtic prefix, and indicates a hollow or low-lying place. This description does not seem applicable to the position of the present house when looked at from the present public road—for the house is built on an eminence which overtops the road. But when seen from the old road above Lumquhat, or from the old Newburgh road, the situation of Pitcairlie appears low. Sibbald
~~~~~~~~~

says "the old tower of Pitcairlie was in a glen." It was the residence of Patrick Leslie, a younger son of the Earl of Rothes. This Patrick was created the first Lord Lindores in 1600. Patrick Lesley was the father, and Pitcairley was the birthplace, of Major-General David Leslie, an eminent general and commander of the forces in Scotland in the days of the Covenant. Like his more distinguished relative, Alexander Leslie Lord Leven, he served in the army of Gustavus Adolphus, and gained his soldiership there. In the battle of Marston Moor, 1644, he fought along with Cromwell against Charles I., and by a dashing charge of cavalry which he commanded, he was prominent in deciding the fate of the battle. In 1645 he discomfited Montrose at Philiphaugh. In 1650 he was appointed Commander-in-Chief, when the Earl of Leven, in consequence of advancing years, resigned. He displayed great generalship in throwing his army betwixt Cromwell and Edinburgh, and afterwards in occupying the heights above Dunbar. But the cool generalship of Leslie was overborne by the imprudence and impetuosity of others.

His army left the hill, "which," says the old Chronicler, "was their strength and forte," and was disastrously routed by Cromwell. David Leslie adhered to the falling fortunes of Charles II. He shared with him the battle and defeat of Worcester in 1651. He was detained as prisoner by Cromwell for a year or two in England. At the Restoration of Charles II. he was created Lord Newark. The ruined tower of Newark Castle, standing on the sea rocks close by St Monance, is the only remaining memento of David Leslie's toils, title, and estates.

MACDUFF'S CROSS.

On the old road betwixt Newburgh and Auchtermuchty, and less than a mile from Newburgh, stands the remains of the famous Cross of Macduff. A small mound of earth, encircled with large whinstone boulders, contains in its centre the pedestal of the cross, and will at once arrest the eye of every passer-by. The old road out of Fife to Perth passes close by it on the south, stretching onwards to the west. The cross thus stood near the western extremity of the county of Fife, on a prominent hill overlooking the Strath of Earn, and thus making visible proclamation of its sanctuary privileges.

The block, which is firmly embedded where it

was placed eight hundred years ago, is of free-stone. Observant eyes have noticed that it is placed so as to indicate the four cardinal points.

De Foe, in his Tour through Great Britain, makes mention of this cross, and says that "the inscription is now worn out, and was in such antiquated terms, mixed with Macaronic or half Latin words, that few men now living would have been able to make it out."

I have before me "An Essay upon the Inscription of Macduff's Cross in Fyfe, by J. C., 1678," in which the author supplies the subjoined, as what was generally given in his day, as "the inscription upon Macduff's Cross, which stands above the Newburgh, near Lindores, upon the confines of Stratherne and Fyfe."

Maldraradrum dragos malairia largia largos
Spalando spados sive nig fig knippite gnaros
Lorea lauriseos lauringen louria luscos
Et coluburtos sic fit tibi bursea burtus
Eritus et blaradrum sive lim, sive lam, sive labrum
Propter Macgidrim et hoc oblatum
Accipe smeleridem super limpide lampida labrum.

The Essayist says—"I had this of an ingenious gentleman, telling me he came by it from the Clerk of Crail, who informed that several succeeding clerks there have for a considerable time engrost this as a true copy in their books, to preserve it from perishing ; for it is now quite worn off the stone—at least, altogether illegible." After giving his own emendations, and conclnding, after a learned analysis, that the language is Saxon, with a few Danish and French words, all thrown into a Latinised form, he thus paraphrases it :—

" Ye Earl of Fyfe, receive for your services as my Lieutenant by right of this Regality, large measures of victual or corn, for the transgression of the laws, as well from those as want or put away their weapons of warfare, as of such as stays away from, or refuses to come to the Host, or those that raises frayes or disturbances therein, or from such as keep, haunt, and frequent unlawful convocations, together with all amercements due to me, for the slaughter of a free liege, or for robbery and theft, or for adultery and fornication within your bounds, with the unlaws of fugitives, and the penalties due by such cowards as deserts the Host, or runs away from their colours, thus shall your gains be the greater. And yet further to witness my kindness I remit to those of your own kindred, all issues of wounds, be it limb, lith, or life, in swa far as for this offering (to wit of nine kyne and a queyoch) they shall be indemnified for limb, lith, or life."

Like many things else, the Essay turns out to be too learned and ingenious to be true. The honest author seems to have suspected this himself, for while it is being " printed by the Heir of Andrew Anderson, Printer to the King's most excellent Majesty," he appends the following note:—"Just now, as it was adoing under the irons (*i.e.*, in the press,), am I told there is an exact coppie, with a true exposition of this inscription at the Newburgh in the hands or books of the Clerk there; and pitie it were, that so old and famous a monument in this our kingdom should be so closlie dormant in a poor country village, without being communicate (for aught I know) to any: But this, however, I hope may invite those of the Newburgh to divulge it, if any such thing they have."

"Those of the Newburgh" had indeed their own version of the inscription, and the true one. Here it is:—

Ara, urget lex quos, lare egentes, atria, lis quos :
Hoc qui laboras, haec fit tibi pactio portus
Mille reum drachmas mulctam de largior agris
Spes tantum pacis, cum nex fit a nepote natis.
Propter Macgidrum, et hoc oblatum accipe semel.
Haeredum super lymphato lapide labem.

The Rev. Walter Wood, of Elie, in whose History of the East Neuk we have found this "exact coppie," convincingly shows, by transposing one or two of the lines, and by placing the one version alongside of the other, that the first is just a corrupted form of the second, and conjectures that the first had been orally communicated by some one who had tried to commit it to memory without understanding Latin. We subjoin Mr Wood's translation :—

"An altar for those whom law pursues, a hall for those whom strife pursues, being without a home. Who makest thy way hither, to thee this paction becomes a harbour. But there is hope of peace only when the murder has been committed by those born of my grandson. I set free the accused, a fine of a thousand drachms from his lands. On account of Macgridin (Mugdrum) and of this offering, take once for all the cleansing of my heirs beneath this stone filled with water."

Spens of Wormiston, who killed a person of the name of Kinninmonth, claimed and enjoyed, as being within the degree of kindred to Macduff, the privilege of sanctuary which the inscription promised.

History tells us how it was that Macduff, "Fife's lion-hearted Thane," had honour and privileges heaped upon himself and his favoured county. It was he who had gone to England and had encouraged Malcolm Canmore to attempt the recovery of his throne and kingdom from the usurper Macbeth. The attempt was made and was successful. Macduff became Malcolm's favourite noble. His thaneship was changed into an earldom—

> " the first that ever Scotland
> In such an honour named."

Great immunities and advantages were conferred on Fife, as Macduff's sheriffdom. As a regality, or territorial possession bestowed by the King, Fife is one of the oldest, and most distinguished by its privileges ; hence, as if it were a distinct principality, it early received and still retains the well-known appellation of THE KINGDOM OF FIFE.

Malcolm Canmore's reign extended from A.D. 1056 to 1093. It marks a crisis in the history of Scotland's religion. The simple worship and doctrine of the Culdees had prevailed for several centuries in Scotland. But Rome had been making her encroachments, and was gradually supplanting the Culdee faith. Malcolm Canmore greatly helped forward this, for his fifteen years' residence in England had familiarised him with the Romish worship, and his Queen, the English Princess Margaret, was a devoted Papist. The crucifix was her favourite symbol. On this account it was that the cross was the form in

which Macduff's sanctuary privileges were published. If it was erected in a time when Popery
was progressing, it was destroyed at a time when
Popery got a death-blow in Scotland, for the
upper part, which contained the inscription, was
cast down and broken in 1559, the era of the
Reformation, when the badges of Popery were
demolished in the land.

We venture no remarks on the hieroglyphic
Cross of Mugdrum.

> " The events it does commemorate
> Are dark, remote, and undistinguishable,
> As are the mystic characters it bears."

BLACK EARN SIDE.

Eastward from Lindores Abbey for several
miles there stretched a wood, which is known in
the histories of Sir William Wallace as Black
Earn Side, or, as it is often falsely spelt, Black
Iron Side. It seem to have been a dark wood
covering the hillsides, and extending to the
river-edge. The name which it bore of Earn
Side Wood favours the idea which geologists entertain, that the river Earn had wound its course
by the foot of the Fife hills, that the river Tay
had swept in by the foot of the Carse of Gowrie
hills, and that the junction of the rivers took

place near Longforgan. Be this as it may, this wood was resorted to by Sir William Wallace, and occasionally afforded him shelter. There is a bridge along which the road passes near the top of the ascent, about two miles east from the Abbey, which is still known as *Wallace's Brig.* The wood gave name to one of Wallace's battles.

> " This wood we'll hold as long as we can stand,
> To the last man we'll fight it, sword in hand
> The right is ours, let's to it manfully ;
> I'll free this land once more before I die."

" This same zeire (1298), also in the month of Junii, the Batell of Black Ironsyde, in Fyfeshire, was fought betwix Sir William Vallace, the Protector, and the Earle of Pembrocke, general of the Englishe armey, in which batell the English wer totally routted and overthrown. Sir Duucane Balfour, Sheriffe of Fyfe, was killed, and Sir John Grhame was hurt, only of the Scotts of quality."—*Balfour's Annals.*

Flisk.

BALLANBREICH CASTLE.

Eastwards from Lindores, and on the western extremity of Flisk parish, is situated the Castle of Ballanbreich. Ballanbreich is derived from two Celtic words—*baile* or *balla*, a town, and *breac* or *brech*, a tront. It signifies the trout-town, and indicates that that part of the river had been favonrable for fishing. This castle, and the barony which is attached to it, now the property of the Earl of Zetland, belonged for many generations to the ancient and noble family of Rothes. Andrew, the fifth Earl of Rothes, lies buried in the churchyard of Flisk. John, the sixth Earl of Rothes, is the one of all the line whose memory a statesman and a Presbyterian delights to honour. The debt of gratitude which is due to him is great, for, when the foundations of British liberty were laid in opposition to the despotism of Charles I., John, Earl of Rothes, was a willing worker in that sacred cause. He was not ashamed to avow himself friendly to Presbytery, when it had to encounter the wrath of the King and the plottings of the Conrt. With counsel, fortitude, and wit he was ever ready ; aud he has bequeathed at once great principles and his own honoured name in trust to posterity.

The Earl of Rothes fignred as an anthor as well as an actor. To his pen we are indebted for a minute account of the doings of these days under the title of "Rothes' Relation." He died in 1641. His son, who was created Duke of Rothes, acted a part clean contrary to his father. He was the willing agent of Charles II. and James II. in oppressing the Church, and overthrowing the principles which his father had so stoutly supported. Yet when death drew nigh, he sought the presence and the prayers of the very ministers he had persecuted, which led the Duke of Hamilton to remark, "When well we banish these men from us, and yet when dying we call for them; this is melancholy work." He died, and was buried; and in Leslie House the curious may see a representation of the splendid yet heartless state which attended his funeral.

The Duke of Rothes, to please King Charles, set up games and sports on the Sabbath afternoon, in conformity with "the Book of Sports." The writer has heard an old man tell, that the existence of these sports was preserved as a tradition in his father's family, and that his great grandfather had played at "cat and dog" on the lawn of Ballanbreich on Sabbath-day.

FLISK MILLAN.

Leaving Ballanbreich and proceeding east-wards, if the traveller delights in magnificent views, he may enjoy one of the finest which Scotland affords, by following the road which turns up by the farm of Flisk Miln—(*Millan*, the bleak height of Flisk.) The scene is girded by the swelling Grampians. Schehallion rises out from among them in pointed grandeur. Ben Lawers and Ben More stand like twin giants in the far west. Benledi sits on her mountain seat overlooking the Trossach beauties which lie scattered at her feet. The Strath of Earn, Merdovn Top, the broken front of Kinnoul Hill, all contribute their varied beauties; the broad acres of the Carse of Gowrie, and their smiling homesteads reflecting the sunbeams; Dundee looking forth from her smoke, and telling of the world's busy bustle; the Tay's broad wave studded with sails; and the plough toiling quietly up the hill on which you stand—fill up the wide and diversified picture.

Our thoughts are recalled from this general survey by the sight of the

MANSE AND CHURCH OF FLISK,

Which stand in near neighbourhood, on a little eminence flanked by a dell, and overlooking the river. This church can rank among its earlier ministers some names of note. John Waddell, minister of Flisk, was rector of the University of St Andrews in 1527, and, as such, was one of the judges who condemned Patrick Hamilton. Sir James Balfour, parson of Flisk, 1561, is characterised by Dr Robertson, " as the most corrupt man of his age." He belonged to the house of Mountquhanie, and was appointed Lord President of the Court of Session, under the title of Lord Pittendriech, having taken the title from a small property in the parish of Portmoak, at the foot of the Western Lomond, which belonged to the Balfours. The course of Sir James does not seem to have been regulated by anything like principle. He sided with the Papist or with the Protestant party, with the Court or with the Congregation, just as it suited his interests. He is accused of being one who compassed the death of Darnley. The house in which the unfortunate Darnley was murdered belonged to Balfour's brother, and among the names which an unknown hand fixed upon the door of St Giles, as having devised the murder, is the name of Mr James Balfour, parson of Flisk, in conjunction with the Earl of Bothwell and others. Knox expresses a most contemptible opinion of this man. He writes in his history, "among those who openly professed the same purity, was he that now rules or else misrules Scotland, viz., Sir James Balfour (sometimes called Master James), the chief and principal Protestant that then was to be found in this realm. This we write because we have heard that the said Master James alleges that he was never of this our religion, but that he was brought up in Martin Luther's opinion of the sacrament, and therefore he cannot communicate with us. But his own conscience and two hundred witnesses beside, know that he lies; and that he was one of the chief that would have given his life, if men might credit his words, for defence of the doctrine that the said John Knox taught. But albeit, that those that never were of us (as none of Mountquhanie's sons have shown themselves to be) depart from us it is no great wonder ; for it is proper and natural that the children follow the father ; and let the godly liver of that race and progeny be shown, for if in

them be either fear of God or love of virtue—
farther than the present commodity persuades
them—men of judgment are deceived."

The Church of Flisk contributed a Principal
to St Leonard's College, St Andrews, in 1592,
in the person of Mr John Wemyss, its minister.

None of the ministers of Flisk displayed any
steadfastness of principle during the times of
trial which passed over the Church. Mr William
Myles conformed to Episcopacy in 1662, and
again at the Revolution in 1688 was ready to
assume a Presbyterian profession.

A little advance on the road which has been
indicated brings us into the PARISH OF

Creich.

SEPULCHRAL MONUMENTS.

Two sepulchral monuments, of great antiquity,
have been brought to light in this parish.

In a field immediately to the back of the Free
Church Manse, when the ploughmen were engaged in ploughing in the spring of 1817, the
plough laid bare a double circle of stones. The
Rev. Alexander Lawson repaired to the spot,
carefully examined the stone circles, took a
drawing of them, and sent a most minute ac-

count of the whole to the *Edinburgh Magazine* of that year. In his communication to the magazine Mr Lawson conjectured that it might be a Druidical temple or oratory. His more recent opinion—which is far more probable, both from the size of the circles and from calcined human bones being found beneath—is that it was a grave. And if so, who can tell the date of that grave? Evidently it was before the time of churchyard burial grounds.

Antiquius quo quid est hoc venerabilius.

To secure the preservation of these stone circles, Mr Lawson got them removed, and placed them in a wood behind his manse in the very form in which they were found.

The other monument is a tombstone in the old church of Creich. It is a flat slab, with the figure of a knight in armour and of his lady engraved on it. The outer edge is sloped and contains an inscription chiselled in deep Saxon characters, which tells in Monkish Latin—

Here lies David Barclay of Luthrie, Baron or Lord of * * * who died on the day of the month —— A.D. 1400.

Here lies Helen de Douglas, the wife of the above-mentioned, who died on the 20th day of the month of January A.D. 1421.

The name of the Barony of David Barclay "has foiled philologists." I have asked the aid of several not unskilled in antiqnarian lore, but none has deciphered the name to his own satisfaction. So that, in the words of the old author, " I shall not stick to say they be no small clerks who should read me distinctly, with one breath, the inscription," and supply the desiderated words.

CASTLE OF CREICH.

One of the principal objects of interest in this neighbourhood is the rnined Castle of Creich. It is a square massy tower open to wind and weather. Part of one of the ronnd flanking towers still stand, and a row of old trees marks out the garden which was attached to it. Within this castle was born Dame Janet Beaton, Lady Bncclench, widow of Sir Walter Scott of Branksome, mentioned in the " Lay of the Last Minstrel"—

> " Of noble race the Ladye came,
>   Her father was a clerk of fame,
>   Of Bethune's line of Piccardi ;
>   He learn'd the art that none may name
>   In Padua, far beyond the sea.

About 1560, when this castle stood in its strength, its halls were gladdened by the residence of Mary Beaton, niece of Archbishop Beaton, and one of the four Maries whose beauty was only inferior to that of their royal mistress, Queen Mary, and who were her maids of honour.

> " Yestreen the Queen had four Maries,
>   The nicht she'll hae but three ;
>   There was Marie Seaton, and Marie Beaton,
>   And Marie Carmichael and me."

Mary Beaton was the daughter of Robert Beaton, Laird of Creich. Her mother was Madame Gresmere, who was a maid of honour to Mary of Guise, Queen of James V. In an entry in the Household Book of King James V., under date May 1538, there is mention made of a gown of red " Crammossy velvet" given to Madame Gresmere for her marriage. The cost of the gown is set down at lib 188. In 1541 there is this additional entry :—" Augt. 27. Item to the Laird of Creich in parte payment of his tocher with Madame Gresmere at the King's command, iij cxxx iij lib vj⁸ viijᵈ."

The last of the lairds of Creich was a steady supporter of the Presbyterian Church. He bore office in her communion, for among the Commissioners for the Public Affairs of the Kirk chosen by the General Assembly of 1644, there is the name of David Beton of Creigh as one of the

c

elders.   His name occurs again in the Commission of the General Assembly of 1648. Anna, the sister of David Beton, was married to Sir John Moncrieff of Moncrieff, a zealous Presbyterian, to whom Samuel Rutherford addressed one of his famous letters. He was no common man to whom Rutherford could write in these terms :—" Now, very worthy Sir, I am glad in the Lord, that the Lord reserveth any of your place and note in this time of common apostacy, to come forth in public to bear Christ's name before men when the great men think Christ a cumbersome neighbour, and that religion carrieth hazards and persecutions with it.

This parish has furnished three eminent witnesses to the truth. Mr ANDREW STRACHAN was minister of Creich about the beginning of the 17th century, when King James was endeavouring to overthrow the liberties of the Kirk, and especially to disallow the General Assemblies, " the bulwark of our Kirk, whereupon dependeth the preservation of the true religion, and of the purity thereof in doctrine and discipline."   In July 1605 Mr Strachan repaired to Aberdeen to attend a meeting of General Assembly, which had been lawfully appointed. The King by an undue stretch of prerogative endeavoured to prevent the meeting from being held. Yet did the ministers, to save the threatened rights of the Church, meet and constitute. For thus acting they incurred the wrath of the King. Mr Strachan was imprisoned in Blackness. He, along with other five brethren, imprisoned for the same offence, were tried at Linlithgow, when thirty ministers assembled to accompany them to the bar. Ultimately he was driven from his country to languish in banishment, and to find a grave in Middleburgh in the Netherlands

In this parish was born the celebrated ALEX-ANDER HENDERSON. The parish has substantial reason to hold in continued remembrance the name of this distinguished man, as the following extract from the Minute of Session, Oct. 1712, shows—"There was a bond of 2000 merks secured on the lands of Creich, which Mr Alexander Henderson, late minister of Leuchars, and afterwards of Edinburgh, had mortified for the encouragement of a schoolmaster in the parish. The said Mr Alexander Henderson being born in the town of Luthrie." This boy, who played by the Moutray Burn, and rambled amid the unbroken pastures of Creich, became afterwards the companion of nobles and the counsellor of kings. In the most memorable Assemblies of the Church of Scotland he presided. He originated the idea of the Westminster Assembly, and of the Westminster Standards. He sat at the council table with Rothes and Loudon. He was closeted with King Charles. His grave eloquence was addressed to Lords and Commons. No man lived more laboriously or more nobly, for his life was spent in contending for the rights of the Church of Christ against the encroachments of the Civil Power, and in advancing the Covenanted Reformation of Scotland. He died regretted in 1646, "in great modesty, piety, and faith."

Mr JOHN ALEXANDER, minister of Creich, is mentioned by Wodrow as one of the noble band of Presbyterian nonconformists. He would not renounce the validity of Presbyterian ordination and receive admission at the hand of a Prelatist, and therefore he was outed by the act of Council at Glasgow 1662.

This parish, which gave to Presbytery one of its most eminent ministers, in the person of Alexander Henderson, also supplied to Scottish Episcopacy one of the most respectable of its Bishops. It was in Creich that BISHOP SAGE was born in 1652. In Ballingry and Tibermuir he officiated as a schoolmaster. He was admitted into priest's orders in 1684, and appointed to one of the churches in Glasgow. In 1705 he was consecrated a Bishop, and died in 1711. A strict Royalist and Episcopalian, he wrote on the controversies of his day, and his writings were much valued by his own party. Some of Bishop Sage's writings have been reprinted by the Spottiswoode Club.

LUTHRIE.

Luthrie, which is mentioned as the birth-place of Alexander Henderson, derives its name from *lith*, a pool or morass, and *righ*, properly, a king, but employed as a termination to denote anything marked or prominent. Luthrie, the morass of the king, or, the large morass. There are those still alive who remember that in their early day stagnant water overspread in winter all the ground betwixt Starr and Kinsleath, and who in frosty weather have often enjoyed sliding betwixt these two places.

CARPHIN.

Carphin, the name of the property which adjoins Luthrie, is composed of *caer*, a fort, and

Finn, a Northman—the fort of the Northmen. It is just another rendering of Norman or North-man's Law, which forms the background of Carphin, and to the fort on the top of which the Danes were accustomed to carry their booty, before conveying it on board their ships, which anchored in the Tay.

PARBROATH.

A fragment of an arch and a line of old elms indicate the situation of the old house of Parbroath. The house links itself with the Seaton family. They were firm adherents of Queen Mary and Popery. David Seaton held the office at Court of Comptroller in 1589. Sir John Scott of Scotstarvit says of them—"The memory of that family is extinguished, albeit it was very numerous, and brave men descended thereof."

Balmerino.

CORBIEHILL.

Entering Balmerino parish from the west we meet with Corbiehill, called also Birkhill. "Laurentius de Abernethie, son of Orm," says

Keith in his Catalogue, " gave Corbie, called
also Birkhill (from a park of birks surrounding
the house), to the Monastery of Balmerino ; and
in his charter is expressed the reason of his
donation, viz., because Queen Emergarda, dying
on the 3d of February, in the year 1233, and
being buried in the Church of Balmerino before
the great altar (ante magnum altare), had, by
her testament, left him 200 merks ster ing."
Corbiehill manifestly received that name because
it had been a favourite resort of the corbies or
crows. Very likely a rookery had been there.
Now only an old ash stands here and there, on
which the crows alight as a halting-place in
coming and going to their nests in the woods.

BALMERINO VILLAGE.

The Parish of Balmerino is so called from the
hamlet which nestles in the curve of the hills,
and runs out its small pier into the Tay. Balmerino signifies the town by the sea. Fordoun
calls it *Habitaculum ad Mare*. The situation is
pleasant, and as it is sheltered by the hills, and
yet not shaded from the sunshine, the air is regarded as very salubrious. The Scottish physicians recommended Balmerino as the residence

of Madeline, James V.'s first wife, when she was sinking in consumption.

ABBEY.

Little remains to indicate the extent and magnificence of the once famed Abbey of Balmerinoch.   Once the choice residence of royalty, the abode of learning, and the dwelling-place of nobles, it is now a shed for cattle. Close by, there is the decaying stem of a gigantic chestnut-tree which adorned the Abbey in the days of its glory, and now in the day of desolation increases the ruined grandeur which still lingers here.

The author of Robinson Crusoe, in his tour through Scotland, has this note regarding Balmerino: "I turned to the north-east part of the county to see the ruins of the famous Monastery of Balmerinoch, of which Mr Camden takes notice, but saw nothing worth observation, the very ruins being almost eaten up by time. The Monastery was founded by Queen Ermangred, wife of King William of Scotland." Any one studious of the "Antiquities of Balmerino," will find in the volume which relates to Balmerino Abbey, published by the Abbotsford Club, and edited by the late W. B. D. Turnbull, all materials ready prepared for him.

Mr James Elphinstone, parson of Inverarity, was the first who bore the title of Lord Balmerino. He was Secretary to King James VI., and got the two Abbacies of Balmerino and Cupar erected into two temporal lordships.

His son John, second Lord Balmerino, was a prominent supporter of the Presbyterian cause, alike by his countenance, his counsel, and his means. Rutherford addresses one of his Aberdeen letters to him " as his very noble and truly honourable Lord." Balmerino's bold signature is conspicuous in the National Covenant subscribed in 1638.

When in 1633 King Charles I. came down to Scotland to be crowned, he manifested a great desire to push the royal prerogative to unwarrantable lengths, converting Parliament into a piece of pageantry, and managing everything by his own will. His royal influence he used in enforcing an act which had reference to the apparel of Churchmen, and which Charles intended to use against hated Presbyterianism. Yet was there spirit and principle enough in the nobles of Scotland to resist these encroachments upon their own privileges, and the liberties of their Church. The indignation of the nobles was moved to a just severity when the King refused to hear the sentiments of the peers, and when the state of the vote was openly falsified to meet the King's wishes. The Lords met to consider their grievances, and to seek their redress. A petition was drawn out expressive of their feelings. This petition Lord Balmerino was desirous to soften in some of its expressions. For this purpose it was committed to him. His lordship showed the petition to a lawyer from Dundee, of the name of Dunmore, allowed him to carry it home, but charged him to show it to no man and to take no copy of it. Dunmore went from the Abbey to Hay's of Naughton, with whom he spent the night. During their evening converse, when Naughton's wine had probably unlocked the secret chambers of the lawyer's mind, he spoke of this petition. Naughton's curiosity was excited. By night, it is said, he abstracted the paper from Dunmore's chamber and carried it direct to Spottiswoode, Archbishop of St Andrews. Spottiswoode, alarmed at its contents, started with it to London, " beginning his journey as he often did," says Burnet, " on a Sunday, which was a very serious thing in that country,"

The paper gave rise to a trial. When the

jury retired, there was a striking incident which happened. Gordon of Buckie, now an old man, and who, forty-three-years before, had assisted in the murder of the Earl of Murray, addressed his fellow-jurors: "This is a matter of blood and they would feel the weight of it as long as they lived. He had in his youth been drawn in to shed blood for which he had the King's pardon; but it cost him more to obtain God's pardon. This had given him many sorrowful hours both day and night." As he spoke, the tears ran down his face.

Notwithstanding this affecting appeal, when it came to the vote, after many hours' arguing, seven voted acquit, and eight voted condemn. The result of the trial excited great commotion. Meetings were held, and it was proposed to force the prison, and to secure Lord Balmerino's liberty; or, if the sentence was executed to avenge his death, both upon the court and the jurors. Traquair hastened to the court, explained the state of public feeling, and obtained the King's pardon. Yet, says Burnet, the ruin of King Charles's affairs in Scotland was in a great manner owing to that persecution.

Lord Balmerino's death is thus recorded by

Sir James Balfour :—" The last of this mounthe of Febuarii, 1649, Johne Elphinstone, Lord Balmerinoche, deyed of ane apoplexie in his owen chamber in Edinburghe, one Thursday, about 3 in the morning, being the first of Marche, having supped with the Marques of Argyle, gone weill to bed, but fond himselve seekie after his first sleeipe, called to a servaut for some sacke, but before the servant coulde returne with the wyne he was gone."

The later wearers of the Balmerino title did not inherit the high qualities of their ancestors. The phrase, " Balmerino's eik," tells of the jolly propensities of one of them. It means an eik which knew no end, for the punch-bowl was constantly replenished and thus was never emptied.

The last Lord took part with the Pretender in 1745. He was executed in 1747, when the title was attainted.

Connected with this parish there were men of low degree, but of noble spirit, who, in their own sphere, testified for the principles of the persecuted Church of Scotland. One of them was ANDREW GULLAND, weaver in Balmerino. He was present at the murder of Archbishop Sharpe at Magus Muir. He took no active part in the murder, but only held the horses of those who were engaged in it. So hot was the search after all who were in the least connected with this tragedy, that Andrew thought it prudent to go away to a different part of the country, and there to gain his livelihood as an *orrie* man about farm-towns. While at his work in the parish of Cockpen, the curate happened to pass, and asked him whether he attended the Parish Church on the Lord's-day. Andrew's Presbyterian blood rose, and he said that he did not own the curate, and refused to give any account of himself. At the curate's instigation he was seized, carried to Dalkeith to prison, and thereafter to Edinburgh. While lying in the prison at Edinburgh, the report broke out that he had been present at the Archbishop's death. No evidence of this was adduced, but the advocate trepanned him, says Wodrow, into a confession in the following manner. At one of the examinations, the advocate, addressing himself to Andrew, aggravated the circumstances of the Archbishop's murder in a most moving way, and as the most horrible part of it represented that it was while upon his knees praying, that the bloody deed was done. This touched the simple countryman so, that he got up his hands and cried out, 'O dreadful, he would not pray one word for all that could be said to him.' Andrew was tried on the charge of being concerned in the Bishop's death, was found guilty, and was condemned to execution —his head to be set up at Cupar, and his body at Magus Muir. He died heroically, denying that he died as a murderer, though he was accidentally joined with those who executed justice upon a Judas, who sold the Kirk of Scotland for 51,000 merks a-year.

There lived in this parish another obscure person, whose name history takes not up, although he was a sufferer in the covenanted reformation of Scotland. Yet does it live in tradition. WILLIAM MURDOCH was a blacksmith in Gauldry in these trying times. He boldly professed himself a Presbyterian, and attended their field preachings. For his steadfastness he was apprehended. It was in his own house he was seized, and while leaving it for prison he passed through his smithy, and when, unobserved by his conductor, he quietly lifted a file and hid it about his clothes. He was brought to Cupar and lodged in the common prison, where there were many fellow-prisoners suffering for the same cause. Whenever night fell, he commenced filing through the iron stancheons which secured the window, and, before morning, he and all his companions in tribulation were seeking the shelter which unfrequented paths afforded them from the rage of their persecutors.

In Wodrow's lists, Mr Walter Greg of this parish is mentioned as one of the ministers who were confined to their own parishes, as underlying the suspicions of a tyrannical Government.

On Newton Hill, which rises to the west of Newton farm, on the borders of this parish, tradition points out a place where, in days of persecution, the Covenanters were wont to meet. It is a sequestered spot, where the hare may lurk secure, and where the plover, in its circling flight, utters its lonely scream. This solitary place has seen multitudes gathered together, and listening, when it was treason to do so, to the Gospel, preached by Mr Thomas Hogg, of Kiltearn, by Mr John Welsh, of Irongray, and by Mr Donald Cargill.

PEASEHILL.

We cannot pass the farm of Peasehill without

animadverting on the sad transmutation to which its name has been subjected. Near this was a battle fought with the Danes, and on this hill the terms of peace were arranged. Hence was it called the Hill of Peace, or Peace-hill. But now it has passed into Peasehill!

> " O what a fall was there, my countrymen !"

From war and peace to pease and beans! The only method to rescue the name from this degrading corruption is for landlord and tenant to encase it in a language which Lowland lips are less likely to pervert, and call it Dunipace, which means the Hill of Peace.

There is a public road which winds round the base of Newton Hill, and carries the traveller into the PARISH OF

Kilmany.

This road passes the farm of Kinnaird, which belonged, in Popish times, to the Nunnery of Elcho, and the fields of Little Kinnear, which formed part of the church lands of Balmerino Abbey. Should Popery regain the supremacy to which it is fast rising, there will be a settlement of a long account of these church lands.

The square tower of the old Castle of Cruivie is also seen on the side of the hill, considerably to the east of the present farm of Cruivie. It is in the parish of Logie, and belonged to the Ramsays of Colluthie.

In passing along we catch a sight, on a terrace on the hill-side, of Forret, also in the parish of Logie. To the house of the Laird of Forret belonged the meek, the gentle, but firm martyr, Dean Thomas Forret, Vicar of Dollar, who was burned for the truth in 1538.

MOUNTQUHANIE.

To the back of the present modern mansion-house of Mountquhanie, a dark pile of ruin rises amid rows of venerable trees. This is the remains of the Old house of Mountquhanie. The name of one who was once its owner figures in an interesting chapter of Scottish history. Among those who, in 1546, plotted and perpetrated the murder of Cardinal Beaton, was David Balfour, son to the Laird of Mountquhanie. The conspirators being declared rebels, gallantly

D

defended the Castle of St Andrews. When every attempt to reduce the Castle had failed, recourse was had to treachery, "that, under truth, they might get the Castle betrayed." In this perfidious service was the Laird of Mountquhanie, Sir Michael Balfour, employed. His own son being one of the conspirators, his designs were the less suspected. But, after he had "laboured by foot and hand" in the dishonourable work, he failed of success, "God not appointing," says Knox, "so many to be betrayed."

The Lady of Mountquhanie, in the troublous times of 1638 and onwards, took part with the Covenanters. Livingstone, whose mention is praise, names her as the Lady Monwhanny, along with the Lady Halhill, the Lady Raith, the Lady Innertiel, all ladies of the Covenant belonging to Fife, " whose memory was very precious and refreshing."

RATHILLET

Is a place familiar to every reader of the Scottish Worthies, and it is at once associated with the name of Hackston or Halkerstone, who made it famous. Tall beeches, with their glossy stems and brown branches inclose the place " which once knew him."

As the properties of Mountquhanie and Rathillet stand close to each other, so a similarity of enterprise conjoins their former proprietors. Balfour of Mountquhanie was concerned in the murder of Archbishop Beaton. Hackston of Rathillet was connected with the murder of Archbishop Sharpe. Little did Sharpe dread the near approach of a violent death, when, on the 3d of May 1679, he turned aside to smoke a forenoon pipe with the curate of Ceres. And little did the nine gentlemen who were the actors think, when they went forth that morning in search of Carmichael, whose oppression was intolerable, that instead of the servant the master should be thrown in their way. Of all the nine, Hackston was the only one who was unresolved in his own mind regarding the deed on which they determined. He used remonstrances, and kept aloof from any active participation in the act. " I shall never lay a hand upon you," was Hackston's reply to the Archbishop's appeal ; and when Sharpe did fall under the redoubled strokes, Hackston had rode a little off. It is a curious coincidence, that it was the same day in May that Cardinal Beaton was assassinated.

At the battle of Bothwell Bridge Hackston was present, conducting himself with great bravery. At Airs Moss, in 1680, he commanded, and being overpowered by numbers was taken captive by Bruce of Earlshall, and carried to Edinburgh. Every one knows the unheard of cruelties to which this good man was subjected at his execution, and how his heart was cut out of his breast and presented to the spectators on the point of a knife, while yet it was throbbing with the lingerings of life—the executioner pronouncing aloud the words, " Here is the heart of a traitor."

It was the heart of a brave man and a Christian. " I am told," says Wodrow, " he was without any sense of religion in his younger days, but getting good of the Gospel preached in the fields, and having thereby a real and thorough change wrought upon him, he left all to follow it, and at last sealed it with his blood." Nor was the servant behind his master, for in the list of those denounced in 1684 as rebels and fugitives because of their faithful adherence to the cause of the persecuted Church of Scotland, we find the name of *James Kinnier, servant to Hackston of Rathillet.*

The family of Hackston exhibits one of those strange reactions by which the son is thrown into a position clean contrary, in all respects, to that occupied by the father. Young Hackston became, in his last years, a supporter of the Pretender. The influence of his wife effected this. He had married Lady Gibson, who was first the widow of Sir Edward Gibson of Kinloch, and secondly the widow of Mr Balllie of Luthrie, and the mother of Colonel Baillie, and last of all the wife of Mr Hackston of Rathillet. Lady Gibson was a determined Jacobite. The explanation is thus very plain. The poor man "cared for the things that are of the world, how he might please his wife;" he forgot the claims of truth and of patriotism, and lent his little influence to support a scion of the Stuart House which had cruelly murdered his own father.

MURDOCHCAIRNIE.

A little to the west of Rathillet is Murdochcairnie. Sir Robert Melville of Murdochcairnie was a man of some note in his day. He was King's Commissioner to the General Assembly in 1594, and one of the members of the Secret Council.

In connection with Murdochcairnie we may here mention the death of Aytoun, younger of Inchdairnie, when on his way to visit his aunt, Lady Murdochcairnie. This young gentleman, when a student in St Andrews, was remarkable for his piety. At the age of 17 he was intercommuned because of his attachment to the persecuted Presbyterian ministers, and forced to leave his father's house. Thus wandering about without a sure abode, he was proposing to shelter himself in the house of his relative. He had got beyond Auchtermuchty when he saw a party of the King's dragoons riding furiously towards Cupar. With the view of escaping them he quickened his horse's pace; but one of the troopers, despatched by his commander, overtook him, and wounded him mortally. The wounded man could scarcely keep his seat until he reached the nearest cottage. There he was sheltered, and Sir John Ayton of Ayton, his relative, was sent for. Sir John Ayton despatched a servant to Cupar for a surgeon. By the interference of the dragoons the surgeon was hindered from going. Some of their number were sent for the wounded man, Despite of all remonstrance on the part of Sir John, the wounded man was hurried to Cupar. Four times he fainted by the way, and on the morrow he died in a lodging-house in peace and security, forgiving the soldier who mortally wounded him. This happened in 1672.

STARR.

From Murdochcairnie we may look across to Starr farm, for the sake of remarking on the name. One wonders, how has that name dropped from the clouds on this place? What does Starr mean? Starr is an old Scotch word, and signifies a " sedge." The place was evidently named Starr, the Place of Sedges, from the sedges which grew thickly there when, in former days, the Luthrie marsh extended from Starr to Kins-leith. It is for the same reason that the village of Starr, in Markinch parish, got its name. That village stands close by the site of an old swamp, where the sedges, having found for themselves an appropriate habitat, had grown profusely. It is of consequence to preserve the correct spelling of Starr. A place which in older days would have been called Starr, is in later times named Seggie.

Of this parish was Mr JOHN SHARP minister in 1605.   He was one of the members who kept the meeting of Assembly at Aberdeen, and was chosen their clerk.   For this he was imprisoned, and latterly banished.   He was appointed Professor of Divinity in the University of Die in Dauphine.

In Wodrow's lists, Mr George Thompson is entered as one of the ministers outed by the Glasgow Act, 1662.

When time has mossed over with hoary age the years in which we live, it will be mentioned as one of the most interesting circumstances connected with this parish, that for twelve years Dr Chalmers was its minister.

____

We now enter the little PARISH OF

Moonzie.

The hill-top situation of Moonzie is expressed in the name Monadh, in Gaelic signifying a Hill. It is also preserved in popular rhyme—

> " Gae ye east or gae ye wast,
> Or gae ye ony way ye will,
> Ye winna get to Moonzie Kirk,
> Unless ye do gae up the hill.

LORDSCAIRNIE

Is the principal object which attracts the observation of the passer-by. Its strong donjon and one of its flanking towers have withstood the decay of centuries. It is, and has been for many generations, the property of the Earls of Crawfurd.

Alexander, Earl of Crawfurd, who is still known in the locality from the nicknames he bore of " The Tiger," and " Earl Beardie," married about 1450 a daughter of the Earl of March, through whom he came into possession of the lands of Auchter Moonzie and Cairnie. It was by him that this old Castle was built.

Calderwood relates, that after the discomfiture of his army by the English at the Solway, King James V., melancholy and dejected, " visited the Castle of Cairnie pertaining to the Earl of Crawfurd, where the said Earl's daughter, one of his royal mistresses, was. He returned to Falkland and took bed." When the news had reached him that the Queen had given birth to a daughter, he turned from such as he spake with and said, " It will end as it began, it came with a woman and it will end with a woman." He died 13th December 1542.

One of the Lords of Cairnie—the Earl of Crawfurd of 1690—was a firm-hearted Presbyterian. He was desirous when the Revolution of 1688 came round, that the government of the Church should be entirely in the hands of those who had been Nonconformist or Presbyterian. He leaves it as a warning when he is silent in the dust, "that if any of the prelatic party are permitted to have the government, of the Church, it will bring ruin to the Church and disappointment to the nation."

COLLUTHIE.

The Ramsays and the Carnegies, both families of distinction, were connected with Colluthie, and took their title from it. Under the year 1356, Balfour records that Archibald Douglas, son of the noble Sir James, and who afterwards was Earl of Douglas, was taken " by the Englishe, with Johne, King of France, in the batell of Poictiers, but by the means of Sir William Ramsay of Colluthey made his escape, and so fred himselve of their hands."

David Carnegie, Laird of Colluthie, was one of the King's Commissioners in the General Assembly which met at Edinburgh April 1583.

This same David Carnegie of Colluthie, in

1591, signs, as first witness, Mr Patrick Adamson's, of St Andrews, commonly called Archbishop Adamson's, confession, declaration, and recantation.

Mr James Wedderburn, minister of Moonzie, was one of the noble band of 400 who were ejected in 1662. He was appointed assistant to his father in 1659, and when his father died in 1661 he became sole minister. He gained a high character as an ardent and faithful preacher of Christ. It was this which acquired for him the appellation of "The Angel of Moonzie." His brethren spoke of him generally under this title; and they said of him that although there were many ministers who were possessed of higher abilities and of greater learning, yet were there few who were more successful in their Master's work than the Angel of Moonzie.

Mr Wedderburn died on the 23d of July 1687, in the fifty-second year of his age. Had he lived but a year longer he would have seen the glorious Revolution of 1688, under William, Prince of Orange, and would have been brought back again to his much-loved parish. He was buried in the churchyard of Cupar. In the Latin inscription on his tombstone in the wall, which affection had laboriously ornamented, and which time has now obliterated, he is called, " Ecclesiæ Munsiæ fidelissimi pastoris "—The most faithful Pastor of the Church of Moonzie.

Dunbog.

COLLAIRNIE.

In entering the parish of Dunbog from the east, the old Castle of Collairney, now in ruins, is seen rising on the sloping sides of Dunbog hill.

Sir David Barclay was a member and office-bearer of the Church of Scotland in the high days of the Covenant. Indeed, almost all the landed proprietors in the north of Fife were so. Beaton of Creich, Sir David Barclay of Collairney, Arnot of Fernie, Erskine of Scotscraig, are all named as elders in the Acts of Assembly. Blessed days for a land, when squire and tenant and hind worship together in the undivided Church of their country !

Some of the descendants of the Collairney family were not ashamed to attach themselves to the cause of Christ in the day of tribulation, as appears from the following notice :—On the 9th of January 1679, Mrs MARGARET BARCLAY, niece of *Sir David Barclay of Collairnie*, who had for some time been in prison in Edinburgh for being at private meetings, was set at liberty for the recovery of her health, upon giving security for 500 merks to return to jail by the 20th, if called, or when called, and meanwhile to confine herself to her room, under the same penalty.

By letters of intercommuning, of date August 5, 1675, we find *Lady Collarney*, with many others, denounced a rebel for inviting and countenancing outed ministers in their invasion and intrusion upon the kirks and pulpits of Balmarinoch, Collessie, Moonzie, and Auchtermuchty, and hearing them preach and pray therein, and for resetting and entertaining Mr John Welsh, a declared and proclaimed traitor.

Mr WILLIAM TULLIDAFF, minister of Dunbog, appears prominent in the histories of these stormy times in the seventeenth century. In March 1664 died Mr James Wood, Principal of the College of St Andrews, a learned and eminently pious man. On his death-bed Archbishop Sharpe visited him, and circulated the report that, in the prospect of death, Mr Wood considered the matter of Church Government as a very small thing, and that he was as much for Episcopacy as for Presbytery. These reports being communicated to Mr Wood, vexed him much, and, to counteract them, he determined to leave behind him a public testimony declaring his unqualified attachment " to the Presbyterian Government as the ordinance of God, appointed by Jesus Christ for ordering his visible Church, and that if he was to live, he would account it his glory to seal this word of his testimony with his blood." This declaration Mr Wood subscribed in presence of three witnesses of whom Mr Wm. Tullidaff, minister at Dunbog, was one. The other two were public notaries. Sharpe stormed when this was known. The witnesses were thrown into prison. When the trial came, all the witnesses swore to Mr Wood's dying testimony. The Archbishop was proved a spreader of lying calumnies, and Mr Tullidaff and his fellow-witnesses were liberated.

Mr Tullidaff was outed in 1662. He and Mr Wm. Rowe, of Ceres, were the only two of the outed ministers in the Presbytery of Cupar who were spared to witness the blessed Revolution of 1688.

Monimail.

THE MOUNT.

On the south side of the hill which is sur-mounted by the Hopetoun Monument, there grow a few old trees, irregularly placed. These trees mark the site where stood, in the beginning of the sixteenth century, the dwelling-place of SIR DAVID LINDSAY OF THE MOUNT, Lord-Lyon-King-at-Arms. He was a " special servant" at the Court of King James IV., having been employed as a confidential companion of the Prince, afterwards James V. His own pen records this in an address to the King—

> When thou was young, I bore thee in mine arm
>   Full tenderly, till thou begouth to gang ;
> And in thy bed oft happit thee full warm—
>   With lute in hand softly to thee sang ;
>   Sometimes in dancing, fairly I flang,
> And sometimes playing farces on the floor,
> And sometimes on mine office taking care.

On the summit of the hill tradition points out a place which was known as " Sir David's Walk." Here he walked in solitary meditation, cherish-ing poetic ardours, and constructing those poems and dramas which, from the one mind on the Mounthill diffused their influence to many ; and being read in the palace and the baron's hall, and exhibited before men of all estates, helped forward powerfully the then advancing Reformation.   From this tendency of his writings, Lindsay has been styled the Poet of the Reformation.   He was employed in embassies to different Courts, and is supposed to have died about 1558.

Dame Janet Douglass, his wife, died not long after him.   The poet was succeeded in the office of Lyon-King-at-Arms by his nephew, Sir David Lyndsay, of Rathillet and Luthrie.   He was succeeded in the heritage of the Mount by his brother Alexander, whose son, the third Sir David, became Lyon-King in 1592.   He continued in office until 1621, when he resigned in favour of his son-in-law Jerome Lindsay.   In 1630 Sir Jerome Lindsay ceased to be Lyon-King, when Sir James Balfour of Kinnaird was appointed.   In the Old Church of Monimail there was a family pew belonging to the Lindsays of The Mount.   Its carved oaken canopy is still preserved as an heir-loom at Kinnaird.   The Lindsay Arms, J. L. (the initials of Jerome

Lindsay), the date 1645, are engraved on it, as also the following quaint couplet :—

Thy hairt prepair, thy God in Chryst ador,
Mount up by grace, and then thous com to glor.

MELVILLE HOUSE.

In Melville House there hang two paintings of much interest to the Protestant and to the Presbyterian. The first is an original full-length portrait of Gustavus Adolphus, King of Sweden, dressed in a buff jerkin and trousers, resembling modern mud-boots. A pair of immense spurs are attached to his heels, a broad lace collar decorates the neck, and a trusty sword hangs by his side. His features are large, his hair close clipt, and a look of gravity sits on the countenance, which well becomes the Leader of the Protestants in the Thirty Years' War. The second is the portrait of Sir Alexander Leslie, who was Lieutenant-General, and afterwards Field-Marshal of the forces of Gustavus. To Sir Alexander did Gustavus give the portrait of himself, which we have described above, in testimony of the regard he bore him. After gaining many military honours abroad, Sir Alexander was

E

called home to command the army of the Covenanters in their struggles against Charles I. for civil and religious liberty. The banner under which he fought was the bravest which was ever unfurled, for it bore enstamped on it the Scottish arms, and had these words engraved in golden letters—" For Christ's Crown and Covenant." "Such," says Baillie, " was the wisdom and authority of that old, little, crooked soldier, that all, with an incredible submission, gave over themselves to be guided by him, as if he had been great Solyman. Such was the man's understanding of our Scots humours, that he gave out not only to the noblemen, but to very mean gentlemen, his directions in a very homely and simple form, as if they had been but the advices of their neighbour and companion." Sir Alexander was created Earl of Leven in 1641, for his important services. In the portrait, the crookedness of his figure is hid by a kind of loose black dress. His figure and his features are small. His hair of a sandy colour, and his beard is pointed. He is the founder of the House of Leven, and a nobler founder no family could have, for the title was gained in fighting for the great principles of civil liberty, and for the pure principles of Presbyterianism—the Presbyterianism of 1638-50, to which every right-hearted son of Scotland looks as the period of the purest development of the principles of the Reformed Church of Scotland. The grandson of the first Lord Leven left an only child, a daughter. In this daughter the honours and estate of Leven met, and as she married George Earl of Melville, the titles of Leven and Melville were united. This George Lord Melville was a sufferer for his religion during the trying times of James II., and fled to Holland. He rejoiced in the Revolution of 1688, and was appointed by King William to be High Commissioner to the Parliament of 1690, when the Confession of Faith was ratified, patronage abolished, and the Presbyterian Church restored to her liberties.

UPPER RANKEILOUR

Was the ancestral home of Sir ROBERT SIBBALD. His father was Mr David Sibbald, third brother to Sir James Sibbald, "Knight-Baronet of Rankellor."

Every one interested in the antiquities of Fife will be curious to know something of Sir Robert, the historian of Fife. An Autobiography, of which only thirty copies were printed in 1833, enables me to supply the following account.

Sir Robert was born in Edinburgh 15th April 1641. After finishing his philosophy studies at the College of Edinburgh, his mother " would have had him study divinity," but the distractions of the Church deterred him. The influence of Archbishop Leighton, who was Principal of Edinburgh College during the five years that young Sibbald studied there, was greatly instrumental in determining his choice apart from the Presbyterian Church. "The impressions I retained from Mr Leighton his discourses, disposed me to affect charity for all good men of any persuasion, and I preferred a quiet life, wherein I might not be ingadged in factions of Church or State." Medicine became his chosen profession. He prosecuted his studies at Leyden, then the first medical school in Europe. At Angiers he 'got his patent of doctor," and returned to Scotland in 1662. In company with Sir Andrew Balfour he founded the Botanical Gardens of Edinburgh, getting " ane lease of the garden belonging to Trinity Hospital, embellishing the fabric of the garden, and importing into it plants

from all places." Charles II. gave him a patent
to be his geographer for the kingdom of Scotland,
and another to be his physician there, together
with his commands to publish the natural history
of the country, and the geographical description
of the kingdom. It was in fulfilment of this
appointment that he prepared "The History,
Ancient and Modern, of the Sheriffdoms of Fife
and Kinross, with a description of both." In
1681, chiefly through his exertions, the Edinburgh Royal College of Physicians was established, and in 1684 he was chosen its President.
The story of his being knighted he thus tells :—
" In the beginning of the year 1682 I was adver-
tised on a Saturday night to bring with me next
day Dr Stanson and Dr Balfour, to wait upon
His Royal Highness, James Duke of York, after
the forenoon sermon. To our surprisall, there
was ane carpet layed, and we were ordered to
kneel, and were each of us knighted by His
Royal Highness, then Commissioner."

Now we come to what Sir Robert calls " the
difficultest passage of his life." The Earl of
Perth, his patron and friend, had turned Papist.
" One Sunday the Earl had taken physick, he
took the opportunity, we being alone, to tell me,

weeping, that he was of that persuasion. This did occasion odd thoughts in my mind. In September 1685 he carried me along with him to Drummond to see his Lady, who was then dying. I knew nothing of it, but he told me afterwards, that the very next day after her arrival he brought her over to the Romish persuasion. The next day after I arrived at Drummond he had given me the Life of Gregory Lopez and of Father Davila to read. One day about 11 o'clock he called me up to his study to read to me a paper that the Duchess of York had writ upon her embracing that religion, and discoursed very pathetically upon it. I know not how it came about, I felt a great warmness of my affections while he was reading and discoursing, and thereupon, as I thought oestro quodam pietatis motus in this, I said I would embrace that religion, upon which he took me in his arms and thanked God for it." Thus are converts made. This " broad-school disciple of Archbishop Leighton, who refused to take any part in the Presbyterian contendings for truth, lest his charity should suffer, yields up his Protestantism

"At the fascination of a high-born smile.'

When Sir Robert returned to Edinburgh the

townspeople, hearing that he and the Earl of Perth had become Papists, laid the blame of the Earl's perversion on Sir Robert, broke into his house, and threatened to " Rathillet" him. He escaped by the garden, lay hid in the fields all night, and " was conveyed down to the Abbey by Lieutenant-General Drummond in his coach, with Claverhouse, who was then Viscount of Dundee." Shortly afterwards he set out for London. On " the night after his arrival there, he was carried to Court to kiss the King's hand."

" The air of London river and city did not agree with him," so that he resolved to return to Scotland. But he had shrewdness enough to see, during his eight or nine weeks' sojourn in London, that matters were hastening to a Revolution—" that the Jesuits were pressing the king to illegal and unaccountable undertakings"—and that the · gathering wrath of the nation would overturn the Government.

On his return home in 1686, he wrote to the Earl of Perth telling him of his purpose to return to the Protestant faith. In September he was received by the Bishop of Edinburgh upon acknowledgment of his rashness, took the Sacrament according to the way of the Church of England, and kept constantly his parish church.

Collessie.

HALHILL.

Within Melville Park, and in that portion which lies in the parish of Collessie, near to an erect block of whinstone, is the site of the Old House of Halhill.

Mr HENRY BALNAVES of Hallhill is well known to the reader of Knox's history. He was an advocate by profession, and was appointed a Lord of Session in 1538. He was a warm adherent to the infant Reformation, and suffered along with John Knox a long imprisonment on board the French galleys, as also in the old castle of Rouen. While there he composed a book, of which the following is the title—" The Confession of Faith, containing how the Troubled Man should seek Refuge at his God, thereto led by Faith ; with the Declaration of the Article of Justification, &c., compiled by Mr Henry Balnaves of Halhill, and one of the Lords of Session and Council of Scotland, being a prisoner within the old palace of Roan, in the year of our Lord 1548."

Sir JAMES MELVILLE, son of the Laird of Raith, succeeded as proprietor of the lands of Halhill, and his tombstone, conspicuous on the wall of the churchyard, summons "the pilgrim passing along this way" to

"Repent, amend, on Christ the burden cast of your sad sins."

Sir James Melville was the founder of the Melville Family. John Livingstone tells us that Sir James "professed that he had got assurance from the Lord that himself, wife, and children should meet in heaven."

Sir James and his brother, Sir Robert Melville of Murdochcairnie, were distinguished as ambassadors and statesmen in the reigns of Queen Mary and King James VI. As might be expected from statesmen in those days, they gave a steady but modified support to the Presbyterian cause. The zeal which was awanting on Sir James' part was conspicuous in his daughter, Lady Culross. She was highly accomplished, but still more eminent for her piety, and for her stout adherence to the persecuted Church of her country.   She employed her pen in encouraging imprisoned and banished witnesses for the truth. It was she who wrote to Rigg of Athernie, when he was confined to Blackness Castle, that "the darkness of Blackness was not the blackness of darkness."

Lady Halhill, the wife of the second Sir James Melville, was a devoted friend of the Covenanted Church of Scotland, and an honoured correspondent of Samuel Rutherford.

RANKEILOUR-MAKGILL.

Looking from the high grounds in Collessie, the eye fixes on the House of Rankeilour-Makgill, raising its pavilion roof from amid its surrounding wood.   Mr James Macgill of Rankeilour, Clerk Register in the reigns of Mary and James, took an active part in the transactions of these stirring times.   Among the lists of fines for Nonconformity imposed by Middleton in 1662, we find Macgill of Rankeilour, £3000.   Since then this House has sent forth those who have contended and suffered for the right.

KINLOCH,

Half-hid by its trees and its many undulations, is celebrated as the residence of JOHN BALFOUR. He was brother-in-law to Hackston of Rathillet, and took a public part in field conventicles, and in opposing the despotic measures of the Court. From incidental notices in the histories of the times, it would appear that Balfour of Kinloch, called Captain Burleigh, was moved to the part he acted rather from political than from religious feelings. Whatever his motives were, the part he acted was a prominent one. In 1677, in an October afternoon, a small company of gentlemen, not exceeding six or seven, had met at dinner in Kinloch House. They were suddenly surprised by the appearance of Capt. Carstairs, who, solely on the warrant of the Archbishop, had taken upon himself to inflict hardships and cruelties throughout the East of Fife on all Nonconformists. Carstairs' company amounted in number to ten or twelve, and announced their arrival by discharging their fire-arms through the windows. The gentlemen boldly repelled the assault, and discomfitted Carstairs and his men. Yet was this act of self-defence magnified into a heinous misdemeanour, and because, when summoned before the Council, they consulted their safety and appeared not, they were denounced as rebels, and the transaction used as a handle against the whole Presbyterian cause.

JOHN BALFOUR was one of those who took a prominent part in the murder of Archbishop Sharpe in 1679. In the same year he was present at the battle of Bothwell Brig, and commanded some regiments of infantry. A reward of 10,000 merks is offered to whoever shall apprehend John Balfour of Kinloch, and David Hackston of Rathillet, and present them to the Council dead or alive. Balfour fled to Holland for safety, and in 1683 he is adjudged by the Lords of Council "to be executed and demeaned as a traitor when apprehended, and his name, fame, and memory, to be extinct, and his lands to fall to his Majesty as in common form."

The name of Balfour of Burleigh is still honourably represented in Holland. In the Brussels newspaper of 28th July 1828, Lieut.-Colonel Balfour de Burleigh is named Commandant of the troops of the Netherlands in the West Indies. The family of Wemysshall are the representatives of Balfour, through Barbara Balfour, the granddaughter of John Balfour, and their ancestor. The late Colonel Wemyss wrote in 1817, "I am too proud of my great progenitor to refuse my name to his life."

" Among some of the ministers of Christ, in the Church of Scotland, eminent for grace and gifts, for faithfulness and success, whom he had known and had acquaintance of, who were before the blessed Second Reformation in the year 1638," John Livingstone mentions Mr John Moncrieff, minister at Collessie, in Fife, and after at Kinghorn.

ROSSIE HOUSE.

The names of Rossie and Kinloch are to be ascribed to the same source. A broad sheet of water overspread the low grounds, and was known as Rossie Loch. Rossie, a derivation from the Gaelic *ros*, signifies a little promontory or piece of land projecting into water. Kinloch means the head of the loch. You find the two words meeting in Kinross, which just means the head of the promontory.

In a plantation a little to the east of Rossie

House there is a decaying building, with its roof uncovered and the door torn off its hinges. This Is the burial place of Sir John Brown. Sir John was proprietor of Fordell, in the parish of Arngask. He sat as Commissioner from Perth in the Committee of Estates, was Major-General of a Horse Brigade, and during his short career distinguished himself as an active officer. He married Marie Scott, eldest daughter, and one of the co-heirs of Sir James Scott of Rossie, in Fife. On Sabbath, 20th July 1651, betwixt Dunfermline and Inverkeithing he encountered a detachment of Oliver Cromwell's army, led on by Major-General Lambert and Colonel Overton. There is as great a conflict betwixt the Scotch and English accounts of the numbers engaged as there was in the battle itself! In the despatch which Oliver Cromwell addressed to the Parliament, and dated " Lithgow, July 21," he writes, " that the number of the English troops were three regiments of foot, two regiments of horse, and about 400 horse and dragoons more," and that the Scotch " had five regiments of foot, and four or five of horse." " The number of Scotch killed was near 2000, some say more." Sir James Balfour's account is that the number of the Scotch was 2500 horse and foot, and that they encountered 10,000 of the English. The number slain was almost alike on each side, being about 800. Sir John Brown is named in Cromwell's despatch as taken prisoner, and Sir James Balfour says that Sir John fought gallantly.

Sir John did not long survive his captivity. He died in September, of fever, in Leith Garrison, where he was imprisoned. "His corps," says Lamont, "was brought over to Rossie, in Fyfe." Sir James Balfour records, "His corpes wer interred amongst his ancestors at Arngascke." Local tradition supports Lamont's statement, and points to this building in the wood as his tomb.

Auchtermuchty.

MYRES.

We know of no other place to which an historical interest attaches until we arrive at the *Castellated* House of Myres. In former days the property of the Moucrieffs of Readie, it gave a safe harbour to some of the saints of

God when hunted down by wicked men. It is related as a tradition among the descendants of that family, that there was, in what now appears as a recess at the foot of the dining-room, a close press with concealed doors, communicating with the cellar, and that there, in times of strict search, the persecuted minister was frequently hid. One distinguished sufferer there was who, oftener than once, found refuge in this hiding-place. It was Mr John Welch, of Irongray, and grandson of the celebrated Mr John Welch, of Ayr. Dear hospitality that was! Because, it appears, he harboured Mr John Welch, a declared traitor, the Council fined the Laird of Readie in 2000 merks. Yet it was a safe and a profitable investment; for Christ says, inasmuch as ye do it to the least of my little ones, ye do it unto me, and the repayment may yet be running on, even unto the third and fourth generation. Among those that were summoned before the Conncil for being present at conventicles, the Laird of Readie is farther mentioned as one, and an additional fine of 850 ponnds is laid upon him. Auchtermuchty comes in for its share of honour in these shaking times, for the name of its chief magistrate—Maxwell,

Provost of Auchtermuchty—stands with a fine of 250 pounds attached to it, because he faithfully served God rather than man, and sought the safety and well-being of his soul at the hazard of man's displeasure and man's wrongous penalties. In the same condemnation, a neighbouring proprietor, Pitcairn of Pitlour, was involved, having been fined 1100 pounds for his attachment to the Presbyterian ministers.

Although I do not find any minister of Auchtermuchty renowned for his adherence to the cause of Presbytery in the days of its distress, I find, in the proclamations of the Council, Auchtermuchty itself mentioned—"its kirk and pulpit being one into which outed ministers were invited and countenanced."

Strathmiglo.

We shall conclude these sketches with two other notices.

In the adjoining village of Strathmiglo, in the possession of one who is lineally descended from the sister of the Rev. Donald Cargill, is the Bible which he carried with him to the scaffold when he was executed in 1681. It is a very beautiful Cambridge edition, printed in 1657, with red marginal lines, ornamentally bound and strengthened with silver clasps, which the respect of its subsequent owners has added. This venerable volume shows on some of its pages the weather marks which it received, when, on the lonely hill-side, or on the naked moor, Cargill held it in his hand, and under the passing storm, proclaimed to those who received no mercy from man the sovereign and abundant mercy of God.

On the western Lomond, where the top rises above the main ridge there is a sequestered glen. It is a lonely spot, known only to the shepherd or adventurous explorer.

> There the bird of the hill makes its nest in the fern,
> There the dark purple heather and bonny blue bells,
> Deck the mountain.

Its name is Glen-vale. Often was it the retreat of the hunted covenanter. Wellwood preached in this solitude, and so did Blackadder. Great multitudes assembled here, and heard the word gladly. Amongst those who frequented this desert place was Lady Leys, wife of Hay of Mugdrum, who, for his wife's piety, was subjected to the penalty of heavy fines.

A brave old place was this Strathmiglo in the witnessing times of Scotland. It was like one of the villages in Israel in the days of Deborah, which offered its inhabitants willingly. But our space prevents us from entering into particulars regarding those who, in their day, fought the good fight for conscience and constitutional law, for the freedom of the Church and the glory of Christ.

Frequently in parks are seen trees of old growth in straggling rows. These mark the place where has stood some dwelling of man—it may have been a humble cottage, or an imposing mansion. The dwelling has disappeared; but the old trees remain pointing out and adorning the spot. So happens it with those who have lived and acted in the world. The earthly house of this tabernacle is dissolved, but the graces and the virtuous deeds which distinguished their lives remain and flourish after they are gone, and benefit to latest ages the land which gave them birth.

END OF PART I.

PART II.

〜〜〜〜〜

Cupar and its Neighbourhood.

PLAN OF CUPAR, 1642.

By M.ʳ JAMES GORDON, Minister of Rotheymay,
Son of Rob.ᵗ Gordon of Straloch.

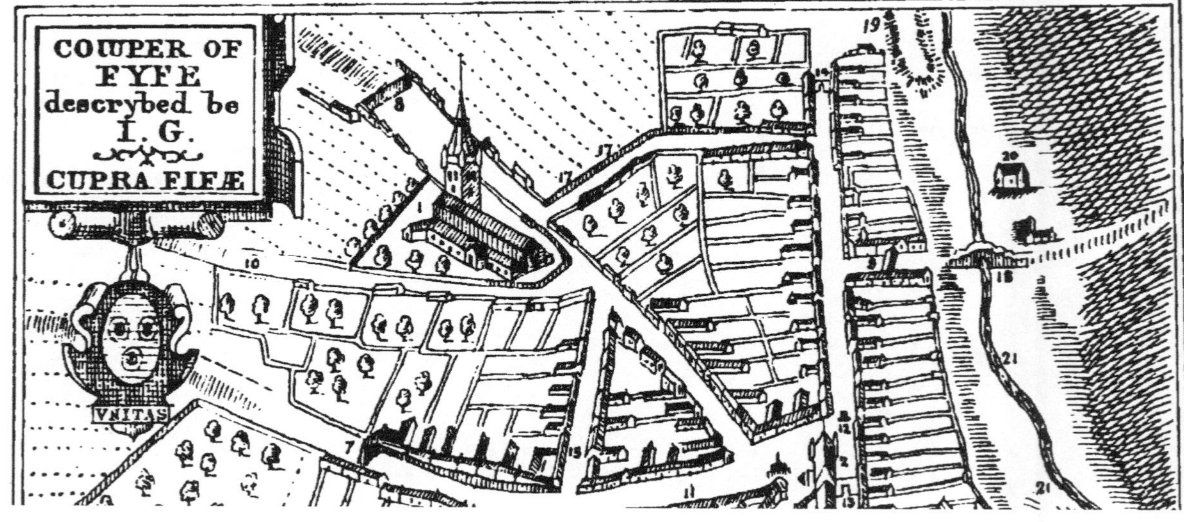

No.	Place	No.	Place	No.	Place
1	The Church	8	The Kirkgate Port	15	Short Wynde
2	Tollbuith	9	Lady Port & Wynd	16	Bober Wynde
3	The Castell	10	Ashler Gate Street	17.17	Provosts Wynde
4	Bridge Wynd	11	Cross Street	18	Lady Bridge
5	Bridge Port	12.12	Bonnygate Street	19	Mute Hill
6.6	The Barony	13	East Port	20	Well Tower
7	The Mill Port	14	West Port	21.21	Lady Burne

Parish of Cupar.

AT length, after weeks of mist and sickly vapour, a bright day breaks in the late October. Autumn sheds one of her melancholy smiles before she resigns herself to gloomy winter.

The sun is darting its golden rays through the clear and unclouded sky. The tinted trees stand motionless, as if lost in silent meditation. The gnats dance merrily, enjoying the last sunshine of the season. The gossamer web, loosened from its grassy moorings, floats on the still air, showing the course of the imperceptible current. The curling smoke rises above the embosoming woods, and where the glade opens into the level fields, the ploughman may be seen bending over the plough, and again stirring up the earth which has but newly resigned its abundance.

Let us embrace such a day, and resume our

rambles,—historical and antiquarian,—taking Cupar as our starting point.

Situated midway betwixt St Andrews and Falkland, Cupar seems to have been, in the early days of Scottish history, rather a place of transit than the scene of memorable events. It was in the royal Palace of Falkland, or in the Arch-episcopal Palace of St Andrews, that eventful doings were accomplished, and Cupar served but as a halting place of rest and refreshment to the actors.

Yet is not Cupar without its passages of interest. Miscellaneous the account must necessarily be.

Cupar ranks among the oldest of Scottish Royal Burghs. In the Index of Charters by King David II., somewhere about the year 1356, there is a charter to William Ramsay, Earl of Fyfe, of the erection of Coupar in ane free burgh.

Change of name generally indicates a change of idea and of condition. That eminence at the east of Cupar, on which the Madras Academy buildings stand, formerly a stronghold of the Earls of Fife, and long known as the Castle-hill, now bears the more peaceful designation of School-hill, thus intimating that the semi-barbarous days of baronial consequence have given place to times of more general education and intelligence. One of the slopes of this Castle-hill was called, before the Reformation, the Playfield. Here were exhibited plays, which, under the name of *mysteries* and *moralities*, were professedly intended to communicate religious instruction to the people. These performances supplied the place of pulpit, of book, and of newspaper, and exercised a powerful influence on the multitudes who assembled to witness them.

As the Mount, the residence of Sir David Lindsay, is only about three miles from Cupar, the playfield was often called into requisition for the exhibition of the Knight's plays. Here is the proclamation which himself gives to summon to one of those scenic performances:—

> " Fail not to be upon the Castle hill,
>> Beside the place where we purpose to play,
>> With gude stark wine your flaggons see you fill,
>> And had yourselves the merriest that you may."

It was here that the " Satire of the Three Estates," and " The tragedy of the Cardinal" were first acted.

The effect which " the theatrical plays and comedies, and notable histories" of Lyndsay had in exposing the corruptions in State and Church which then prevailed, and in helping onwards the advent of the Reformation, was widely influential.   In illustration of this, Row states that Sir David Lindsay's "Four Monarchies" was the means of introducing the Reformation Spirit among "all the scholars of the grammar school of Perth, taught by Mr Andrew Simson, to the number of three hundred and above," and that the reading of this poem was the very first step to the making of Mr Simson himself a Protestant.   We may also quote as an evidence in the same direction, the following passage from James Melville's autobiography : "I remember the benefit of David Lindsay's book, quhilk my eldest sistere, Isbel, wold reid and sing, namelie, concerning the latter judgment, the pains of hell, and the joyes of heavin, whereby sche wold cause me baith greit and be glad."   The popular power of Sir David Lindsay's writings in Scotland was very great, and continued long. The common people could repeat large portions by memory, and so great was their confidence in what he had written, that it was a proverbial expression applied by them to any thing they did not credit, "*That's no in Davie Lindsay.*"

Pitscottie, in his chronicles, mentions that in a Council of the Popish Clergy, an "act was made that Sir David Lindsay's buik be abolished and burnt:" and that Coupar of Fyfe "was among the earliest places in Scotland where the Popis religion was abolished, and the images thairof caused to be castin down." This was as early as 1558.

Cupar seems to have ofttimes received passing visits of Royalty. In 1540, Mary of Guise, Queen of James V., having landed from France at the East Neuk of Fife, was there met by the King, and conducted to St Andrews. There, says the chronicler, "the King and Queine remained the space of fourteen dayes, with gritt merrines, sich as justing on horss, and running at the lists, archerie, and hunting, and all other princelie games. Thairafter, the King, and Queine went to Couper in Fyfe, and dyned thair, and syne passed to Falkland."

Twenty-one years after this, on the 21st March 1561, were the streets of Cupar enlivened by the presence of their daughter, the beautiful Mary, Queen of Scotland. It was her first passage through her kingdom. Only four months had passed since she had arrived from France, and taken possession of the throne of her ancestors. Then too was she in the opening bloom of her unrivalled beauty, for she had not completed her nineteenth year.

In 1560, Knox preached to the Lords of the Congregation in Cupar, when their spirits were dejected by the temporary success, the cruel oppression, and the arrogant boasting of the Queen Regent. Her French troops had come from Stirling to Fife, "at which they had greatest indignation." They gained some small victories on the coast, and fiercely spoiled the district, sparing neither sheep, oxen, kye, nor horse. The Queen's spirit was elated, and in her pride, she profanely asked, "Where is now John Knox's God? My God is now stronger than his, yea even in Fife!" Knox repaired to the Lords at Cupar in their greatest dejection, and made a comfortable sermon to them, upon the danger wherein the disciples stood when they were in the midst of the sea, and Jesus upon the mountain. He exhorted them not to faint, but to row against contrarious blasts, till Jesus Christ should come: "For I am assuredly persuaded, said he, that God shall deliver us from this extreme trouble, as I am assured that this is the Gospel of Jesus Christ which I preach to you this day. The fourth watch is not yet come. Abide a little, the boat shall be saved, and Peter, who hath left the boat, shall not drown, I am assured; albeit I cannot assure you by reason of this present rage."

Sir James Melville, in his Memoirs, tells us, that in 1583 James VI. held Court at Cupar. The minion, James Stewart, Earl of Arran, was then rising into power with the King, and making himself odious with the Nobility. " By his insolency," says Melville, " he drove the Earl of Gowrie from Court, far against his Majesty's intention, who sent me for him to his house to bring him again to Court, which was for the time at Couper in Fyfe, where his Majesty agreed him and the Earl of Arran."

About this time might be seen in Cupar, and frequently in the company of Sir James Melville, a person of some political importance. It was Davison, one of England's chief secretaries, and for the present Elizabeth's accredited commissioner to the Scottish king. " His Majesty was for the time at Falkland," writes Melville, " and wrote for me, to be directed to ride and meet the said Davison, whom I was commanded to convoy to Coupar, there to remain till his Majesty had time to give him audience. Afterward I conveyed him to my own house," at Halhill. This secretary Davison is connected with a passage in history of tragical interest. When Queen Elizabeth, after assuming for a time an ill-counterfeited reluctance to do anything against Queen Mary, whom she had long detained a prisoner, at length consented to sign Mary's death warrant; she professed that this was meant only as a terror to Mary's partizans, and as a means of suppressing those dangerous plots which were ever and anon contrived for Mary's deliverance. The death sentence, after being signed, was committed to the keeping of Secretary Davison. The English Council knowing what was agreeable to Elizabeth, succeeded in gaining possession of the sentence, gave to poor Mary but the short warning of one night to prepare for death, and next day hurried her to execution. Elizabeth was enabled, from the circumstances of the transaction, to act the part which she had assigned to herself. She feigned great indignation, wrote to James a letter in which she cast the blame of his mother's death

on the Council; and committed Davison to the
Tower of London.

We shall close these notices of royal visits by
mentioniug the reception given by the town of
Cupar to Charles II. Through the impatient
loyalty of the Scots, and his own perfidiousness
in solemnly swearing to engagements which he
never meant to keep, Charles found himself
again, after years of exile, on Scottish ground.
On the 1st of July 1650, he landed at Dundee,
aud thence he passed to St Andrews. "'The 6th
of July, leaving St Andrews, he came to Couper,
where he gatt some desert to his foure-houres ;
the place where he satte downe to eate was the
Tolboothe. The towne had appointed Mr
Andro Andersone, Scholemaster ther for the
tyme, to give a musicke song or two whille he
was att tabell. Mr David Douglysse had a speach
to him at his entrie to the tounc. After this he
went to Falkland all night.   All this tyme the
most pairt of the gentelmen of the Shyre did goe
alongs with him."   Lamont.

A visit to the burying-ground will lead the
thoughts from these passing pageants to subjects
of graver concern. Built into the west wall is
an elaborately sculptured monument, which is

weather-worn and obliterated—for time buries tomb stones and effaces epitaphs. This monument is said to have been chiselled in Holland, and it covers the dust of the Rev. Mr William Scot, who was surpassed by few in his day "for piety, gravity, learning, solidity in judgment, and faithful adherence to the principles of the Scottish Church." By birth, Mr Scot was connected with the family of Balwearie, and this accounts for the ample patrimonial means he enjoyed. Both his words and deeds prove that while he had the liberal means, he also had the liberal heart, which deviseth liberal things. When far advanced in life, he gave this account of himself in one of the defences he was forced to make against the solicitations made to him by the Archbishop of St Andrews—"I have continued in my ministrie manie yeers, spending more goods nor ever I gained thereby." The spire which surmounts the church tower and the shadow of which falls daily on his tomb, is a conspicuous monument of his public-spiritedness and liberality, for it was erected at his sole expense.

Mr Scot's ministry extended from 1595 to 1642. The greater part of this period was embittered to the faithful ministers and people of

Scotland by the attempts of James VI. and
Charles I. to substitute Episcopacy in the place
of Presbytery.   In struggles and sufferings Mr
Scot was associated with Andrew and James
Melville, with Alexander Henderson and Samuel
Rutherford.   He had to confront the King at
Hampton Court, and at home to resist the insidious proposals of Archbishops Gladstanes and
Spottiswoode of St Andrews.   He united the
courteousness of the gentleman with the constancy of the martyr.   His courteousness and
his birth connexions probably saved him from
the extremity of trial to which many of his
brethren were subjected, while his constancy led
him firmly to say " before I embrace these things
that are urged, I am readie to undergo his Majesty's will" and to be silenced.

It is somewhat consolatory to know that before
his lengthened day of usefulness closed—a day the
opening and high noon of which were so gloomily
obscured—a brightening ray broke forth.   His
monumental inscription makes reference to the
altered and more hopeful state of ecclesiastical
matters at the time of his death.   This inscription, now illegible on the stone, has been preserved in a curious book, entitled " An Theatre

of Mortality, or a further Collection of Funeral
Inscriptions over Scotland, gathered by Robert
Monteith," and published in 1713. It is as
follows :—

Scotis resuscitatis, Anglis excitatis, renovato
faedere, reparata religione, prostrata hierarchia,
restituto presbyterio, succenturiantibus illustris-
simis prima nobilitate et ministerio bene meritis
in Ecclesiam, nunquam Satis memorandis, con-
firmante Caesare Britannico, adstipulantibus,
regni ordinibus, obiit placidissime in Do-
mino unus, qui nobis cunctando restituit rem,
Gulielmus Scotus, Ecclesiae Cuprensis pastor,
ex illustri et antiquissima familia Scoto-Balviri-
ana 84º anno aerae Christi M.DC.XLII A D. Cal.
Junii 13.

The indulgent reader will accept the following
translation as embodying the spirit of the inscription:—"When the hopes of Scotland were
revived, when England was excited to activity,
when the covenant was renewed, when religion was repaired, when Prelacy was overthrown, when Presbytery was restored, when
the most illustrious of the chief nobility und
of the most eminent ministers in the church,
who are worthy to be held in perpetual re-

membrance co-operated, when his British Majesty confirmed this happy change, and the estates of the kingdom concurred in it—then quietly died in the Lord, one who, by his counsel, helped to restore to us this happy condition of affairs, viz., William Scot, minister of the church at Cupar, descended from the illustrious and very old family of Scot of Balwearie, in the year of his age 84, and of the year of Christ 1642, 20th May."

Mr Scot was the writer of a work entitled, " Apologetical Narration of the State of the Kirk of Scotland."

Fronting the gate of entrance to the churchyard, and a little to the south of the church, the visitant may see an erect cleanly painted tombstone. The top of it is ensculptured with two heads facing each other, and an hand in the centre. This inscription records what the stone was erected to commemorate. " Here lies interred the heads of Lawrence Hay, and Andrew Pitulloch, who suffered martyrdom at Edinburgh, July 13, 1681, for adhering to the Word of God, and Scotland's covenanted work of reformation; and also one of the hands of David Hackston of Rathillet, who was most cruelly murdered at Edinburgh, July 30, 1680, for the same cause."

We have been unable to discover any particulars of the personal history of Lawrence Hay and Andrew Pitulloch, save that Andrew Pitulloch was a common land labourer. Even Wodrow, indefatigable in his inquiries, although he alludes to them, supplies us with no information. But their obscure names have found a place in " a cloud of witnesses for the royal prerogatives of Jesus Christ; or the last speeches and testimonies of those who have suffered for the truth in Scotland since the year 1680." As we are thus led to mention " the cloud of witnesses," we may add that there are two works which no other country in the world save Scotland could have furnished. The one of them is " Naphtali, or the wrestlings of the Church of Scotland for the Kingdom of Christ, together with the last speeches and testimonies of some who have died for the truth since 1660 to 1667." The other is the " cloud of witnesses extending from 1680 to 1688." An honest criticism will see in these works, extreme statements with which it cannot sympathize, but which from the state of the times and the suffering of the parties, it can easily explain, and modes of expression which will cause it to remember, that they were uttered nearly 200 years ago, and by persons in the hnmblest walks of life, but it will pass over these accidental abatements, and will rejoice in surveying that heroic array of noblemen and learned men, of lairds, of ploughmen, of artizans, of soldiers and sailors, who in the face of oppression, and torture, and death, firmly adhered to what they could intelligently defend as the canse of Christ.

The testimony of Lawrence Hay is dated " At the Iron House." In it be says—" O Sirs, give him much credit, for he hath disappointed me of my fears in that wherein I feared appearing before men, and helped me to stand before them, so that I had no terror or amazement, more than they had been the meanest of creatures. Although I can not say that I have fought the good fight, as that eminent Apostle said, yet I can say, praised be God, he hath given me tlle victory through Jesus Christ my Lord."

Andrew Pittulloch in his last speech " leaves his testimony against them that say we hold our principles of men, and that we die for pleasing men ; but it is not so, for I never thought that little of my life as to lay it down for the pleasing of any." "We hold our principles of none but of God and his Word." In another place he says—"My head shall be a standing witness against them and preach to them from Cupar Tolbooth." And so it did. The heads of both of these martyrs, and the hand of Hackston remained affixed to the Tolbooth, until the Revolution came and consigned the skeletonised remains to their present resting-place.

The Records of the Synod of Fife supply us with notes illustrative of the Presbytery of Cupar. Under the year 1657, the Presbytery is recommended to have a care of their Register, for the Register "is written with verie small writt, it is hardly legible, with base ink for the most pairt, and without a competent margine, and in verie many places interlyned." It would appear that the members of Presbytery were very fond of protesting, and that the business was not carried on in the most brotherly spirit. The Synod warns the Presbytery against this, and recommends the brethren to dine together after business, that the ill humours of the meeting may evaporate amid the fumes of Scotch broth and beef, and in the easy interchange of after-dinner pleasantries. There is much of the philosophy of common sense in the minute. Here is part of it—"That the Presbitrie will endeavour by all meanes ane peaciable carriage of thair affairs, and to shun by all means entring of protestations about matters of smaller importance, quhairin thair is difference of judgement amongst them. And that for intertainment of kyndliness amongst them, they will tak thair refreshment togidder the day of thair Presbyteriall meeting, after the dissolving thairof."

Before passing away from Cupar we subjoin what seems to us as the truest explanation of the oft-quoted local proverb, "*Them to Cupar maun to Cupar.*" The explanation has at least the merit of being classical, for it is founded on the following quotation from Buchanan's History of Scotland. " Inland, and almost in the centre of the county, lies Cupar, whither the rest of the Fifeans come for the administration of justice." Them to Cupar are wilful, litigious persons who will have their own way, and who, contrary to the persuasion of all their friends, are resolutely set on going to Cupar, and entering on a law suit. Such obstinate, wilful persons must just be left to themselves.

Leaving Cupar, and proceeding about a mile and a half westward, we arrive at CUPAR MUIR. A few scattered cottages, a free-stone quarry, and a busy pottery, mark out the place. But Cupar Muir and the fields around it shewed another sight 300 years ago. The Eden was not then, as it is now, an embanked river, having its course prescribed to it. It spread its straggling waters over the low fields, which are known as "the Wards," and which now yield luxuriant harvests. The mode of crossing it was by regular ferries, and the name of Ferrybank still remains to remind us of this.

On the morning of Wednesday, 13th June 1559, a thick mist enveloped the landscape. As the mist began to dissipate, two armies were dimly seen occupying the different sides of the river. The army of the Congregation occupied the sloping fields above the farm of Retreat, and the present village of Cupar Muir. On the opposite side the Queen Regent's forces stretched, (Pitscottie, who knew the locality, says,) as far as Tarvit Mill along by the foot of Scottarvit Hill, and up by the Garlie Bank.

It is needful shortly to explain the circumstances which arrayed these two contending armies against each other. John Knox had come to St Andrews on the invitation of the Earl of Argyle and Lord James Stewart. On his own responsibility, in the face of Archbishop Hamilton's threatening, and contrary to the opinion of his friends, he was left to preach on Sabbath, 10th June. His subject was, " Christ casting the buyers and sellers out of the Temple." As the result, the Provost, the bailies, and the " commonalitie of the town, for the most part," declared on behalf of the Reformation, and " agreed to remove all monuments of idolatry." That Sabbath evening the Archbishop stole out of St Andrews, and rode post to Falkland, where the Queen Regent was residing. His representations aroused the Queen. Proclamations were issued for the assembling of the army. Vengeance was vowed against Cupar and St Andrews. By the morning of the 13th, 3000 armed men were on the march, 2000 of them French soldiers, commanded by Gen. D'Oisel, and 1000 Scottish troops, led by James, Duke of Hamilton.

The Earl of Argyle and Lord James Stewart were apprized of the Queen's designs. With the view of opposing them the two young noblemen set out to Cupar, after despatching messengers throughout the country to make their danger known. On the night they arrived at Cupar they numbered only 100 horse and a company of foot soldiers from the coast. But by midday of Tuesday the muster rose to 3000 men. And still their friends arrive, Lord Ruthven from Perth, and the Earl of Rothes with 1000 spears. Dundee sends a regiment of its citizens with the martial Provost, Mr James Halyburton at their head ; and from St Andrews, and Cupar as being most directly in danger, new companies of fighting burghers continue to offer themselves. Knox says, " God did so multiply our numbers that it appeared as men had rained from the clouds."

The numbers that thus flocked to the uplifted standard of the congregation, and the mediation of Lord Lindsay prevented battle and bloodshed. When Lord Lindsay, after holding parley with the Lords of the Congregation, crossed the Eden, and conferred with the Duke of Hamilton and General D'Oisel, he found the Duke desirous to avoid fighting with his own conntrymen, and D'Oisel, although " choleric and hasty" was not so fool-hardy as to risk an engagement with an enemy which greatly outnumbered his troops, and whose hearts were roused to courage by the greatness of the interest they were called to defend. "He moved up to the hill-head of Tarvit with certane of his captanes, to spy and see if the congregation was sick ane number as my Lord Lindsay said they were." The sight satisfied him, and he referred the matter to Lindsay for settlement. On the *Houlet Hill*, on Garlie Bank, a treaty was drawn out and signed by the Duke and D'Oisel, whose signature has proved a standing puzzle to the antiquarian. The treaty was carried to the congregation. "This secured," says Knox, "we departed first, because we war thereto requeasted by the Duke, and so we returned to Couper, lauding and praising God for his mercie shewed, and thairafter everie man departed to his dwelling place."

Knox, who was present with the army at Cupar Muir, often alludes to the feelings of anxiety he experienced both there and in the other places, where the fate of the infant reformation seemed to be brought to the issue of a battle. "I have not forgotten what was the dolour and anguishe of my ain heart at Sanct Johnston, Couper Mure, and Edinburgh Crags."

On the evening of that memorable 13th of

June, Sir James Melville of Halhill had his first interview with the Queen Regent, and he tells us how the doings at Cupar Muir affected her. " I found the Queen Regent within the old tower of Falkland ; because that same day her army under Duke Hamilton and Monsieur D'Oisel was ranged in battel upon Cupar Moor, against the Lords of the Congregation ; at what time her Majesty made a hard complaint unto me of her disobedient subjects.   And even as I was speaking with her, the Duke and Monsieur D'Oisel returned from the said Muir without battel. Whereat the Queen was much offended, thinking they had lost a very fair occasion."

Parish of Ceres.

THE name of Ceres has no connection with Ceres, the Roman Goddess of corn and husbandry. Its name is derived from St Cyr, who was assigned to the parish as its patron saint in the days of Popery. The old method of spelling the name was Cyrus, Cyras, and Seres. Its present form may have been assumed to distinguish it from St Cyrus near Montrose.

An honr's walk conveys us from Cupar Muir
to Scottarvit Tower. There it stands like an old
warden, looking forth from its site, which commands at one glance the double straths of Eden
and of Ceres. From numberless points does this
venerable Tower meet the eye, awakening the
mind's curiosity and interest.

Above the door of the round turret, which ad-
mits to the battlement, there is a stone with the
subjoined inscription :—

These initials indicate the names of the members of the family in 1627, when the turret was
built. S I S is Sir John Scot, D A D is Dame
Anne Drummond of Hawthornden—Lady Scot,
and I S is John Scot their son.

The name of Sir John Scot is inseparably connected with Scottarvit. It was in this stable
tower that he wrote his "Staggering State of
Scottish Statesmen"—a small volume of 190
pages, in which he gives a short gossiping account of the chief officers of State in Scotland.
In these stone-arched rooms he enjoyed with the

bard of Hawthornden " the feast of reason and the flow of soul," and held discussions with the learned men of the day. From these small windows he surveyed the broad lands of Fife, and as he gazed, it may have been, that then the first conception of a Statistical account of Scotland suggested itself to his mind.

We wonder this fact has been lost sight of, and that the claims of Sir John Scot of Scottarvit as the first designer of a Statistical Account of Scotland have been allowed to lie dormant. The evidence is abundant and incontestible. We adduce a portion of it.

Baillie in his journal of the General Assembly 1643, has this short notice, "Sir John Scot's bill, for pressing Presbyteries to describe their own bounds, was not so much regarded."

The Records of the Synod of Fife are more copious and minute. At a provincial Assembly or Synod, holden at St Andrews, April 5, 1642, the following deliverance was given :—" Anent the bill given in by my Lord Scotstarvit to the Assemblie (Synod) complaining that, notwithstanding of ane act of the last General Assemblie holden at Edinburgh, appointing *all the severall Presbyteries of this kingdom to sett down the de-*

scriptions of their severall parishes, according to
the alphabet then given to the several Commissioners to deliver to their Presbyteries, and to
report the same to the Chancellerie, betwixt
and the first day of Januar last bypast, yet none
of the ministrie of this province, except nyne of
the Presbyterie of Kirkcaldie has obeyed the
samen : thereupon the Assemblie (Synod) consi-
dering the worthiness of the work, tending to the
honour of the nation, appointed the moderators
of the severall Presbyteries to urge the fulfilling
of the foresaid act, betwixt this and the first of
May next precelslie."

The term " Statistics," we are told, was first
introduced by Sir John Sinclair from the German into the English language. But here we
have in the above extracts, substantially the
idea and plan of the statistical account.

In thus claiming for Sir John Scot the honour
of having in 1642 designed and publicly announced the plan of the great National Work
which Sir John Sinclair executed in 1798, we
but state a fact. We leave intact the high and
merited praise which is due to Sir John Sinclair
for the energy, the perseverance, and labour with
which he completed a publication which extends

to twenty-one volumes—which involved the editor in seven years, seven months, and seven days of ceaseless labour and anxiety—which in those days of high postage called forth a correspondence of 20,000 letters—and which set in motion the minds and pens of 900 contributors. With this, as with many other great works, the conception and fulfilment wss separated by a wide interval. Broached by a Fife Baronet in 1642, it was taken up and carried out by a Caithness Baronet 158 years after.

How interesting would it be, to recover some of the accounts which were then prepared, for it is evident from the snbjoined minnte Oct. 1642, that considerable progress had been made. " Anent the reference concerning Sir John Scot, his bill, given in to the last Assemblie (Synod) requiring the description of the severall paroches within the province, the Assemblie (Synod) schewes they have done diligence, whilk hes bein delivered be some, and is in readiness to be delivered be others."

In addition to the projecting of the Statistical Account, Sir John Scot had much to do in promoting the Survey of Scotland by Timothy Pont, and in the preparation of the Maps of Scotland

by Sir Robert Gordon of Straloch, and his son
Mr James Gordon, minister of Rothiemay ; and
in the publishing of Arthur Johnstone's Edition
of the Scots Poets. He was appointed a Lord
of Session, under the title of Lord Scottarvit, and
filled the office of Director of Chancery.

The old man closes the pages of his " Staggering State," with this sad recital of the evil
fortunes, to which himself was subjected in the
unprincipled reign of Charles II. " Albeit he
was possessor of the said place of Chancery
above 40 years, and doer of great services to the
King and country, yet by the power and malice
of his enemies, he has been at last thrust out of
the said places in his old age, and likeways fined
in £500 sterling, and one altogether unskilled
placed to be Director. He had been a Counsellor since the year of God 1620, and for his
Majesty's and predecessor's service, been twenty-
four times in London—being 14,400 miles—and
twice in the Low Countries for printing the
Scots Poets, and the Atlas ; and paid to John
Bleau a hundred double pieces for printing the
poets."

One of Sir John Scot's descendants deserves
honourable mention for his steadfast adherence

to the Presbyterian Church of Scotland in the days of her persecution. It is George Scot of Pitlochie. For adhering to principle and for frequenting conventicles he was fined, imprisoned on the Bass, and ultimately driven to leave his native land. In 1685, the merciless fury of James VII.'s persecuting Government was at its height. Many of the best of Scotland's inhabitants despaired of deliverance, and were looking for refuge to the distant and uncivilised colonies. Amongst these were Pitlochie and his lady, and several of the Riggs of Athernie, to whom by marriage, the Scottarvit family were related.

Early in September 1655, a ship lay in Leith Roads, receiving its passengers and provisions for a distant voyage. This ship had been chartered by Pitlochie. The jails of Edinburgh, Glasgow, Stirling, and even the noisome dungeons of Dunnottar Castle had been opened, to allow those who had been imprisoned for worshipping God in the fields, to exchange imprisonment for perpetual banishment. Pitlochie's ship was warranted to receive such, and upwards of a hundred prisoners were escorted on board by a company of soldiers. The passengers had scarcely lost sight of the receding shores of Scotland, before a miserable fate overtook them. Putrid fever broke out in the ship. Three or four bodies were daily cast into the deep. "Upwards of sixty died," says Frazer of Brea, "whose blood will be found in the skirts of enemies, as really as if they had died at the Cross and Grassmarket of Edinburgh." In the list of those who died are the names of Pitlochie and his lady, of Lady Athernie, her son, and daughter. After enduring much severity from a cruel Captain, the survivors landed on the shores of New Jersey, and some returned again to Scotland, when three years afterwards, William Prince of Orange unfurled the banner of the Revolution on the shores of England.

Passing south-west through the nestling village of Craigrothie, whose name indicates that the hills surround it like a wheel, we arrive at the ruinous house of STRUTHERS. The little stream, which rises out of the adjoining morass, and runs eastward, may have supplied the place with the name of Struthers, for Sruth in Gaelic signifies a stream. Once this ivy-clad ruin had its prosperity. A noble park surrounded it; rows of stately beeches shaded it; turret and arch adorned it; and under its roof prince and peer have reposed.   In the time when Royalty kept frequent Court at Falkland, a Fife residence was an object of ambition to every courtier. With this view, Lord Lindsay of the Byres acquired Struthers. The family of Lindsay afterwards succeeded to the peerage of Crawford, and Struthers became their favourite residence.

Struthers is connected with " ane noble and valiant Squire, William Meldrum, umquhile Laird of Cliesh and Binns."

" Meek in chalmer like a lamb
But in the field ane campion."

This noble and valiant Squire, after performing feats of chivalry in France returned in great honour to Scotland. His company was much desired by Patrick Lord Lyndsay of the Byres, and with him Squire Meldrum took up his abode at Struthers, as his man of affairs. Under Lord Lindsay, he was made Sheriff-Depute of Fife.

Pitscottie relates how that betwixt Leith and Edinburgh Squire Meldrum was murderously attacked by Stirling of Keir, in consequence of his attachment to a lady in Strathearn, whom Keir wished to marry a relation of his own. Meldrum was " evil martyred, for his hochis war

cutted, and the knappis of his elbows war
strikin off, and was strikin through the bodie, so
thair was no sign of lyff in him. Yitt be the
mightie power of God, he eschapped the death,
and leived fyftie yeirs thairafter."

Squire Meldrum was a great favourite in the
cottages of the poor, and at the tables of the rich.
He had the good fortune to become the frequent
companion of Sir David Lindsay, who took a
great liking to him, and who wrote his life as a
ballad of romance, which was for long in the
months of many. It was at Struthers that Squire
Meldrum died.

> " Adew, my Lords ! I may na langer tarrie—
>   My Lord Lindsay, adew above all other ;
> I pray to God and to the Virgin Marie
>   With your Lady to live lang in the Struther."

From 1653, during the time of the Commonwealth, " the Struthers" seems to have been
occupied by an English force which was stationed
there, that in co-operation with other English
troops at Burntisland and Falkland, they might
hold Fife subject to Cromwell.

In the life of Robert Blair we are told that
the Presbytery of Cupar were molested by the
leaguers at Struthers. In 1653, two of the offi-

cers at the Struthers took up their names, and commanded them to disperse, and not to meet again. That day Mr Blair sat with the Presbytery of Cupar as correspondent from the Presbytery of St Andrews. He spoke freely and boldly, yet prudently, to the English officers. The next day some few of the Presbytery of Cupar convened. After prayer and adjourning of their meeting, one of their number, Mr Wm. Row, being found on the street, was carried up to their camp at the Strnthers, but presently dismissed. Thereafter they convened in their Presbyterial meetings and were not troubled.

Two names stand out from the noble line of Crawford, and invest Struthers with an honourable interest. The Restoration of 1660 furnishes the one. The Revolution of 1688 supplies the other. In contemplating their lives we are entertained with the high spectacle of men struggling in unsettling times to maintain their uprightness.

The first of these was John, 17th Earl of Crawford Lindsay. A firm Presbyterian, he was also an inflexible supporter of Charles II. It was he who bore the sceptre on January 1st, 1651, when Charles II. was crowned at Scone, putting it into the King's hands with these weighty words which in every particular Charles' whole reign contradicted. " Sire, receive this sceptre, the sign of the royal honour of the kingdom, that you may govern yourself aright, and defend all Christian people committed by God to your charge, punishing the wicked and protecting the just."

On 15th February we found Earl Crawford entertaining Charles II. at " the Struthers," where he remained until Monday 17th—" Mr Duncan and the minister of the Parish preaching on the Sabbath in the hall of 'the Struthers.' " Before 1651 closed, Crawford was surprised by Cromwell's soldiers, carried to the Tower of London, and there kept a prisoner for nine years because of his attachment to the King. With the Restoration in 1660 Crawford was set at liberty and reinstated in the offices of High Treasurer and President of the Council. His return to Scotland was hailed with every demonstration of gladness. But this did not last long. Archbishop Sharpe was bent on his removal from office and from Court. Sharpe enforced it on the King that he was not secure, so long as any who supported the Covenant were about him, and urged him to try Crawford whether he would renounce the Covenant. The King did so, and found Crawford resolute. "No," said he, "I have endured much for your Majesty, and I am resolved to remain loyal, but to renounce the Covenant is what I caunot do with a good con- science." The consequence was that he laid down his Treasurership, retained his integrity, and retired to Struthers.

On his way thither, in the street of Kirkcaldy, he met Mr Robert Blair who had been banished from St Andrews, and conversed with him. This was reported to Sharpe. Mr Blair was subjected to closer confinement in the Parish of Aberdour, and the Earl was the more narrowly watched. From 1663 to the year of his death he lived quietly at Struthers, receiving outed ministers to the hospitalities of his house, and using his influence to get for them as much freedom as could be extorted from the tender mercies of Persecutors.

He died in 1678, aged 81. Samuel Ruther- ford dedicated to this Earl of Crawford, "A peaceable and temperate Plea for Paul's Presby- tery in Scotland," published in 1642. To him also he wrote one of his Aberdeen letters. The moral of the life which the Earl deliberately chose, is sufficiently indicated in the following sentences. " O my dear Lord, consider that our Master, eternity, and judgment, and the last reckoning will be upon us in the twinkling of an eye. There will shortly be a proclamation by One standing in the clouds that prisons, confinements, forfeitures of nobles, wrath of kings, hazard of lands, houses and name for Christ shall be no more. At the day of Christ, truth shall be truth and not treason."

The Countess of Crawford failed not her Lord in any thing that was good. Robert Blair, mentioning the Countess on his death-bed, said of her, " My Lady Crawford set her alone, set her alone among women."

His son William succeeded him in the peerage as Eighteenth Earl, and inherited his decided principles as a Presbyterian, his high feelings as a Christian, and his patient endurance of persecution for conscience' sake. One little sentence in a letter of his preserved by Wodrow discovers the honest nature of the man, and the life-long nobility of principle which guided him. " I wish," he writes, " to be confirmed in what is real duty, without the least regard to ease and shifting of suffering."

In another letter he says, " As I never had a sixpence from my father besides what was employed in my education, so I divested myself of all I had in any other title for the payment of his debt, that the memory of so good a man and so kind a father might not suffer by the neglect of a son that owed all things to him in gratitude as well as duty."   Such a display of home piety in the requiting of parents is not very common in any rank of life.

Another extract shews the straits to which this peer of the realm was reduced in the days of persecution for his adherence to principle. " The means of my subsistence," he writes from Struthers in 1685, " even in my own country, are so inconsiderable that I have in the midst of my friends hardly any redundancy above the meanest of food and raiment."

These are marks of solid worth which may be known and read of all men, yet Macaulay, drawing this nobleman's character upwards of 160 years after he has been in his grave, is pleased to stigmatize him as a hypocitical religionist.

The Earl's intelligent, patriotic, and consistent

preference of Presbyterianism has exposed him to the unjust censures of Bishop Burnet, and other Episcopalian writers. Yet the body of evidence extant has only to be honestly examined to satisfy any one how great was the forbearance and moderation of the Earl in the settling of Scottish ecclesiastical affairs at the Revolution. We subjoin a few extracts from letters written at the time.

State of feeling in Scotland regarding Episcopacy and Presbytery.—"This is beyond all doubt to me, there is not a member in the house, yea, I may say, nor subject in the nation, who are thoroughly for King William's interest, who are not disgusted at prelacie and wishes Presbyterie were established in its puritie."

Disloyalty of the Episcopal Clergy to King William.—"Most of them have expressly prayed against our King (William), and for the late King (James VII.), and have hounded out their people to rise in arms."

Effect of the maintaining of Episcopacy.—"I would reckon Scotland as effectually lost as Ireland once seemed to be."

Lenity of the Earl's procedure to the Episcopal Clergy.—"We have been tender in our examinations and sentences as if we had been judging men for their lives." "I shall once more repeat, what I have oft said on this subject, that no Episcopal man, since the late happy revolution, whether laic or of the clergy, hath suffered by the Council upon the account of his opinion of church matters, but allenarly (solely) for their disowning the civil authority, and setting up for a cross interest."

Numberless additional extracts to the same effect might be given, but enough has been produced. Presbyterianism had just emerged from 28 years of bitter persecution waged in the interests of Episcopacy, during which time 18,000 of the choicest of Scotland's inhabitants had suffered cruel deaths, prolonged imprisonment, enforced exile, and ruinous fines. Yet when the blessed Revolution of 1688 came restoring power to Presbyterianism, Presbyterianism retaliated not. By the grace of God her annals are unstained with blood and violence.

Notwithstanding the incessant reproaches of party writers, William Earl of Crawford was deservedly entitled by his countrymen "the great and the good Earl." After using his influence to obtain for the Church of Scotland as secure a settlement as he could, he died in 1698, full of years and honour.

Here is a goodly quarto of 400 pages, with all the pomp of large type, a broad margin, and adorned frontispiece. It contains " Memoirs of the life of the late Right Honourable John Lindesay, Earl of Crawford and Lindesay, Lord Lindesay of Glenesk, and Lord Lyndesay of the Byres, one of the sixteen Peers of Scotland, Lieutenant-General of his Majesty's Forces, and Colonel of the North British Grey Dragoons, by Richard Rolt, author of the ' History of the late War.' 1753." It is a somewhat diffuse and inflated account of a brave soldier and distinguished general. We have an account of his Lordship from 1705, when he was committed to the care of an " old governante at the family seat at Struthers, in Fifeshire," onward during his studies at Glasgow University, where he acted as the champion of his fellow collegians, heading them in their encounters with the citizens ; in making enterprises on fruit gardens ; and in redressing their affronts ; and throughout the various campaigns in which a chivalrous love of arms led him to engage. His first service was as a volunteer under Prince Eugene, in 1733, when Austria resisted the progress of French power in Germany. In 1738, Lord Crawford joined the Russian army under the famed Count Munich, and fought against the Turks in several battles, in those Principalities with which recent warfare has familiarised us. At the battle of Grotska in 1739, he was engaged with the Austrian army against the Turks. In this battle he had his favourite Spanish steed shot under him, and his thigh bone splintered with a ball. Despite of this wound, which invalided him for a year, and lamed him for life, he lost not his martial ardour. At the battle of Dettingen, 1743, where for the last time a King of Great Britain (George II.) appeared in fight, Lord Crawford bravely commanded a detachment. He skilfully conducted the retreat at Fontenoy in 1745. In the rebellion of 1746, he commanded the Hessian troops which guarded the important passes to the Lowlands at Stirling and ·Perth, while the Duke of Cumberland routed the rebels at Culloden. Again, we find him in the Netherlands taking part in marches and skirmishes until the peace of Aix-la-Chapelle, 1748, terminated the war.

The Earl of Crawford had married, in 1747, a daughter of the Duke of Athole, but before the year had closed she died of fever. Nor was the Earl long of following her. The wound he had received at Grotzka carried death with it. It broke out anew, and after causing him much torment it terminated his life in London, 25th December 1749, at the age of 47.

His burial and that of his Countess connect them both with Ceres. The visitor of the churchyard may see two coronetted coffins with faded crimson and soiled mountings in "the desolate place," which the Crawfords had builded for themselves. These contain the mortal remains of this Lord and Lady Crawford.

Southward and eastward from Struthers, is seen the broken outline of the ruins of CRAIGHALL. The name is taken from the site, for Craighall stands on the ridge of a craig, which overlooks a small ravine.

Honoured in the lists of Scottish lawyers ever be the name of Sir Thomas Hope, who, upwards of 200 years ago, possessed this estate of Craighall. Seldom has there been a nobler entrance on professional life than his.

Fourteen ministers having, in 1606, held a

General Assembly at Aberdeen, in defence of the freedom of the Church, against the despotic interference of King James, were thrown into different prisons. Six of them, four of whom belonged to Fife,* were incarcerated in Blackness. A day was appointed for their trial at Linlithgow. When the day arrived, in consequence of the strong feeling expressed against them by the king, no lawyer could be found to undertake their defence. Even the Church's paid procurator, Mr Thomas Craig, awed by the fear of the king's wrath, forgot his duty, and declined to advocate the case. When the ministers were thus deserted, two youthful advocates bravely stepped forward, and offered to conduct the defence. These young advocates were Mr Thomas Hope, and Mr Thomas Gray. For two hours did Mr Hope stoutly maintain the cause of the empannelled ministers, against the charges of Sir Thomas Hamilton, the Lord Advocate. His advocacy, powerful though it was felt to be, failed in obtaining justice to his clients, for they were

---

* The names of the six are worthy of remembrance ; they were Mr James Forbes of Alford, Mr John Welsh of Ayr, Mr Alexander Strachan of Creich, Mr John Sharp of Kilmany, Mr Robert Durie of Anstruther, and Mr Andrew Duncan of Crail.

all banished; but it succeeded in attracting
notice to himself. Calderwood says, "his plead-
ing that day procured him great estimation and
manie clients; and his credit has ever growne
sen syne."

So great did his credit grow, that in 1626,
Charles I. made him king's advocate. Bishop
Burnet mentions him in these terms,—"Sir
Thomas Hope, a subtle lawyer, though in all
respects he was a zealous Puritan, was made the
king's advocate." But the favour of the court
was powerless in causing this high principled
man to swerve from his principles. Throughout the difficulties of that testing time, he remained the firm friend of the Presbyterian
Church. He felt that the true interests of the
Crown can never be separated from the liberties
of the nation and the rights of the Church. When
consulted as a crown lawyer, regarding the introduction of Episcopacy and a Liturgy, he can-
didly declared his opinion in favour of the Presbyterian Church, and did not hesitate to express
his sympathy with her. "We are informed,"
writes Baillie, in 1637, "that the best lawyers,
Hope, Nicolson, and Stewart, being consulted by
the king, declared all our by past proceedings

to be legal," Before the famous Glasgow As- sembly of 1638, the Marquis of Hamilton the Commissioner, laboured hard at the Conncil table, to have a resolntion passed, that in conformity with the king's will a modified Episcopacy should not be questioned in the approaching Assembly. Many of the Conncil went into this, bnt Sir Thomas Hope, then Lord Advocate, like a patriotic Presbyterian, stontly resisted it, and got the resolution defeated. " For this contra- diction, adds Baillie, " the advocate was per- fumed by the Commissioner with many unkind words." In conseqnence of this unbending firm- ness, "the Advocate's service was no more re- quired by the Commissioner, and Sir Lewis Stewart was used in his room." In 1643 King Charles addressed his commission "to onr trusty and well-beloved Sir Thomas Hope, of Craig- hall," and Sir Thomas sat as Lord High Com- missioner in the General Assembly of that year.

By reason of his great practice at the bar, Sir Thomas Hope acquired a large fortune. He be- came proprietor by purchase of the lands of Granton in Mid-Lothian, of Prestongrange in East Lothian, of Kerse near Grangemouth, of

Merton in the Merse, and of Craighall and its barony in Fife.

Most of the older families in Scotland, whether in the noble rank of Lords, or in the honourable rank of Lairds, can read the names of their ancestors in the lists of those who contended with national spirit for the interests of the Presbyterian Church. The families of Hope and Hopetoun may be proud to claim as their founder this distinguished lawyer and true-hearted Presbyterian Sir Thomas Hope. His death took place in 1646.

Two of his sons, at the time of his death, sat as Lords of Session. One of them bore the title of Lord Craighall, and the other that of Lord Hopetoun.

Returning to the village of Ceres, we enter it by a narrow bridge, by which, tradition says, the men of Ceres marched out to join King Robert the Bruce on the eventful field of Bannockburn, and along which the lumbering coach of Archbishop Sharpe rumbled on that fatal day when he met his death on Magus Muir.

Ceres has in its list of ministers many names of historical celebrity.

Mr Patrick Constan or Adamson was the first minister after the Reformation, having been ordained in 1563. It was he who made the threefold distinction of Bishop. " My Lord Bishop" was a title essentially Popish. "My Lord's Bishop" was the *tulchan* Bishop who held the title, that my Lord might draw the fruits of the benefice. " The Lord's Bishop" was the true minister of the Gospel. Yet did Mr Patrick forget his own distinctions. He dissembled with his brethren, and in 1576 " griped the Bishopric of St Andrews." But, as his own published recantation shews, his worldly pomp and pre-eminence" afforded him but small consolation. He was relieved in extreme poverty by the very brethren whose cause he had betrayed, and died in 1577 in great dolour.

Mr Thomas Buchanan was ordained 1578, and died 1599. He was cousin to the learned George Buchanan. James Melville relates an affecting interview which brings the two cousins together. " That September," he writes, "in time of vacans, my uncle, Mr Andrew, Mr Thomas Buchanan, and I, hearing that Mr George Buchanan was weak, and his historie under the press, past ower to Edinbruche annes errand, to visit

him and sie the wark. When we came to his
chalmer, we fand him sitting in his chair, teaching his young man that servit him to spell *a*, *b*,
ab; e, b, eb, &c." After salutation, Mr Andrew
says, ' I sie, Sir, ye are nocht idle.' ' Better
this,' quoth he, ' nor stealing sheep, or sitting
idle, quhilk is as ill.' Thereafter he showed us
the Epistle Dedicatorie to the King; the quhilk,
when Mr Andrew had read, he tauld him that it
was obscure in some places, and wanted certean
words to perfect the sentence. Says he ' I may
do nae mair for thinking on another mater.'
' What is that?' says Mr Andrew. ' To die,'
quoth he, ' but I leave that and manie ma
things fur you to helpe.'

  " We went from him to the printer's work-
house, whom we fund at a place, quhilk might
be an occasion of steying the haill wark, anent
the burial of David Rizzio. Therefore, steying
the printer, we cam to Mr George and fund him
bedfast by (contrary to) his custome, and asking him how he did? ' Even going the way of
weelfare,' says he. Mr Thomas, his cusin,
shows him of the hardnes of that part of his
storie, that the king wuld be offendit with it, and
it might stey all the wark. ' Tell me, man,'

says he, 'giff I have tauld the truth.' 'Yes,'
says Mr Thomas, 'I think sae.' 'I will byd
his fead (feud) and all his kins then,' quoth he,
'pray, pray to God for me and let him direct
all.' Sae bi the printing of his historie was
endit, that maist lerned, wyse, and godlie man
endit this mortal life."

Although Mr Thomas differed in his views of
some college transactions with Mr Andrew Melville, one of the greatest faults in the estimation of James Melville, James speaks of him in
the following terms of high respect :—"This was
Mr Thomas Buchanan, first schulemaister in
Stirling, and then Provost of Kirkheugh in St
Andrews, and minister of Syres, a man of notable gifts of learning, naturall wit, and uprightness in the cause of the Kirk against the Bishops,
but had his awin imperfections, viz., of extream
partiality in the cause of his friends, which maid
him to alter (differ) with Mr Andrew."

Another distinguished minister of Ceres, who
was also a sufferer in the kingdom and patience
of Jesus Christ, was Mr William Row. He
was younger son of Mr John Row of Carnock,
and son-in-law to the well-known Mr Robert
Blair of St Andrews. In 1607 he acted as mo-

derator of the Synod of Perth.   In consequence
of his acting in this capacity against the views of
Sir David Murray, Lord of Scoue, who threatened
and brawled, and insisted to have Mr Alexander Lindsay, Bishop of Dunkeld, chosen as
constant moderator, Mr Row was put to the
horn, and forced to lurk in concealment here
and there among his friends.   In 1608 he is
named in a petition of the General Assembly as
one of the "banished and confined ministers."
Under 1665, April 4, Lamont writes in his
diary, "The diocesian Synod satt att St Andrews,
where Mr Sharpe, the Archbishop, himself was
Moderator, and did preach that day.   Those
ministers of the Presbyterie of St Andrews that
were suspended this tyme twelve months, wer
now deposed, with Mr William Row, minister of
Cyres.

"April 21 and 22.—The sentence of deposition
was intimatt to the fornamed persons, with this
provision, if they keiped not the next Presbyterie day, and acknowledged their fawlt, and
were submissive to the present ecclesiastick government, they sould remove their abode from
ther respective congregations."

Mr Row outlived the persecuting times of

Charles II. and James VII., and was restored to the church and parish of Ceres in 1689. He was one of sixty ministers whom, out of 350 ejected to make way for Prelacy, the Revolution still found alive, and to whom the rule of the Church was re-entrusted. Mr Row died in 1698.

Mr Thomas Halyburton succeeded Mr Row as minister of Ceres in 1700. The memoirs of his life have long been a cottage book in Scotland, and a common engraving of him has made us familiar with the light gracefulness and vivacity of his appearance. After labouring three years in Ceres, he recorded this as what he found, " that of 300 or 400 persons, there were not above 40 who had not at one time or other been more or less awakened by the word. All who were thus convinced did declare that any awakenings ever they had were either under the preachers in the fields, or since the Revolution. There was never one that said he was touched by the Curates." In 1710, Mr Halyburton was translated from Ceres to St Mary's College, St Andrews, as Professor of Divinity. His health, never robust, with difficulty carried him through the duties of but one session. To a student who visited him in his last illness, he said, "If I had you lads all about me now, I would give you a lesson of divinity.   By the power of that grace revealed in those truths I taught you, here I lie pained without pain, without strength yet strong. I think it would not be a lost session this though you were all here."   Mr Halyburton died in the morning of the 23d September 1712, aged 38. "What a loss," says a contemporary writer, "may we justly reckon the death of this great little man to the poor wrestling Church of Scotland."

Leaving Ceres and passing eastwards we arrive at PITSCOTTIE. Pitscottie means the little hollow. It stands at the entrance to Dura Den, and as the rising ground on two sides appear to meet, when seen from the west, the name is descriptive of the place.   On the little table land which is at present occupied by the modern steading of Pitscottie farm, there stood three centuries ago a " narrow countrie hous covered with strae and ried."   In this house there lived " in guid civilitie," Robert Lindsay of Pitscottie, the author of "The Chronicles of Scotland." As we look on the place of his habitation, imagination readily enters into the daily life of the old chronicler as he "sought, gathered, collected, and wrote" the notable acts which he records. Going one day to Struthers to gather information from Lord Lindsay, and another to St Andrews to Mr John Mayor, Doctor of Theology, or away to Sir William Bruce of Earlshall, where he met Sir Andrew Wood of Largo, Sir David Lindsay of the Mount, Andrew Fernie of that Ilk, ane nobleman of recent memory, and Sir William Scott of Balwirie, and after having been "instructed and learned and laitly informed by thir authors," coming home to Pitscottie like a bee laden with its sweet burden.   Here it was in this garden, along these fields, and by the side of that rippling stream that he sauntered, ruminating on what he had gathered, and reducing it to form in the pages of his history.   There are some arrogant critics who have written disparagingly of " the Chronicles of Scotland," but let any one begin the perusal, and soon will he confess to a fascination, which binds him to the quaint and graphic narration, and which carries him unweariedly to the end.   It is matter of regret that so little is known of the personal history of old Pitscottie.

PITSCOTTIE MUIR is named in a decreet against

some onted ministers in 1671 ; as a place where field-preachings were held ; and in many after acts against conventicles we find it specified.

Taking the road which passes Pitscottie Farm, and leads to Cnpar, we come about half-a-mile on to the decaying homstead of a small farm. That is DURAQUAIR, or as it is popnlarly.called, Little Dnra. On the opposite side of the road, where a thriving wood climbs the hill, there was held a celebrated conventicle in 1674, at which Mr John Welsh of Irongray preached. Howie, the author of the Scots Worthies, knew of Duraquair, and thns in his little garden amid the moorlands of Lochgoin he writes regarding it :—
" Among Mr Welsh's converts in Fife was the Countess of Crawford. She was danghter to the Earl of Annandale, and sister to the Duke of Hamilton. This took place at Dnraquair, near Cnpar, and hard by her own house, where the power of God was manifested, to the checkiug the conscience and awakening the hearts of many. On that occasion there were abont 8000 persons present, and the Honourable Lady declared she was constrained to close with the offer then made. This impression was lasting, and evinced by mnch fruit of piety, which shone

forth in all her walk as a Christian."   We are elsewhere told that "Mr Blackadder had this information from herself, who told him with great majesty and seriousness in presence of her lord."

On the day when Mr Welsh preached at Duraquair, Adam Masterton, younger of Grange, was scouring the country with a party of Life Guards.   After disturbing a field-preaching by Mr Wellwood in the Lomond Hill, young Grange marched straight to Duraquair; " but the people had got notice and hurried Mr Welsh away. A great body of them escorted him as far as Largo, where they hired a boat. Mr Welsh, with his wife and some others, landed safely under night in Aberlady Bay, and got to his own house in Edinburgh."

Parish of Kemback.

Let us retrace our steps to Pitscottie, that we may enjoy entire the walk through Dura Den. As we approach Pitscottie, a full view is got of the house of BLEBO, standing amid the woods and swelling protuberances of its own hill. On the walls of this house hang two portraits of ecclesiastical interest. The one is a painting of Cardinal Beaton in his flaming scarlet. The other is a likeness of Archbishop Sharpe, taken by his own daughter.

This DURA DEN meets the traveller like a delightful episode amid common-place things. It is a vale of beauty, doubly sweet because unexpected, amid red-roofed villages, and railway lines, and toil-wrought fields. He who has geological tastes may here gratify them to the full bent, in reading the lessons which the rocks supply ; and he who wants these tastes, need not feel the want, for he can let his senses luxuriate amid the sweet sound of falling waters and singing birds, and the sight of wild flowers growing in sheltered nooks, and the scent and cool shade of overhanging woods, and "the breath of Heaven, fresh blowing, pure and sweet."

But there are few favoured spots where the lover of the picturesque does not meet with some abatements to his pleasure. Here are many-storied mills, and rows of low-roofed cottages, showing that this sweet stream, formed to sing its own songs in its own valley, is doomed to the servile toil of driving spinning jennies. It is as if a poet were chained to a counting-room desk, and his pen, whose numbers had delighted many, was employed all day in registering bales of cotton and yarn. Had it been the old meal mill with its dark wheel standing out against its white powdered walls, and turning its grindstones " to the water's dash and din," it might, like Oliver Basselins in the valley of the Vire, have symbolised with the landscape.

In the valley of the Vire,
Still is seen an ancient mill,
With its gables quaint and queer,
And beneath the window sill
On the stone
These words alone,
Oliver Basselins lived here.

By the time we had settled this question of taste, or to keep pace with the times, and use the phrase of the day, this aesthetic point, we find ourselves opposite to Kemback House. This reminds us that the stream gives to the Den through which it flows the name of Dura. Dur in Gaelic, like *hudor* in Greek, means water. Dura Den is the den of the water. It also bears the name of the Kem. Thus it is able to divide its favours on both sides with impartiality—giving to the property on the left bank the designa-

tion of Dura, and to the property on the right
that of Kemback.

KEMBACK, reposing under the shadows of the
hill, has its reminiscences of the past to tell.
In the fifteenth century it belonged to a cadet of
the house of Graham. The family of Graham
was conspicuous in assassinating at Perth, the
first and noblest and best beloved of the James's
—one of the foremost in his dominions as
scholar, poet, and musician. The ballad lines
impale the principal of the name who took a
chief part in that bloody deed—

> " Robert Graham,
> Wha kill'd our king,
> God gie him shame."

The laird of Kemback was present and joined in
the murder.

This property afterwards passed into possession of a family of the name of Schives, and was
long held by them. Lamont, nnder date 1655,
November 21, thus relates the melancholy end
of one of the proprietors :—" Mr Jhone Sives,
laird of Kembocke, in Fyfe, was found dead att
the water syde of Eden, in the place called the
Haugh, near to Edrie's lodging. The most pairt
of the day before, he was drinking ale and

strong waters at George Trumbell's house in Cupar, near the Tolbooth, with Sir George Moresone, laird of Dairsie, Achannachie, the laird of Mount, and divers others. He was a great oposer of the Presbyterie of St Andrews anent the planting of Kembo Kirk with a minister."

There is a local tradition, that after the year 1662, a member of the family of Schives suffered persecution for non-conformity. He was obliged to leave the house, and to hide himself in a cave in the neighbourhood. His place of concealment was discovered by tracing in the snow the footsteps of a sister who carried food to him.

In 1667 the estates of Kemback became the property of the family to whom at present it belongs. Lamont thus journalizes—"Mr John Makgill, late minister of Coupar in Fyffe, and now Dr Makgill, a mediciner, bought the lands of Kemback in Fyffe, from the Lady Kemboke surnamed Sivves. It stood him about twenty-five thousand merkes Scots money, and is estimatte to be about 7 chalders of victuall, and seven hundred merkes of money yearly—14 in all ; beside the casualities, which are a libertie of

salmond fishing in a pairt of Eden water, 80 of
sheeps grasse on the hill to goe with the tennants
flocks, 2 horse grasse, and 2 kay to be keeped
with the tennant, both summer and winter, 15
dissone of Kean fowls," &c.

This Mr John Makgill was admitted minister
of Dunbog in 1646, and was translated to Cupar
in 1654. In 1662 he was outed because " he
would not submit to Episcopal Government."
In 1663 he went to France, studied medicine,
and graduated as Doctor. " He came home,"
says Lamont, " in a grey sute, but went abroad
in black apparrell." His profession was changed,
but not his principles. To these he nobly adhered, and suffered for them once and again in
fines and penalties.

Parish of Dairsie.

At the northern extremity of the Den are seen
the Church and ruined Castle of Dairsie. They
stand upon a wooded bank, the base of which is
swept by the winding Eden.

The estate of Dairsie was acquired by David
Leirmonth, of Clatto, in 1520. His son, Sir

James Leirmonth, of Balcomy and Dairsie, acted a prominent part in the eventful times of the dawning Reformation.   He was Master of the Household in the reign of James V., and was one of the commissioners sent to treat with Henry VIII. regarding the marriage of Edward VI. and the infant Mary of Scotland.   He was Provost of St Andrews from 1532 to 1547, and was thus officially in the focus of the great events which were then adoing.   He was a favourer of the Reformation, and this secured for him the hatred of Cardinal. Beaton.   His name was in the doomed roll of noblemen and gentlemen which was presented to James V. by the Cardinal and Prelates in 1542.   Foiled in this attempt, the rage of the Cardinal still dogged Sir James, and it was found, after the Cardinal had himself been put to death, in May 1546, that a plot had been prepared by him whereby Sir John Melville of Raith, Kirkcaldy, laird of Grange, Normand Lesley, and Sir James Leirmonth of Dairsie, were "either to have been slain, or else taen, and after to have been used at the Cardinal's pleasure."

Sir James died peacefully in 1547.

This old castle was very much rebuilt by Arch-

bishop Spottiswoode, and within it he fonnd a
calm retreat from the nngracious service he had
nndertaken of opposing his conntry's faith, that
he might enjoy the Conrt smiles of James VI.
and his son Charles. Born the son of an eminent Presbyterian minister, Archbishop Spottiswoode set himself to destroy what his father
had painfully and prayerfully built up, and the
Chnrch of Scotland, galled by his Episcopal in-
novations and the severities with which they
were enforced, like the wonnded eagle, saw that
the arrow which had pierced her was feathered
with a pinion nursed in her own side. But his
efforts to establish Episcopacy against a nation's
conscience, though permitted for a time to suc-
ceed, proved at last hopelessly ineffectnal. From
before 1609, Bishop Spottiswoode had laboured
hard to supersede Presbytery, but when he saw
the reaction of national feeling in the memorable
year 1638, he fled to London. His exclamation
was, " Now, all that we have been doing these
thirty years is undone." He became dejected in
spirit, and died 22d November 1639.

In this Castle of Dairsie, tradition says that
he prepared his history.

The adjoining church was erected by Archbishop Spottiswoode in 1622. As it was intended both as a Parish Church and Archepiscopal Chapel, its outward architecture and internal upfitting were meant to embody all those devices and sermons in stone and wood in which Puseyism delights. Every one admires the church. It is beautiful for situation. Its massive Gothic windows and outward proportions and many-sided tower make the building not unfit for the site.

When we see the commotion which even in this nineteenth century the insidious introduction of the mummeries of Puseyism into some of the Episcopalian congregations in England awakens, we need not feel surprised at the zeal which the Presbyterian Church Courts manifested 200 years ago, to have this old Church of Dairsie cleared of all " superstitious monuments and kirk burial." In the records of the Synod of Fife there are various entries on this subject anent the Kirk of Dairsie. It was found that throughout this Church, " crosiar staffes were emblazoned not as a sign or cognizance common in the arms of the family of Spottiswoode, but merely a sign of his degree hierarchical." Further it was found that there was " a glorious partition wall with a degree ascending thereto, dividing the body of the kirk frae their qnoir, as it is ordinarily called in Papistrie, and among them that follow Papists." All this was ordered to be removed, and that "nothing remains but shoulder height to be for backs of seats adjoining thereto." Kirk burial was discharged altogether.

The bridge which crosses the Eden here was built by Archbishop Spottiswoode to facilitate his communication with St Andrews.

We shall close these sketches with the mention of one whose name is still affectionately remembered in this parish. Dr Robert Macculloch, ordained in 1771, fulfilled here the long ministry of fifty years and upwards. He was the son of the Rev. William Macculloch, whose labours were so signally owned at Cambuslang in 1742. Full of the impressions which the great work in his native parish had left behind, he came to Dairsie, and there he laboured on abundantly, helped and cheered by many a valued visit at communion and other seasons, of such men as Dr Erskine, Dr Webster, Mr M'Laren, Dr Gillies, and Dr Balfour. His manners were stern; his love of order was excessive. He could not have slept if he knew that his hat was not in its right place. His adherence to time was most rigid.

Every thing must go on with the regularity of clock-work. Those who knew him tell, as most characteristic of him, that some years before his death he had his coffin provided, and this he did, not as Charles V., that he might lay himself down in it and look forth on the vanity of earthly things, but simply that he might protect his family against the hazard of being overcharged at his death, as he thought he himself had been at the funeral of some of his family.

He published lectures on the Prophecies of Isaiah, in four sturdy volumes. They are chiefly valuable as containing the spirit and substance of Vitringa's commentary. But his greatest works, and they are still following him, were not " with ink and pen," but by the living voice on the hearts of men. We have heard aged persons particularise with emotion some of his ministrations. Many quiet undemonstrative cottagers will silently respond to this reference, and those who have the best means and who are most capable of judging, are forward to acknowledge how much of what is good in the district is to be traced to the prolonged and owned ministry of Dr Macculloch.

END OF PART II.

PART III.

Falkland, Kettle, and Leslie.

Falkland.

~~~~~~~~~

CHAPTER I.

A French Author has the following reflection : —" I confess it would be impossible for me to reside, or even to travel with pleasure, in any country where there were neither archives nor antiquities. That which gives interest and beauty to things is the trace of man having passed there, lived there, suffered there." To any one with the tastes of this author, Falkland will be full of interest. Everything is here mossed over with antiquity. Everything is suggestive of the actions and events of former times.

It is the Palace, uplifting its grey walls and roof in the old burgh, which lends all its importance and attraction to the place. What distin-
~~~~~~~~~

guished persons has that Palace received within its portals! What momentous consultations have been held within its halls! Events which, in their issues, have involved the interests of nations and of churches, have here had their rude beginnings in the thoughts and converse of a few individuals.

Originally, this Palace of Falkland was but a tower and stronghold of the Macduffs, Thanes of Fife. In the times of James I. it came into possession of the Crown, and continued to grow in favour with all the James's as a Hunting Lodge. It became, under James V. and James VI., the Fountainbleau of Scotland.

Noways would it repay the trouble to attempt recounting its tales

> " Of old, unhappy, far off things,
> And battles long ago."

These times of " sturt and strife" have long since exhausted themselves. They contributed but few of the living forces which go to the formation of a nation's greatness, and supply the elements of modern history. The most interesting, and the most picturesque point of view in history is where the barbarous and the civilised touch each other; just as in natural scenery,

the most striking landscape is formed where cul-
tivated and grain-bearing fields meet the unbroken upland, rough with grey rocks, and
variegated with the whin, the broom, and the
heather.

The mid-reign of James V. is such an era in
history, and there we will commence. Falkland
Palace was then known as the " Old Tower of
Falkland." The hunting forest which surrounded
it stretched from Strathmiglo throughout the
Howe of Fife. This forest had been nursed and
protected by successive monarchs, for when
James IV. built " ane verrie monstruous great
schip," named the Great Michael, " it tuik so
meikle timber, that she wasted all the woodis of
Fife, except Falkland Wood." Enclosed by this
forest, and surrounding the Palace, was a deer
park. Sir David Lindsay alludes to it as a
noticeable feature in the landscape :

" Farewell, Falkland, the fortress of Fyfe
    Thy polite park under the Lawmound Law,
  Sum tyme in thee I led a lusty lyfe.
    The fallow deer, to see them raik on' raw.'

This old tower often resounded with the merry
feats produced by the disguises and wanderings
of James IV. and James V. Pitscottie writes

of James IV., " He would ride out through any part of the realm, him all alone, unknown that he was king, and would lodge in puir men's housis, as he had been ane traveller through the countrie." This description applies equally to James IV. and James V., and it is difficult to assign to each of them respectively the traditional stories which are given of their wanderings. The two following may be taken as specimens of their Fife adventures.

One of the roads from Falkland to Cupar crossed the Keilour, at a ford a little below Rankeilour. Close to the ford was the mill of Ballamill. The King, happening to be overtaken there by a storm and by nightfall, sought shelter from the miller. The miller, a kind jolly man, was taken by the frank bearing of the stranger, and gave orders to his wife to slaughter the hen that roosted next the cock, and prepare it for supper. When the supper was set on the table, the miller assigned the board-head to the stranger. The stranger declined it, wishing the miller to be gudeman in his own house, but the miller's word was resolute, " Sit up, for I will ha'e strangers honoured here." The night was spent happily, and on the morning, the King prevailed on the miller to give him a convoy. They had not gone far until the miller discovered that his companion was no other than the king. Fain would he have returned, but the King insisted that he should go on to Falkland. At dinner, a seat of honour was appointed to the miller, and when he declined it, the King reminded him of his own rule, "Sit up, for I will ha'e strangers honoured here." The miller remained a few days the king's guest, every day making him long, amid the honours and restraint of the palace, for the freedom of his own cottage and the clatter of his own mill. At parting, the King asked him whether he would have the "twa" parts or the "aught" parts cf Ballamill. The honest miller, thinking that eight was more than two, named the eight. He got what he wanted, and returned home right glad; not merely the tenant, but now the proprietor of the eighth of the lands of Ballamill.

On another occasion, when out a hunting, to the west of Falkland, the King was separated from his company. He entered a wayside alehouse near to Milnathort, and there found a tinker regaling himself. The King joined him in a tankard of ale. In their conversation the tinker expressed a great desire to see the King, whom he knew to be out hunting that day. The King offered to help him to the sight he desired, and got the tinker, wallet and all, placed on the horse behind him. "But how will I distinguish the king from the other nobles?" asked the tinker, as they rode along. He was told that all the nobles would be unbonneted in the king's presence. When they came to the place which had been appointed for meeting, and when the hunt was over, they saw a company of nobles awaiting his Majesty. Every bonnet was raised, and every head remained uncovered, as they drew near. "Which is the King?" asked the tinker, "for they are all unbonneted." The King humorously answered, "It must be either you or I." In a moment, the astounded tinker slid off the horse, and falling on his knees, offered his homage to the King. What became of the tinker we cannot tell. Not unlikely he may have had a home given him in Kingskettle, and "by special appointment" been constituted tinker to his Majesty.

James V. ever loved Falkland, for it was the scene of his first adventure. When a lad of fifteen he here planned and executed his escape from the powerful Douglas, Earl of Angus. Long had Angus held possession of his Majesty, employing the king's authority according to his own pleasure, for his own influence and aggrandisement. James was impatient under the restraint, and once and again had moved different of the nobles to attempts at his rescue, which had proved unsuccessful. The King's own quickness and energy stood him in better stead than the stout valour of his nobles. Watching his opportunity, when the Earl of Angus had gone to Tantallon, and when his Argus-eyed keeper, George Douglas, the Earl's brother, was absent for the day on his own business, the King set forward to Falkland accompanied by James Douglas of Parkhead, the captain of the guard, and about an hundred gentlemen. On their way they called on the Laird of Fernie, the forester of Falkland Park, and ordered him to summon the gentlemen of the county to assemble, with their "speediest dogs," at Falkland at seven next morning, "to chase the deer with hound and horn."

When the King had retired to his own chamber after supper, he called for James Douglas, the captain of the guard, and drinking to him and talking of to-morrow's sport, he undressed and went to bed. The captain thus seeing the King in bed withdrew, thinking all was " sicker enough." The watch is set, and all is still, when the King arose, and by the help of Jockie Hart, " ane yeoman of the stable and ane other secret servant," mounted prepared horses, and riding up the vale of Devon, at break of day entered the town and castle of Stirling.

Next morning the King was missed, the cry of treason was raised, George Douglas was spurring onwards to Balmbreich, for word was that the King had gone there. But the King was safe within the enclosing walls of Stirling Castle, and soon did he issue his proclamation, that no one bearing the hated name of Douglas should approach him within six miles, under the pain of treason.

It was in June of 1527 that this successful escape was effected.

James V. had a decided taste for architecture. " He did many gude acts, sick as bigging of palaces and castles." He had enlarged and decorated Holyrood for the reception of his first bride, Magdalene of Valois. For the entertainment of his second, the designing Mary of Lorraine, he converted the old tower of Falkland

into a palace. It must have been sadly dilapi-
dated when James undertook its repair, or rather
reconstruction. Beaton of Creich, who was its
keeper, in a report which he made to the Scottish
Parliament in 1525, says that it " was riven, and
the thak y^rof brokin." Great was the transfor-
mation under the architectural taste of the King.
The pillared buttresses, the medallioned walls,
the mullioned windows, all characterise the florid
style which James loved, and indicate him as
distinctly as the mouldering and alternating
initials of J. R. (James Rex) and M. R. (Maria
Regina). The Holyrood-like appearance, which
the round towers with their conical tops impart
to this palace, will strike a stranger.

In this palace, which himself had greatly built
and beautified, James V. breathed his last in
1542. That eager politician, Kirkcaldy of
Grange, the brave old seaman, Sir Andrew Wood
of Largo, were near him ; and so was the crafty
Cardinal Beaton, with the forged will, all ready
for the King's signature. They told him of the
birth of his daughter, but the King spoke little,
and at length turning his back to his lords, and
his face to the wall, he died.

His body was conveyed to Holyrood, and

L

there buried beside his first Queen in the Abbey Church.   His tomb is inscribed thus :—

" Illustris Scotorum Rex, Jacobus, ejus nominis 5, aetatis suæ anno 31, Regni vero 30, mortem obiit in Palacio de Falkland, 14 Decembir. A.D. 1542.   Cujus corpus est traditum sepulturæ."

In consequence of James V.'s double French marriage, " the great and ancient friendship and alliance" which existed betwixt France and Scotland was much strengthened.   During the regency of his widow, Mary of Guise, and the reign of his daughter, Mary Queen of Scots, the Scoto-French alliance was even more intimate, for then Frenchmen abounded in Scotland, and were much employed about the Court.   The thistle and the lily were then intertwined as the thistle and the rose are now.   It is curious to observe how this historical circumstance has left its mark on the language of Scotland.   Names of persons in Scotland are taken from the French, as Dalziel, which is the Scotch rendering of D'Oysel.   Names of places in Scotland are Scotticised French, as Pettycur, which is just *petit corps*, because a small French party of soldiers landed there in the days of the Regent Mary, to assist in putting down the rising Reformation. In Cupar there is a lane called the Mouse Wynd ; the original of this is Mews, a place for stabling, because when Cupar, as the county town, received passing visits of royalty, it was in that wynd where were the mews, or royal stables. The Mouse Wynd in Cupar is matched by the Rotten Row in Glasgow, which is just the Routine Row by which the bishop and chapter walked in procession to the Cathedral. The daily Scotch exclamations, " Ou Aye," " Oh Yes," is just the French " *Oui.*"

Jockteleg, the name which a Scotchman gives to the clasp-knife which he carries in his pocket, is a Scottish version of *Jacques de Leige*, the name of a celebrated foreign cutler who manufactured them.

The aumrie, by which, in Scottish cottages the cupboard is known, is nothing but the French *aumoire.* It were easy to go on multiplying examples.

CHAPTER II.

After the death of James V., his widow, Mary of Guise, the Queen Regent, was but seldom at Falkland.   The rise of the Protestant religion in the country, and her desire to put it down, so engaged her that she had little leisure for the quiet and retirement which Falkland supplies.

The only occasion of importance on which we meet with her at Falkland was June 1559; when on the night of the 12th her French troops, under D'Oysel lay all night at Falkland, and on the morning of the 13th marched along the front of Cult Hills to meet the Protestant forces at Cupar Muir. Sir James Melville, in his Memoirs, says that when he was sent from France to the Queen Regent, the Constable of France, in giving him his instructions, informed him that the object of the King of France in sending troops to Scotland, was only to secure civil obedience from the Scots unto their lawful Queen—adding, " If it be only religion which moves them, we must commit Scotsmen's souls unto God, for we have difficulty enough to rule the consciences of Frenchmen."

It was "only religion which then moved Scotsmen," and moved them to the very heart.
Scotsmen were engaged in those struggles which
a year later secured for the land the glorious
Reformation. The authority of the Queen
Regent was on one side, and the religion and
liberty of the country were on the other ; and,
notwithstanding the Constable's protestation, the
influence of France was ever arrayed with
unerring instinct against the rising cause of
Protestantism.

Here, in the earlier and happier days of her
reign, the favourite of romance—Mary, Queen
of Scots—often resorted, hunting and hawking
in the forest, beguiling the wet day with her
needlework ; and, as she gazed through the stone-
shafted window on the mist-covered Lomonds,
recalling with fondness the sunnier plains of
beautiful France.

It was, however, in the reign of " the Most
High and Mighty Prince, James VI.," that
historical events gathered thickly around Falkland, investing it ever afterwards with national
interest. The first occasion worthy of being
noticed on which he came to Falkland was, when
a lad of sixteen, he escaped from the Lords who

had detained him at Ruthven Tower. He was fretting and fuming under the indignity he had suffered, and was meditating vengeance against all the abettors of the Ruthven Raid. But, amid this ebullition of boyish passion, he had the good sense to send across to Collessie, to Hallhill, and summon to his aid the sagacious counsel of Sir James Melville.

Sir James was one, arrayed in soft apparel, and in King's Courts, whom yet it is worth the trouble to go forth to see. From the early age of fourteen, when he had been sent to France as a page of honour to wait upon the young Queen of Scots, he had breathed the air of courts, and yet he retained his integrity. Hear the spirit in which he received the King's commission: "I had determined to be no more concerned in public affairs, but to lead a quiet and contemplative life the rest of my days. This desire of my Prince and Master was like to put me from this resolution. In this perplexity, I had recourse in humble prayer to God, so to direct my actings as they might tend to his glory, and to the weal of my Prince and country. And, thereafter, according to my dutiful obedience, I went unto his Majesty."

When he came to Falkland he soothed the King by his sage converse and counsels, advising him to a general act of oblivion to all who had been engaged in the Raid of Ruthven. Honour to the good man's memory! he preferred the interest of the King and country to his own. "He perilled himself rather than conceal the truth which endangered his Majesty." For, some weeks after, the King, "taking him to the Gallery of Falkland," asks his mind regarding the bringing back of that worthless favourite, James Stuart, Earl of Arran. "The Earl of Arran is one of the worst instruments which can come about you," was his reply. Bravely and honestly said, Sir James! but your faithfulness will cost you your place. And so it was. Arran was reinstated as the favourite, and Sir James' place in the Privy Council was supplied by another. "So," writes he, "I was shut out of doors, and had no more place to do good."

The influence of the Church was exerted in the same direction as Sir James'. A deputation appointed by the Presbytery of Edinburgh, and consisting of Mr Robert Pont, Mr David Lindsay, Mr John Davidson, and Mr David Fergusson, came to Falkland 18th July 1583. They were brought into the King's cabinet, and there they endeavoured to convey to the King the Church's counsel against the minions who swayed his ear and heart. Mr David Fergusson commended the King for his "paraphrase in meeter" of the Hundred-First Psalm, and insinuated the admonition that, as he had rendered so faithfully David's meaning, he should follow David's example:

"Mines eyes shall on the faithful look, that they may
    dwell with me,
Who walketh in a perfect way, he shall my servant
    be."—KING JAMES' *Version.*

Others spake more boldly. But "after some fair speeches, as they took their leave the King layed his hands upon everie one of them."

And now comes into view the historical feature which distinctively characterises Falkland. It was in Scotland what Hampton Court afterwards was in England, the place where James held his conferences regarding the Church. A very short digression will enable the thoughtful reader to understand the bearing of these conferences.

The Scottish Kirk did in 1560 what the Swedish nation do now. At every coronation in Sweden, the herald calls aloud, " *Carl is crowned King*. HE AND NONE ELSE." The Reformed Church of Scotland proclaimed, *Jesus Christ is the Head and Monarch of the Church*. HE AND NONE ELSE. The Scottish Church acknowledged the lawful authority of the King in all things civil. But in things ecclesiastical they refused to obey any one " but only Christ, the only spiritual King and Governor in his Kirk,"—a great principle this, which has ever gathered around it the spiritual life of the country, and all the true and effectual contending for national freedom.

This *policie* of the Kirk political statesmen have ever " mislyked," calling it " a devout imagination." The able but worldly Regent Morton opposed it in its infancy. James VI. at the outset was not inclined to resist it, until his mind and feelings were misled by minions. When Sir James Melville came to James after the Raid of Ruthven, he found the King resolved " that he would give satisfaction to the Church in their desires, as the fittest and most effectual way for settling peace in the country." But no sooner did a profligate favourite gain an influence over James, than all his better aspirations forsook him : "At the advice of Arran the King forbade the free Assemblies of the Kirk, the same being one of the occasions of all the following troubles."   These favourites succeeded in fastening in the King's mind, " as a nail in a sure place," that "free assemblies" and " free monarchy" could never agree, and thus it became the life work of the King to overthrow Presbyterian Church Government.

On May 18, 1584, a packed Parliament was convened at Edinburgh, and held with closed doors.   Arran, and Patrick Adamson, Archbishop of St Andrews, were the ruling spirits, and the rest were obsequious to the Royal pleasure.   They met on three separate days, and during their sittings they overthrew the whole platform of church government, which had been established by previous acts of Parliament, and which had existed for twenty-four years, to the contentment of the nation and the comfort of the church.   They said "Let us take to ourselves the house of God in possession."   The only voice raised against these tyrannical and unconstitutional doings was the voice of the church.   Mr David Lyndsey, minister of Leith, was sent to remonstrate in the name of the church.   All access was denied him, and he was cast into Blackness Castle. James Lawson and Walter Balcomquhall, ministers in Edinburgh, protested in the pulpit, and again at the Market Cross, against these proceedings; and to prevent themselves being cast "into sure and fast prison," they fled to England.

Meanwhile, after the rising of the Parliament, the King had returned to Falkland, to watch the effect of what had been done in Edinburgh. The ministers, from their exile in England, had written their flocks, explaining the grounds of their flight, and counselling the people to faithfulness. The King, to counteract these letters of the exiled ministers, had a reply in name of the people, penned by Patrick Adamson, defending the King's prerogative and the Parliament's doings, renouncing the ministry, and expressing a hope that his Majesty would provide in their room "good and quiet spirited pastors." Arran was despatched divers times to Edinburgh to urge the people to subscribe this reply. Some of "the baser sort" did subscribe, but the great body of the people boldly refused; and for refusing many an honest citizen was imprisoned, and two brothers, of the name of Cathkin and Robert Mark, were banished.

Nor had this storm yet passed away. Eleven Edinburgh elders and deacons were summoned to Falkland before the King on June 24th 1584. The King inquired of them why they had not subscribed the reply which had been prepared by Adamson, in answer to the letter of their exiled ministers. John Blackburn readily replied, "Because it was against the Word of God and his conscience." The King in his own little way tried to turn the man into ridicule, and to make mirth out of him. Hitching in his chair and laughing, he said, "Here we have gottin a Scripturar." Arran stormed and endeavoured to browbeat the man. He called him a proud knave, and asked him, "If the sinews of his craig yuiked?" In other words, if he wished to be hanged. But Blackburn was firm. He repeated his statement, that he was willing to submit his judgment to the light of God's Word. "The King riseth, and goeth quickly to the foot of the board, and took the pen, inkhorn, and paper from the Clerk, and gave him and put him to a bye-board." But the bye-board was soon exchanged for the guard-room. He is respited from the iron chains until night, that he might stand and catch the light from the high window to prepare his answer. For six days was the poor man detained in the guard-room, with the shackles on his feet. For a month was he kept at Falkland, and for another month at Dunfermline, on his own charges, until his case was disposed of. By such brave contendings and endurings on the part of obscure and poor men has Scottish freedom, civil and religious, been won!

From 1588 to 1603, the Reformed Church of Scotland's "bonds in Christ were manifest in all the palace." The rooms and courts of this old palace witnessed the plottings of James and of his flatterers, and the assembling ofttimes of grave Divines, summoned by the call of the King, or by the exigency of the occasion, to defend the inalienable rights of the Church of Christ. Sometimes there were what was known in after stages of church history as *blinks*—outbursts of sunshine amid the clouds. It was one of these sudden and short blinks when James, after his return from Denmark with his young Queen, appeared in the General Assembly of 1590, and broke forth, " in praising God that he was born in such a time as the time of the light of the Gospel, to such a place as to be King in such a kirk, the sincerest kirk in the world. The kirk of Geneva," continued he, " keepeth Pash and Yule. What have they for them? They have no institution. As for our neighbour kirk in England, it is an evil-said mass in English, wanting nothing but the liftings." The reader may well be astonished, and ask what great change is this that has come over the King? Is James also among the prophets? It is nothing more than the workings of a capricious mind guided by no right principle, but moved to a fit of good humour, and in the humour of the moment uttering for the selfish object of pleasing others, sentiments which his heated imagination can picture, but which his heart feels not. Remember the proverb, King James! *Ne quid nimis.* It is too great a leap this of yours! The words were good, but your heart was not sincere; and twenty years of petty persecution on your part witness your insincerity.

There was one man who, in these years, impressed the stamp of his name, his image, and his words on this Falkland Palace, and history has rendered the impression indelible. That man was Andrew Melville. There was no one in his dominions whom the King disliked and dreaded more. James regarded Melville with the aver-

sion with which a base spirit regards a noble and
generous one.   The courtiers, of course, reflected
the feelings of the King. Melville knew how ·
unwelcome he was, when he was kept standing
long in the corridor awaiting an audience, and
when courtier and servant alike cast upon him,
as they passed, their cold and disdainful look.
But when a man has a work to do for God, he
feels his heart uplifted above the petty annoy-
ances which men can occasion.   Melville had a
work to do, and he did it well, " purchasing to
himself a good degree, and great boldness in the
faith which is in Christ Jesus."   Within this
Palace, in September 1596, Melville told the
King that "In Scotland there were two kings,
two kingdoms, and two jurisdictions.   There
was the civil king, James the Sixth. There was
Christ Jesus the King, and his kingdom the Kirk,
whose subject King James the Sixth is, and of
whose kingdom King James was not a king, nor
a lord, nor a head, but a member."   Most memorable words ! whose echo centuries have not
silenced, for still do they ring through every corner of Scotland as distinctly as they did through
the four corners of that room where, with great
" vehemence," they were uttered.

In 1592 there had been an attempt to surprise and seize the King as he lived securely at Falkland, and this was known at the time, and named in history, as the Raid of Falkland. Earl Bothwell had spurred across the East Lomond with a company of his retainers, thinking to take the King at unawares; but Robert Affleck, servitor to Sir Robert Melville, meeting the company on the Lomond heights, " when it was already dark night," turned, and joined himself with them as if he had been one of them, and knowing the near roads on the hill, he contrived to reach the Palace in time to give the alarm, and to get the gates secured. The country about rose, and the Earl and his accomplices fled, " so wearied with ryding night and day, that they fainted for want of meate and sleepe."

Sir James Melville, writing of this alarm, says, " We gave his Majesty counsel to ride quietly to Bambrigh, on the Tay, that there he might, when he pleased, take a boat and go over to Angus, where he would have leisure to convene the towns of Perth and Dundee. That same night I lay in my boots upon my bed (at Halhill), expecting word from Falkland, where there was one left to be ready for that effect."

Falkland links into a more important episode of Scottish history. It connects itself with the dark and mysterious Gowrie conspiracy. On an autumn morning in 1600, Alexander Ruthven, brother of the Earl of Gowrie, rode into Falkland, attended by his two servants, Andrew Henryson and Andrew Ruthven. They had rode from Perth. It was only betwixt six and seven o'clock when they arrived, and put up at " aue Law's house." Very soon after their arrival, Alexander Ruthven is seen in close converse with the King, beside the Palace stables. The King lays his hand graciously on Alexander's shoulder, and their talk seems very eager. Alexander is telling the King a story, which rouses at once his curiosity and his avarice. The evening before, he said, he had been taking a quiet walk in the environs of Perth, when in a secluded spot he met a suspicious-looking man, with his face muffled in his cloak. On asking him his name and errand, the man answered confusedly. His confusion excited Alexander's suspicions. He examined the man more closely, and found beneath his cloak a pot full of foreign gold coins. He ordered the man to accompany him, and going back to the town, he locked him up in a secure place unknown to any one.   And the object of his early ride that morning was to acquaint the King, and to get the King to accompany him to Perth, and personally examine the matter.

But, for the present, their converse must be stopped, for all was impatience for the chase. The hounds and huntsmen were out, the courtiers were in their saddles, and the morning was bright.   The King mounted his horse, and joined in the hunt, his imagination all the time filled and busied with the strange story.   The chase was a long one; "it lasted from seven hours in the morning until eleven, and more, being one of the greatest and sorest chases that ever his Majesty was at."

No sooner is the buck run down, than an order is given for fresh horses, and the King and his sixteen attendants start off with Alexander Ruthven to Perth.   When they were within about a mile of the town, Alexander Ruthven posted on to forewarn the Earl of his Majesty's near approach.   The Earl had commenced his dinner, but leaving it unfinished, and gathering together about sixty of his retainers, he set forth on foot, and met the King at the Inch.

It was about one o'clock when the King and

his company entered Gowrie House. There was
no provision made for his entertainment, "and
the longsomeness of the preparing and the bad-
ness of the cheer" fretted the hungry King, and
the hungry courtiers. Two o'clock had passed
until dinner was served. After the King had
dined in the dining-room, and while his court
were dining in the hall, Alexander Ruthven conducted the King through the hall, and up a turnpike, and through different rooms, locking each
door behind them. At length he brought him to
a chamber which entered into a turret, where, to
the King's dismay, instead of meeting with the
strange man and the pot of gold, he saw a man
in armour with a dagger at his girdle. Alexander
locks the turret door, draws the dagger, and
threatens the King with death should he attempt
the least alarm, at the same time urging him to
bethink himself of his father's, the late Earl of
Gowrie's murder. The King dreading death
remonstrated eagerly, but Alexander swore
solemnly, that it was not his life nor his blood
that he craved, but only a promise. "What is
the promise?" asked the King. "My brother
will tell you," said Alexander. "Then bring
your brother," replied the King.

While these things are adoing in the turret, the Duke of Lennox, the Earl of Arran, and the rest of the King's attendants have finished dinner, and going out by a side door were sauntering in the garden, when Mr Thomas Cranstoun entering hurriedly calls to them, that the King is horsed, and away through the Inch. They all rush off in separate ways, in search of their horses.

It was when the Earl of Gowrie, the Earl of Mar, and the Duke of Lennox, had reached the street gate, that a voice was heard from the turret—" That," said the Duke of Lennox, " is the King's voice." Sir John Ramsay, a young page, darts up a staircase, which was known as the Black Turnpike, and at the top of it finds the King and Alexander Ruthven struggling. By one stroke of his dagger he wounds Alexander. A second stroke, from Sir Thomas Erskine, kills him. The last words he uttered were—" Alas, I had not the wyte of it."

The Earl of Gowrie, with a drawn sword in each hand, rushes up the staircase, and stumbles over the dead body of his brother. A scuffle ensues, and the Earl also is killed.

The rumour of the Earl's slaughter soon spread over the town. The burghers gathered tumultu-

ously.   The Earl was their Provost, and they all
loved him. Proceeding in a mass, they surrounded
Gowrie House, calling out " Give us our Provost.
Thou son of Seignor Davie, thou hast slain an
honester man than thyself."   The King had to
appease the tumult, by addressing the crowd
from the windows ; and, summoning the magistrates to the room, he left the house and the
bodies of the two brothers to their care.

It was eight o'clock at night before the King
could leave the town. The night was dark and
wet.   Right glad was he to reach the shelter of
his own palace of Falkland, and to hear its doors
barred behind him. It had been an eventful day
this Tuesday, 5th of August, and much had the
King to think of as he laid his head on the pillow.
It had been a fatal day to the noble house of
Gowrie.

Dead men cannot speak ; and so the King
had the telling of his own story to himself, but
many received his version of it in the same spirit
of hesitancy as the honest countryman to whom
the King related it—" A wonderfu' story, your
Majesty, if its true."

" At that time, being in Falkland," writes
James Melville, " I saw a funambulus (a rope-

dancer) a Frenchman, play strange and incredible pratticks upon stented tackel (stretched rope) in the Palace close, before the King, Queen, and hale court. This was politiklie done to mitigate the Queen and people for Gowrie's slaughter."

The time at last arrived when James was to exchange Holyrood for Whitehall, and Falkland for Hampton Court. Sir Robert Carey had arranged with his sister, Lady Scrope, and was watching beneath the chamber window where in Richmond Palace, Queen Elizabeth was dying. When the Queen had breathed her last, Lady Scrope dropped a signet ring, and Sir Robert, bearing the news was off, as fast as a relay of fleet horses could carry him, to Scotland. On Thursday, March 24, 1603, Queen Elizabeth died, and on Saturday, the 26th, the tidings were conveyed to King James in his bed-chamber at Holyrood. It was the quickest journey that had ever been performed betwixt London and Edinburgh. There is a spurious story, which exists as a popular tradition, that Sir Robert Carey delivered the news to King James at Falkland, and that the King, there and then, bestowed on him the rank and the title of Viscount Falkland. Sir Robert Carey was afterwards created Earl of

Monmouth; but it was Sir Henry Carey who was entitled Viscount Falkland, and that not until 1620. This very circumstance of selecting Falkland so many years afterwards, as a title of nobility in England, shows the lingering attachment which King James still cherished amid the fertile meadows of England for his early hunting home.

The name of Falkland is thus connected with breath, and life, and individual action. It is embalmed in British history by the virtues of Lucius, the second Viscount Falkland, " the generous and the just." Virtues bright in themselves, yet sullied by the direction in which they were exerted, for they were employed on behalf of the unconstitutional and false policy of Charles, and thus they shone like the funeral embellishments of the hearse and the coffin, or like the flowers with which the grave is strewn.

An attempt was made, in 1611, to change the Presbytery seat from Cupar to Falkland. The hated name of Presbytery, the king-pleasing abettors of Episcopacy endeavoured to abolish, by substituting *Exercise* in its place to designate the district meeting of ministers to manage the affairs of the Church. During the short and forced prevalence of Episcopacy, *Exercise*, derived from *exercitus*, an assembly, is uniformly used in all their minutes and documents in this sense. The King's Majesty had intimated his will "Anent the transporting of the Exercise from Coupar to Falkland;" but the brethren "craved a supplication to be sent to his Majesty for continowing the meiting at Coupar for sundry gude caussis and considerations, namelie, that Falkland in winter, or efter greit weittes in sommer is not accessible. In the meantym, to satisffie his Majestie's desire, thae ar orderit to convein at Falkland, the hail brethreine of the Exercise of Coupar, till the Assemblie, and thairefter till his Majestie's answer be returned thairanent."

It was no fault of James if Falkland did not enjoy all the honours civic and ecclesiastical which he had to confer. But this he was willingly ignorant of, that the honour which cometh from above, and exalteth a place and a people, is an honour which kings cannot give, although they have often sought to take it away, and that is loyalty to the royal prerogative of Him who is higher than the kings of the earth, and Whose kingdom is a spiritual kingdom.

CHAPTER III.

It was the Augustan age of Falkland during the early reign of James VI. Its every day life must then have been stirring and gay. What with gatherings of Ambassadors and grave Statesmen; what with *fêtes* in the Palace, and huntings in the hills, the little burgh must have looked very proud and important.

This may, then, be the best time to take a survey of the town. If, as Thackeray says, "the lives of streets are as the lives of men," these streets of Falkland have a tale of their own to tell.

> "You never tread upon them, but you set
> Your feet upon some ancient history."

Nobles in attendance upon the Conrt would, in these days of royalty, have rooms for themselves and for part of their retainers in the Palace. Some of the nobility and gentry had private houses in the town. For some of the principal servants of the King's household there were separate dwellings. And the burgesses of Falkland who were possessed of domiciles, or carried on trade in it, held themselves high as inhabitants of a privileged place.

On the south side of the street, and fronting the Palace, is a substantial two-storeyed house, with its venerable thatched roof and its harled walls.   It bears the following inscription in capital letters :—

> AL PRASE to GOD,
> THANKS TO THE MOST
> EXCELLENT MONARCH OF
> GREAT BRITAINE, OF WHOSE
> PRINCELIE LIBERALITIES
> THIS IS MY PORTIONE.
> DEO LAUS.   ESTO FIDUS.
> ADEST MERCES.   NICHOL MONCRIEFF.
>   1610.

The sentiments with which Mr Moncrieff concludes his inscription, and which he has couched in Latin, may be rendered, "Praise to God. Be faithful. The reward is at hand."

The house adjoining occupies the site of a house which was built in 1607, and which was assigned to the Royal Falconer. A stone of a horse-shoe shape, which belonged to the older house, and which is built into the present one, is thus inscribed :—

J——R——6
GOD SAIF YE KING
OF GRIT BRITAN,
FRANCE, AND IRLAND,
OUR SOVERIAN, FOR OF
HIS LIBERALITY THIS
HOUSE DID I (EDIFY.)

Crossing the street from these two houses, and immediately to the west of the Palace, was the Palace Green. Here stood the royal hostelry, with stables, brewery, and barns. It was the resort of knights and gentlemen, and the lounge of their retainers, where each after his own fashion regaled himself with the wines of France, or with a tankard of home-brewed ale.

Not far from this there lately stood, in a garden, a fragment of wall which was known as "The Burleigh Walls." It was the remains of a dwelling-house which belonged to the Balfours of Burleigh, and which in the times of King James sheltered that stirring and sturdy family, then in the sunshine of their prosperity.

At the corner of the square, from amid roofs of venerable thatch, a round tower raises its conical summit. The round tower, borrowed from the French style of architecture, was adopted as a characteristic of old Scottish baronial homes, and we never look upon it but with delight. Here it forms part of a house, which in its earlier days was occupied by a Baron of Parliament, and now belongs to a family of the name of Halkerston, said to be connected with Hackston of Rathillet, of "Scots' Worthies" memory.

In the main street, and forming as it were part of the south side of the square, there is a three-storeyed house with yellow harled front, and erect chimney, and steep thatched roof, at present used as a co-operative store. This is the house in Falkland on which every true-hearted Scotsman will look with the deepest interest. It is the house in which the godly and youthful Scotch martyr, Richard Cameron, was born and lived. It was the dwelling of a family who, all of them, ultimately, testified for Christ and his cause, two of them to death, and the others to bonds and imprisonments. The present occupant and proprietor thinks that the fore-part of the house is much in the same condition in which it was when inhabited by the family of the Camerons. From an Instrument of Sasine drawn up by Thomas Lawson, clerk to the burgh of Falkland in 1700, we were kindly allowed to make the following extract : — " Compeared personally, Thomas

Watson, burgess of the said burgh, as procurator for umquhile Allan Cameron, Merchant, burgess of Falkland, and Mr Richard Cameron, his eldest lawful son, household proprietors of the tenement of land, and Margaret Paterson, spouse of the said Allan, and mother to the said Mr Richard, and past to the ground of the same with an discreet man, George Coll, one of the present bailies of the said burgh of Falkland, having and holding then in his hands an disposition containing therein an provin of resignation of the dates of the fourt and last days of February, one thousand six hundred and seventy years, granted and subscribed by the said Allan and Mr Richard Cameron and Margaret Paterson, each an of them with consent of another to, and in favour of, the deceast David Fergusson, Merchant, burgess of Kirkaldie," &c.

In the Mill Wynd, and close to the large mill, there is an humble tenement which James VI. bestowed upon one of his grooms of the name of Ramsay, for faithful service. The present proprietor is a Ramsay, and for 260 years have the Ramsays possessed this house, handing it down from sire to son. They hold it on condition of paying to the Sovereign the sum of five bawbees Scots, but for the same the sovereign is obliged to call in person. The popular version of the story, never awanting in pictorial effect, says that the Sovereign must call in a coach-and-six for the five bawbees.

At the foot of this Mill Wynd there stood, where now stands the gas work, what was called *the College*. Probably this was nothing more than a school of an higher class and range, for the instruction of families of upper rank.

About the middle of the Cross Wynd, and on the east side of it, there is a small court, one side of the court is now occupied as a smithy, a second by a stable, and the third by a dwelling-house. This place is dignified with the name of the Parliament Close. In Newton of Falkland, too, there is a Parliament Close, and one also in Freuchie. It is possible that the Baronial Courts may have been held in these closes. Or it may be, that political gossips who thought themselves wiser than even the Scottish Solomon, may have met there to discuss, so far as they dared, the events of the day, and that in burlesque the name of Parliament may have been given to the place of their meeting.

Falkland has her Rotten Row as well as

Glasgow. Rotten is the unfortunate and laughable rendering of the French *routine*. We meet with it in the Glasgow street "the Rotten Row;" and at Cross Regal Abbey, where the path by which the Bishop and the Chaplain walked in procession to the chapel, is popularly known as the Rotten Row. In Falkland, the Rotten Row was the prescribed route by which funerals were conducted to the burial-ground, so that the inmates of the Palace might not be disturbed by seeing these mementoes of mortality passing before the Palace windows.

But it is time to leave these local details, and return to the course of history.

Charles I. visited Falkland on the 4th of July, 1633, and, to quote the words of one of the fulsome addresses with which he was entertained in his progress, "the radiant beams of his sun-like appearance" again recalled its former splendour. June 18 had been the Coronation Day. In the Abbey Church of Edinburgh, Charles had been invested with the Scottish crown and sceptre. He had held a Parliament, wherein many of the noblemen, barons, and burgesses, boldly resisted the encroachments which he had set his heart in making on the

Church. Charles took their opposition ill. He sulked, and let no opportunity pass of marking his displeasure. From Edinburgh he went to Linlithgow, and from thence to Stirling. The Provost of Stirling had been one of the burgesses who opposed the King at the Parliament. The King remembered this, and on the presentation of a piece of plate by the Provost, refused to admit him to kiss hands. Upon Wednesday, 3d, the King went to Dunfermline, his birthplace ; and on Thursday, 4th, came to Falkland. Rushworth, in his Historical Collections, adds this Note, " that the nobility and gentry of Fife had prepared to give a noble reception to his Majesty, but many of them being Dissenters, his Majesty was pleased to take another way, and avoided them." A petty and mean affront this, which only disgraces the monarch that made it, but which men like my Lord Rothes, Lindsay, Balmerinoch, and the gentry of Fife, could afford to despise, when, instead of the countenance of an unconstitutional King, they had the satisfaction in their consciences of having acted a faithful part, at once to their country and their Church.

There, then, walking in the streets of Falkland

is Charles I., with his grave countenance, his lustrous eye, his upturned moustache, his depending tuft, and his long hair falling in curls on his shoulders. He was not allowed to regulate the apparel of Kirkmen in Scotland, but he is master of his own, and he is very careful of it. His collar is broad and profusely embroidered. A broad blue ribbon suspends the most noble Order of the Garter on his breast. He wears a high crowned hat. A cloak is thrown over his shoulders. A knot of ribbons binds his velvet breeches at the knees, and a long staff enables him to steady himself on his high-heeled shoes.

" Friday and Saturday the 6th and 7th of July the King hunted in his park at Falkland, and there, on Sunday, Maxwell, Bishop of Ross, preached before his Majesty."

In the King's company there is one, no less notable than the King himself. That square, short man, with the four-cornered cap, and the dress of a Churchman, and wearing, in imitation of his Royal Master, a moustache and Charlie, is William Laud, at present Bishop of London, and Councillor to his Majesty, but who, in a few weeks will be Archbishop of Canterbury and Primate of England. Laud's is but a monkish mind, which has long dwelt with the moles and the bats, and which delights in medieval darkness. He is the High Priest of the high places of the Church of England. The Church of England, at the Reformation, did that which was right in the sight of the Lord in declaring against Popery and the Pope. Howbeit, the high places were not taken away. The Reformers would have removed these, but the imperious Henry VIII., and the no less imperious Elizabeth, demanded that they should be retained. Laud would have collected and elevated into a system these remnants of Popery which deformed the Anglican Church, and separated her from the other Reformed Churches. He was the Dr Pusey of his time. He would have protected and magnified those semi-popish observances in the Anglican Church which connects her with the Church of Rome, and separates her from the simplicity of Scripture. He has come down to Scotland, with his Royal Master, to enforce the Presbyterian Church into conformity with his pet system.

Here are some of his brief entries into his Diary :—

> July 1, Monday.—I went over Forth to Brunt Island.

> July 2, Tuesday.—To St Andrews.
>
> July 3, Wednesday.—Over Tay to Dundee.
>
> July 4, Thursday.—To Faulkland.
>
> July 7, Sunday.—To St Johnston.
>
> July 8, Monday.—To Dunblane and Stirling, my dangerous and *cruel* journey, crossing part of the Highlands by coach, which was a wonder there.

From these markings it appears that Laud arrived at Falkland on the Thursday, spent Friday and Saturday there, and gave to the inhabitants of Scotland the edifying example of setting out again on his journey on the Sabbath, and travelling on that day from Falkland to Perth.

There are degrees of comparison in everything. In the above extract it is amusing to see the Bishop applying the word *cruel* to a little rough jolting which he got in his cushioned coach, as he crossed the Shirramuir. If the Presbyterians of Scotland had cropped his ears, and slit his nose, and branded his brow with a red hot iron, as was done at his instigation to many a poor Puritan in England, he would have better understood the meaning of *cruel*.

Presbyterian pens have not spared Laud, but their severest sentences are mild compared with the pitiless scorn with which Lord Macaulay, Englishman and Episcopalian, regards him: " For that individual (Laud), indeed we entertain a more unmitigated contempt than for any other character in our history." Such is Macaulay's estimate.

Falkland continues faithfully to reflect the unsettled and changing scenes through which Scotland passes.   Charles II. comes from his asylum in Holland in 1650, and receives for a season Scotland's chivalrous, ineffectual, and ill-requited loyalty.   He comes and goes to Falkland, haunting like a troubled ghost his ancestral halls. On the night of the 6th July the old Palace opens its doors to receive him into his ancestral halls. "The time that he abode at Falkland he went down one day and dined at the Earl of Wemyss' house, and another at Lesly, with the Earl of Rothes." On the 1st of January 1651, he was crowned at Scone. He was crowned, " swearing the national Presbyterian Covenant. He died thirty years after, swallowing the Popish wafer." Back again he comes to Falkland on the 22d, and remains a few days. It was his last visit to Falkland, and the last time that the Palace lodged royalty. A wandering life he led, going hither and thither — a King without a kingdom—until he fled from the battlefield of Worcester, and escaped to Paris.

And now a different actor appears. A letter was written by Oliver Cromwell from Burnt-island, 29th July 1651, which begins thus—"The greatest part of the army is in Fife, waiting what way God will further lead us." Fife had opportunity enough to become acquainted with these soldiers of Cromwell, for garrisons of them were established in different parts of the county, and remained for many years. Under 1652, Lamont has the entry in his Diary—"This yeare the English beganne to cutt doune Fackland Wood; the most pairt of the tries wur oakes." The wood was used by Cromwell in building some forts at Perth. Of date "January 3, 1655, we have this—"There cam ane order from the English garrison that lays att the Palace of Fackland, to the parish of Largo, to briuge 52 loads of coalls, being but a fortnight's purvision of fyre for the garrison."

.Cromwell, the Protector, had the palaces of Kings at his command, and thus did he dispose of them—" Collonell Lockart, who latelie married the Protector's niece, got by gift from the

Protector the Palace of Fackland, with the parke."

Disaster overtakes the palace itself, as well as its former occupants. Somewhere about this time it was, that the north and east wings were destroyed by fire, and were allowed to remain in ruins.

~~~~~~~~~~~~~~~

CHAPTER IV.

Falkland has supplied one of the noble band of "Scots' Worthies" in the youthful Richard Cameron. We have pointed out the house in which he was born, and have seen that his father, Allan Cameron, was a merchant burgess of Falkland. Richard himself was an Episcopalian for many years, and acted as schoolmaster, and as precentor to the curate. This had been his cradle religion, and he gave himself no thought about it until one day he attended a field preaching by some outed Presbyterian minister, when the Word went with power to his heart, and he turned to the Lord.
~~~~~~~~~~~~~~~

After undergoing this heart revolution, Falkland, which was then entirely the dwelling-place
of Court parasites, almost every one of whom
regarded it as treason to countenance anything
that was opposed to the King's religion, became
but an unkindly home to him. He left it about
1662, so far as we can discover, and never returned to Falkland again. His first employment
was in the house of Sir Walter Scott of Harden,
where he served as tutor to the family. Soon
afterwards we find him joining himself to Mr
Welsh, of Irongray, and the other field preachers.
By them he was licensed to preach the Gospel.
While faithfully calling upon all men to repent,
and to turn to the Lord, he lifted up an unwaver-
ing testimony against "the Indulgence." He
regarded the acceptance of *an indulgence* from
any earthly king as derogatory to the commission of Christ to go and preach the Gospel; as
dishonouring to the laws and liberties of the
kingdom, which had already established the right
to preach the Evangel; and as opposed to the
scope and spirit of the National Covenant.

His decided and openly declared sentiments
regarding "the Indulgence" brought upon him
much opposition, and led him in 1678 to retire

to Holland. Here he was welcomed by M'Ward and Brown, two exiled Scottish ministers, and was by them and Mr Coulman, a Dutch minister, solemnly ordained to the holy ministry. When the hands of the Presbytery, which were laid on his head, were removed, Mr M'Ward continued his, and said, "Behold, all ye beholders, here is the head of a faithful minister and servant of Jesus Christ, who shall lose the same for his Master's interest, and shall be set up before sun and moon in the public view of the world."

In the beginning of 1680 Mr Cameron returned to Scotland. Henceforward you find him associated with Donald Cameron and Alexander Peden, and regarded as the representative of the strict Covenanters. One bold act this humble covenanting minister did in this year, 1680, which the two kingdoms of England and Scotland imitated eight years after : He publicly and formally renounced all allegiance to the Stuart dynasty for their tyranny, their perjury, and their profligacy. This, and nothing more, was just what the nation did in the glorious Revolution of 1688. Ignorance and prejudice may deride the Covenants and the Covenanters of Scotland, but he who can read history aright will rejoice to acknowledge that the Scottish Covenants and the Scottish Covenanters, in their leading principles and leading contendings, were, throughout years of oppression, the great and the only assertors of constitutional law and freedom.

July 22, 1680, was Richard Cameron's last day on earth. He had slept all night in the house of William Mitchell, in Meadow-head, at the water of Air. In the morning he was supplied with water to wash, and when he dried his face and hands, he said, "This is their last washing, I have need to make them clean, for there is many to see them." During the day, Bruce of Earlshall, with a troop of dragoons, 120 in number, was seen hovering in the neighhood.' The Covenanters, numbering in all 63, took up their position on the east end of Airsmoss, on a firm piece of land, which was surrounded by morasses. About four o'clock in the afternoon, Bruce with his dragoons assailed them. Cameron prayed, and in his short prayer, his thrice repeated expression was long remembered :—" Lord, spare the green, and take the ripe." Stoutly did the Covenanters fight, but they were overpowered by numbers. Nine of them were left dead on the field, two of whom were Richard Cameron and his brother Michael. Earlshall gave a guinea to one of his troopers to cut off Mr Cameron's head and hands, and with these as his booty; and with Haxton of Rathillet, John Pollock, and William Manuel, as his prisoners, he set out on his march to Edinburgh.

At night Cameron's friends returned, and dug a grave in which they buried his headless body, and the eight who had fallen with him. It was to this grave that Peden repaired, and there before God poured out his lamentations and prayers. In strains worthy of the occasion, the gifted authoress of the "Lays of the Kirk and Covenant," has commemorated that affecting scene:

" There came a worn and weary man to Cameron's
    place of rest,
  He cast him down upon the sod, and smote upon his
    breast;
  He wept, as only strong men weep, when weep they
    must or die,
  And, '*O to be wi' thee, Ritchie*,' was still his bitter cry.
     *   *   *   *   *
" 'I bless Thee for the quiet rest, Thy servant taketh
    now;
  I bless Thee for his blessedness, and for his crowned
    brow;

> For every weary step he trod, in faithful following
>   Thee,
> And for the good fight foughten well, and closed right
>   valiantly.
>   *   *   *   *
> Upon the wild and lone Airsmoss, down sank the
>   twilight grey,
> In storm and cloud the evening closed, upon that
>   cheerless day ;
> But Peden went his way refreshed, for peace and joy
>   were given ;
> And Cameron's grave had proved to him the very gate
>   of Heaven."

Old Patrick Walker, the pedlar, tells us there is "a large grave-stone upon four high pillars, with Cameron's name upon the head of it, and the form of an open Bible before him, and the names of the other eight round the sides of it. And downward upon the same stone was the following inscription, all in very legible letters:

> " Halt, curious passenger, come here and read,
>   Our souls triumph, with Christ our glorious head,
>   In self-defence we murdered here do ly,
>   To witness 'gainst the nation's perjury.'

In the year 1723, when I came from Mr Peden's grave-stone at Cumnock, I came to Airsmoss to that grave-stone, and stayed some time in that bloody spot, and can assert the truth of this."

Close by the old flat grave-stone a modern monument has been raised, to testify that in our day there exists a wide-spread sympathy with Cameron's contendings, and that it is to those principles for which he struggled and died that we owe our boasted privileges and liberties. The modern monument stands a bright object amid the dark muirlands, and the sun as it goes down " beyond the hill where Lugar flows," gilds with slanting beam the fresh chiselled sand-stone ·pinnacles.

The Lord has different kinds of witnesses, and each is needed in his own place.   While Richard Cameron is thus contending on the high places of the field, there is a little girl of good family in Falkland, meekly and firmly maintaining the same testimony, and, like a flower, shedding sweetness all around her.   Her father was proprietor of the estate of Templelands, at present a small pendicle in the neighbourhood of the town, but then an extensive property, and he was clerk to the King's Stewartry of Fife.   Her name was Emilia Geddie.   She was born at Falkland in 1665, and she died in 1681 at the early age of sixteen.   Her precocity, both in parts and in piety, is truly marvellous.   When only about five years of age she said to her teachers, when learning the Shorter Catechism, "*I think the Bible is God's word, and the Catechism is the Bible's word.*" She had a perfect and clear up-taking of the great principles for which the Church was then struggling, and she had the heroic fortitude which faith gives to suffer for them. Her father was plied by some of those *declarations* which Government employed to entrap unwary souls into apostacy, and he was threatened with loss of place, and loss of goods, and with imprisonment in case of refusal. He spoke in the hearing of his daughter of the painful position in which he was placed. This little girl, then only eight years old, with a gracious heroism encouraged her parent. "Don't comply," she said. "Although they take all from us, let us live by faith and God will provide for us. As for herself, she was willing to go and serve some lady, that would give her meat and old clothes, and all her wages she would give for the support of her parents." Thus to its very letter was the word fulfilled, "Out of the mouth of babes and sucklings hast *thou ordained strength because of thine enemies, that thou mightest still the enemy and the avenger.*" And so the enemy and the avenger was stilled by a child's voice. Mr Geddie remained faithful. His prelatic persecutors cast him into prison, but the prayer of. his child prevailed with God, and he was at length liberated.

She had personal as well as relative reproach to bear for her principles. In the ninth year of her age, when going to school, she was assailed by some rude boys, who beat her cruelly, " because she would not swear to them, that she would be no more a Whig, but go to church and hear the curate." If at any time she would speak to any of her companions for breaking the Sabbath, or any other wrong-doing, they would only laugh at her, and call her " a strange young Whig."

Once she was assailed with a temptation of Satan. She was enabled to overcome, and by a natural reaction, joy and gladness took the place of dejection. With a watchful and discriminating tenderness she observed, "Soon after, I was so plagued with lightness of heart, that to be rid of it, I could have wished to be in my former tempted condition."

She had been staying at Kirkcaldy and spending a Sabbath there, when she met with some persons whose religious life consisted merely in hearing sermons. She said, " These people are like to some horses, which pull a great deal of fodder from the rack, and tread it under their feet, eating little or nothing of it. We should be like the horses which eat what they pull down."

She had an innocent delight in contemplating nature, and in watching the instincts and actions of the inferior animals. Her pet employment was to tame and feed birds. This observation she made for herself, which has escaped the notice of many older minds, " that birds drink none before they can fly for it," and in this she saw the wise and wonderful arrangement of God.

But the wind that withereth the flowers passed over her in the end of 1680. Her decline was gradual, although her suffering was often great. " I am not weary of my bed," she said, " for my bed is green, and all that I meet with is perfumed with love to me. The time, night and day, is made sweet to me by the Lord. When it is evening it is pleasant ; and when it is morning I am refreshed."

The year 1681 still found her lingering. At length, on a Sabbath, the call came :—" About eight o'clock at night her attendants, thinking that she was just expiring, called for a light. She smiled, and said, 'I shall not die yet; for I want that promised presence of God which I have long believed I shall have in the moments of death.' She gave solemn counsels to her companions, and about two hours before her death, with her eyes and hands towards heaven, and sitting up in her bed, she pleaded the promises God had spoken to her heart, and implored mercies for herself, her parents, and the suffering church and people of God." She then lay quietly down waiting for death. Thus died this youthful and faithful witness for Christ and his suffering cause.

Two memorials of Emilia Geddie remain in good condition in Falkland. There is the house in which she lived, which belonged to her father. It may be seen in the wynd which bears the name of Sharpe's Close—a substantial three-storeyed house. Inserted beside the door is a deeply sculptured stone with heraldic emblems—with the initials, " W.S. J.W. 1727," and the motto " Diligentia et vigilantia." The initials indicate William Stevenson and Jean Wallace. The latter was related to Mrs Geddie, and seems to have inherited the Geddie property. There is also Emilia's Grave. It is on the east wall of the burial ground. It is surrounded by a low wall and balustrade. On the pillars at the entrance are J.G. (John Geddie) A.W. (Ann Wallace) : 1691. The grave-stone, with its epitaph, seems the erection of William Stevenson and his wife.

Among the persecuted ministers who preached in the neighbourhood of Falkland, in the solitude of the Lomonds, or under the cover of the woods, were Mr John Blackadder, Mr John Wellwood, Mr John Welsh of Irongray, and Mr Donald Cargill. In illustration of the great fatigue which these men often underwent, we may read what Kirkton has written regarding Mr Welsh— "I have known him ride," says Kirkton, "three days and two nights without sleep, and preach on a mountain at midnight on one of the nights." Mr Welsh was often hid in the house of Moncrieff of Reedie at Myres. On one occasion, he and the curate of Falkland had a small encounter. The curate was accustomed to boast of the large number of communicants on his roll—an inglorious boast, seeing that it was brought about entirely by pressure from without, compelling the people by authority to attend his ministry, or seducing them by motives of worldly interest. However, he boasted of it, and was lifted up by it. Nothing would satisfy him but that he would meet Mr Welsh and refute his doctrine. In this vapouring humour he came to the wood of Falkland, where Mr Welsh was preaching to a multitude of people, assembled from different parts of the country. In these days the Word of God was precious to the persecuted Presbyterians; and when the curate attempted to speak, the assembled people, intolerant of the interruption of the service, would have treated him roughly had not Mr Welsh come to his rescue.

Despite of all the attempts to repress a testimony for the cause of Christ in Falkland, some noble instances of individual faithfulness occur. Wodrow mentions the sufferings of Thomas Thomson, in Easter Conland, in Falkland. Because he would not conform to Episcopacy he was fined £100 sterling, soldiers were quartered on him, and at last he was obliged to leave his farm with his wife and family, and to hide and wander until the Revolution came and restored liberty.

Among all the individual portraitures which connect themselves with Falkland, none is more graceful and interesting than that of Lady Catherine Hamilton, Duchess of Athole. She was the pious daughter of a pious mother. While yet "in the prime of earliest youth," at the engaging age of nineteen, her private papers show her dealing closely with the Lord, and covenanting with Him. Her piety she brought with her as her richest dower, when, in her twenty-first year, she was married to the eldest son of the Marquis of Athole, John, Lord Murray, who was created first Duke of Athole. Falkland had about the year of the Restoration, 1660, passed into the power of the Athole family. In room of the sovereignty of the Isle of Man, they had received £70,000 along with the hereditary keepership of the Palace of Falkland, and the Palace bolls, which amounted to the annual value of £1200. In 1689 the Duchess and her husband resided there. Her attachment to the oppressed Presbyterian Church of Scotland was one of principle. Both principle and piety had attached her warmly to the non-conforming Church of Scotland, and when the Revolution of 1688 came, opening the door for the restoration of the faithful Presbyterian ministers to their charges, we find her in her Diary, dated Falkland,

May 9, 1691, manifesting her concern regarding the appointment of a minister to the parish. " O Lord, help me always to remember thy goodness to me. Thou hast many times prevented me with thy mercies and disappointed my fears, and now again lately, I have had another proof of it. Thou only knowest what a burden it was to me, the fear I was in that my husband should have obstructed a good minister being settled in this place, and now, glory to God that has given me to see him the main, nay, I may say the only instrument of bringing a godly minister, the Rev. Mr John Forrest, to this place. O Lord! grant he may, in the first place, reap the benefit of his ministry to himself, and bless it in a special manner to him, that he, finding the good of it, may yet be more instrumental in bringing in good ministers to the places he has interest in." Mr Forrest's connexion with Falkland was a short one, for, in 1692, we find him succeeded by Mr Selkrig.

It is most satisfactory to observe how deeply rooted the faith of this pious lady was in the essential doctrines of grace. Around the " sure covenant" her thoughts and desires were ever hovering, " O Lord, I come unto thee for thou art the Lord my covenanted God. Thou knowest that this day I know not of any fraud or guile in this declaration." Again she writes, "I did, thou knowest, O Lord, with the sincerity of my soul, accept of the Lord as my covenanted God, and did most earnestly entreat the assistance of the Holy Spirit and strength to be with me for ever, that I may never go out of thy way, but be helped to live uprightly and holily all the days of my appointed time."

This well-ordered covenant, which had been her solace through life, was her strength at death. When Mr Findlater, the minister, attended her when she died, at Hamilton in 1707, in the 45th year of her age, he brought the everlasting covenant to her thoughts, as a strong refuge, and the last words he heard her utter were, "That is all my salvation and all my desire."

The excellence of this noble woman is seen in the regard her husband cherished for her memory, and in the influence which her gentle piety had in binding him to the covenanted Church of Scotland, even when he changed his politics and party, and joined the Tories in the reign of Queen Anne.

CHAPTER V.

On the battlements of the Palace, immediately above the gateway, there is a stone with the fast fading but pious inscription, "Deus dat cui vult"—God gives to whom he pleases. This motto was verified when, in 1715, the Palace became the temporary abode of the Highland freebooter, Rob Roy Macgregor. Taking advantage of the unsettled state of the country, occasioned by the rebellion on behalf of the Pretender, Rob, who was no Pretender, thonght it a good time to pay the Lowlands a visit on his own account. He came to Fife, and took np his quarters for a time in the Palace, overawing the neighbonrhood, and making his own exactions.

Rob Roy, in the royal Palace of Falkland, seems as little at home as he is in Wordsworth's poetry. Of Wordsworth's poem we give the only portion for which our readers will thank ns—

" A famous man is Robin Hood,
    The English ballad-singers' joy ;
And Scotland has a thief as good—
An outlaw of as daring mood—
    She has her brave Rob Roy !
Then clear the weeds from off his grave,
And let us chant a passing stave
In honour of that hero brave.
Heaven gave Rob Roy a dauntless heart,
    And wondrous length and strength of arm ;
Nor craved he more to quell his foe,
    Or keep his friends from harm."

The Palace motto saw another strange fulfilment when the Palace became the abode of the Presbyterian minister. Vicissitude most striking ! While the Stuart race are dying out in exile, their ancestral halls cover, and their ancestral hearths warm, an incumbent of that church which they sought to extinguish. As late as 1808 the Palace was used as the dwelling of the parochial minister.

The Falkland of thirty years ago was different from the Falkland of the present day. We can see it now, as we saw it then, for the first time. The shadows were falling on its empty square— the fountain was sending forth its pure waters, not as now in separate jets, but in one vigorous unbroken gush, which made the large stone trough to boil with the agitation, and which filled the otherwise silent square with its mono· tonous and lulling sound.   The old barn-looking church, with its outside stair and brown shuttered windows, stood near it. In passing through the town the eye is struck with the old dates which many of the lintels display.   In the Mill Wynd there is a cottage with 1680 above the door—the year when Charles II. was reigning as an absolute monarch, and when the Parliament of England were discussing a bill to exclude the Duke of York from the succession. In the Cross Wynd there is an old lintel dated 1686 —the year after Charles II. had died, and when James II. was plotting to restore the Popish religion. In the main street there is the well-to-do looking house of the merchant burgess, Lawson, presenting on its front a pair of scales, and the year 1696—when William III., after the death of his beloved Mary, sat securely on the British throne.

The Maspie Burn separates the royal burgh of Falkland from the barony of Balmblae. This barony of old belonged to a family of the name of Carmichael.   The walls that enclosed the garden attached to the family residence still stand, and the arched door-way of entrance is still visible. The people of Falkland say that the Balmblae House contained in its day the finest dining-room in Fife.

Amid these minor items, let us not overlook the fine motto which encircles the town arms—a deer crouching beneath a spreading tree—*Cole temperantiam et non contemne Christum* : Practise temperance, and do not despise Christ.

Leaving Falkland by the east, we may observe, close by the present schoolhouse, a large stone deep sunk in the ground. This stone is known to this day as the " Liquor Stone." On this stone funeral companies were in the habit of placing the coffin, while drink was supplied to refresh them, in bearing the body to the church-yard.

We pass through the sweet-lying village of Newton of Falkland, regaled by the gleam of the Balreavie Burn, and by the cawing of the rooks amid the old trees of Lathrisk, and we arrive at

Freuchie.

A quaint old place is Freuchie. Its frequent squares, and courts, and bullet-paved closes, and tortuous streets, give it a character of its own. Among the villages of Scotland we know no one like it. These twisting, narrow, and orderless streets represent a time when there were no wheel carriages, and when all journeys were performed on horseback, and when all goods were conveyed by pack horses.

Freuchie lay beyond the precincts of the Court at Falkland, and it is to this fact that we are to look for the meaning of the proverbial saying, " Go to Freuchie." The disgraced courtier, when he got his dismissal, was sent there. The good . people of Freuchie have an explanation more complimentary to their village, although we fear it will be regarded as apocryphal by every one but themselves. They say that in the time of the Kings there lived a very wise man at Freuchie, and that the King, when puzzled with any subject that was too much for him, would command some of his attendant courtiers "to go to Freuchie," and get the counsel of the Freuchie sage.

Freuchie has its own memories to record. In what is called the Parliament Close, the walls of an old barn still stand where, during "the killing times" in 1685, a body of Covenanters were lodged, on their way to the dungeons of Dunnottar. There they were held in fast prison, and there many of them died.

Tradition says that Rob Roy's gillies made very free with the goods of the villagers. In one house the very burial bread, which had been prepared for a funeral, was carried off by them. A horse was taken from J. Lumsden's stable to carry Rob's "ill gotten gear" to Perth; but in a fit of honesty, for which Rob often prided himself, the horse was returned.

Two characteristic stories illustrate the differing conditions of Falkland and Freuchie. Falkland, as a "burgh of ancient charter proud," rejoices in her municipal privileges. After an election of bailies, a burgess who had been elected to that high office, enters his byre with all his blushing honours fresh upon him, and approaching his cow addressed her, in the fullness of his heart, " Ah, crummie, crummie, ye're nae a common coo noo, ye're a bailie's coo, ma woman." Freuchie's interests, on the other hand, were with the unfranchised. The hope of her villagers was with forthcoming reform. In those days of high excitement, the Freuchie weaver, getting hold of an all-absorbing news-paper, casts the care of crummie on his wife, " Jenny, attend you here to the coo, and let me attend to the affairs of the nation."

Kettle.

ONE feels relieved in finding that, after all, Kettle has nothing to do with pots and pans. Its original name is Cattul, a compound Celtic word, which signifies the battle of the stream. Very likely the word commemorates some for-gotten battle fought on the banks of the Eden long, long ago, when the fortifications in the East Lomond could tell their own story.

A tradition survives of a battle fought at Hole

Kettle with the Danes, and stone coffins have been found there. Who knows but that this forgotten battle of Cattul may have been the battle in which the incident took place, which gave to Scotland the thistle as the national emblem? It may have been that, coming along from their camp at Daneshelt, or down from their fort at Norman's Law, the Danes, under the silence and the darkness of night, intended to surprise the Scottish army, and that one of their number planting his bare foot on a thistle, cried out under the sudden pain, and so by the alarm saved the Scottish army.

A later tradition explains how the old name of Cattul was modernized into Kettle. The story goes that one of the Kings, hunting in the myres of Kettle came upon a beautiful spring of pure water bubbling up. The King alighted from his horse, and admiring and drinking of the spring, his fancy struck with the resemblance which it had to a boiling pot, and indulging itself in an innocent pun on the name Cattul, dubbed it the King's Kettle.

The east part of the parish of Kettle rises into the wild upland. There, even at this day, a feeling of loneliness takes possession of one. You find yourself amid solitary fields, resounding in early spring with the cry of the plover, diversified only by the ploughman bending over his share, and bounded by a horizon of hill, out of which Clatto Knock, and Down Law, and Glass Law, and the bulkier and more distant Largo Law rise as forts.   Near to the farm house of Clatto, on a grassy bank of uncommon verdure, there are two venerable ash trees, which have survived the storms of many generations. These trees indicate the spot where stood centuries ago the Castle of Clatto. A beautiful situation the castle had, looking down into the den with its tiny streamlet.

It is a spot which might fitly appropriate to itself the exquisite lines of Wordsworth—

> " Meek loveliness is round thee spread,
> A softness still and holy ;
> The grace of forest charms decayed,
> And pastoral melancholy."

Yet, amid these still scenes, there lived in this old tower the lawless family of the Setons—a father and six sons, who were wont to issue forth from the caverns in the den, and rob the passing traveller.

It chanced that James IV. passed that way in

one of his wandering excursions. Two of the young Setons, not knowing him to be the King, rushed forth upon him at a turn of the den. The King, who was an expert swordsman, stoutly defended himself, and in the scuffle cut off the hand of one of his assailants. The wounded man withdrew, and his brother, not thinking it safe to maintain the combat with such an assailant, also made off. The King dismounted and picked up the bloody hand. Next day, returning with a body of attendants he called at the Castle. Old Clatto put on a show of welcome. The King inquired for his sons. Four appeared, one was from home and the other was sick. The King desired to see the sick man, objections and apologies were offered, but the King's word prevailed. Placing himself by the bed, the King wished to feel the sick man's arm. The whole arm is offered. "Let me try the other," said the King. Reluctantly was the maimed arm produced. "Ah!" said the King, "You have lost a hand, probably I can fit you," and out he brings the stiffened hand. The evidence was conclusive. The assize was short. The execution was speedy. In an hour the old laird and his five sons were hanging dead from the ash trees which surrounded their dwelling.

Before the Reformation, and up to the year 1636, the Parish Church was situated at Lathrisk. In the days of Popery the church belonged to the priory of St Andrews, and William Myretown, perpetual Vicar of Lathrisk, founded the Collegiate Church of Crail in 1517. The east part of the parish was supplied by a chapel at Kettle. The Church lands of Chapel were, by James Earl of Murray, when Prior of St Andrews in 1558, "disponed to John Arnot and his heirs, declaring that he and his progenitors had been possessors of those lands past memory of man." Three hundred years are now added to the above date, and still the lands are possessed by an Arnot.

Mr William Cranstoun was minister of Kettle at the time that King James VI. was endeavouring to pave the way for the prelatic power of the bishops, by making them constant moderators of the Presbytery and Synod. At a meeting of the Synod of Fife, held at Dysart on the 18th of August 1607, Mr Cranstoun "did an honest and stout part" in maintaining the liberty of the Church. Lord Lyndsay, Lord Holyrood-

house, and Lord Scoon, had come to attend the
Synod as Commissioners from his Majesty, with
the view of having Bishop Gladstanes appointed
constant moderator. It was Mr Cranstonn's
duty, as the moderator appointed by the last
Synod, to preach the opening sermon. But
Bishop Gladstanes and the King's Commissioners
had determined to push aside the Synod's moderator, and to have a nominee of their own to
preach the sermon. Mr Cranstonn, ignorant of
all this, was in the Session-house composing his
thoughts for the service, while the people were
assembling in the church and the psalms were
singing. Feeling the air in the Session-house
to be close, he went to the pulpit, "partly for
more open air, partly that his affection might be
stirred up with singing the psalms." While he
is sitting in the pulpit a messenger is sent to him
with a letter, but his thoughts are engaged with
the worship, and without opening the letter he
thrusts it into his pocket. Soon after, another
messenger ascends the pulpit with a verbal order
from the Lords the Commissioners to Mr Cranstonn, to leave the pulpit. He replied " that he
came to that place in the name of a greater Lord,
whose message he had not yet discharged."

Next came one of the bailies of the town, whispering to Mr Cranstoun that he was commanded by the Lords to desire him to come down. "And I command you in the name of God," said Mr Cranstoun boldly, "to sit down in your own seat and hear what God will say to you by me." The bailie obeyed. Last of all came the Netherland Consul, saying that the Lords had appointed another to preach. "But the Lord," said Mr Cranstoun resolutely, "and His Kirk have appointed me." And so he entered on prayer and preached.

After sermon, the members of Synod were threatened with a charge of horning, whereby they would be denounced as rebels should they refuse to vote the office of constant Moderator to the Bishop. "The brethren answered severally, that they would rather abide horning, and all that can follow thereupon, then lose the liberty of the Kirk." By such strict and self-denying resistance of Erastian encroachment, has Presbyterianism achieved its scriptural and constitutional freedom in Scotland.

This worthy and faithful minister of Kettle, Mr William Cranstoun, was too uncompromising to escape the wrath of the Bishops. When an old man, he was deprived of his charge by Archbishop Spottiswoode, through the Conrt of High Commission, in 1620.

Near to where the present house of Chapel stands, there stood the old house of Bankton. The old trees, which still grow, cast their shadows over it. On the lintel of the garden door was engraved the significant motto, " A weighty man ne'er wants a weapon." In 1679 James Russell was the proprietor of Bankton and Kettle. He belonged to that class of men of whom Scotland in his day reared many—who feared God and loved the Gospel of Christ, and who esteemed it a duty ever to be maintained in the face of all hardship, to defend the principles of Christ's Church and the liberties of their country. This honse often missed its master, for because of his principles he was often obliged to hide, to escape imprisonment and fines. Often was he driven to associate with resolute spirits like himself, freqnenting the lonely moors to enjoy a preached Gospel, and sometimes drawing the sword when need was, and fighting valiantly as Christian men for liberty and life. Saturday, 3d May 1679, saw a band of these resolute men gathering on the uplands to the south of Cupar.

James Russell was there, and so was his neighbour, John Balfour of Kinloch, known as Burley,
and Balfour's kinsman, Hackston of Rathillet,
and the Hendersons of Kilbrackmont, and George
Fleming of Balbethell, and William Dingwall,
alias Daniel, *alias* Danziel, of Caddam, killed afterwards at Drumclog. They were all well mounted,
and each carried his sword and pistols. The object of their quest was Carmichael, an Edinburgh
bankrupt, who, armed with power from Government to fine and imprison all who attended field
preaching, was like a wolf desolating the county.
They missed the servant, but they found the
master. For when about to separate they were
told that the Archbishop of St Andrews was
near, and soon they saw his lumbering coach
descending the ridge of the hill near Blebo Mains.

Questions of casuistry, which might puzzle
learned clerks in their study, are often unhesitat-
ingly disposed of, in the time of action, by honest
and intrepid minds. They felt the persecution
raised against themselves and their unoffending
brethren throughout the land as not only a
violation of Christianity and law, but as an out-
rage on humanity. They regarded Sharpe and
all his party " by their bloody doings to be

bloodsuckers, murderers, and open-declared enemies to God and man," as at war with their country, and as in time of war, they thought it just to pursue them to death. Sharpe they esteemed as the head and heart of the persecution. Seeing him thus cast nnexpectedly in their way, they made haste and did not delay.

Russell was the first to spur his horse after the retreating coach. He nnclasps his cloak and throws it from him, and coming up to the carriage he fires his pistol into it, and then cuts the traces. It was Russell who, when the deed was done, pronounced with a free drawn breath, " He's dead now."

It is a singular enough fact that all those who were active in putting the Archbishop to death, such as Russell and Burley, escaped with their life; while Hackston of Rathillet, who stood aloof and refused to have any part in it, and poor Andrew Gulland, who was innocently and accidentally present, and who only looked on, were both executed on the charge of being the Archbishop's murderers.

Leslie.

HE who would try the strength of his lungs, may breast the East Lomond on a breezy spring day, and cross to Leslie. This was once the highway betwixt Falkland and Holyrood. Many a footman has run with his message, and many a knight has pushed his charger, across this mountain tract.

The climber will be repaid by a magnificent view on either side. Northward is the Howe of Fife, dark with fir woods, studded with villages and farm steads, begirdled by the Ochils, and traversed by the sounding rail car, with its coiling smoke. Southward is the smiling coast of Fife and the expanding Firth, bright with the dazzling sun gleam.

Leslie lies at our feet, and it is there we are going. How well it looks from this ! Its double line of streets stretching along its own miniature ridge, the Leven coursing past in its dark bed, that fringe of noble beech trees, and the house of Rothes, reflecting its manorial dignity on the village.

It is vain to attempt to connect the name of Leslie with the features of the place. Fetkill was the original and descriptive name of the parish. Leslie is a name brought with the Rothes family, and affixed to the place. Let us avail ourselves in this particular of the help of Christopher Irvine, the faithful adherent of Charles I. In his Scottish nomenclature, Christopher says, "The name Lesly is an old Highland word signifying Lees-lye—the share of a pleasant field. So I believe it is an old Scots name and not an Hungarian, as some do insinuate. Their first lands was the barony of Lees-lye in the Garioch." We have heard two lines of an old ballad quoted as expressing the origin of the name of Leslie, and we give them as an illustration of a loose popular explanation :—

> " Between the less lea and the mere
> He slew a man and left him there."

We leave it with the general antiquarian to decide whether the Old Kirk of Leslie, part of which is built into the mausoleum of the Rothes family, was the original of King James' poem, "Christ's Kirk on the Green." On the green, and not far from the gateway of the burial-ground, may still be seen the Bull Stone, to which the poor animals brought up for the bull fights, were attached; for this was a famous gathering-place for these barbarous fights and games of strength and skill. May it not be from this that the parish was named Fetkill—Féte kill, the Church of the Games. It is true that there is here a combination of the different languages of Gaelic and French. But such heterogeneous combinations are occasionally met with, as in Falkirk —Vallum, a wall, and Kirk, the kirk built on the old Roman wall—Valkirk, Falkirk. A fighting place Leslie seems to have been. The gateway to Leslie House, at the foot of Leslie path, still bears the name of the Barras Yett, or the Gate of Combats. Here cock-fights took place in the presence of the Duke and the villagers. So late as an hundred years ago these games and fights were still practised. Since then, what had flourished under the patronage of noble Dukes, fell under the management of *the chapmen*, who had a society here. They had their rough contests among themselves with bar, and putting-stone, and shinties, and when "the malt got the better of the meal," with fists. By degrees the fight extended to the neighbouring towns, and scenes were enacted worthy of Donnybrook. Mediæval sports and games look well in the fancy pages of a novelist, but they brutalise the people by whom they are practised. Better far is the modern volunteer movement, which gathers np and disciplines for the country's defence the fighting prowess and propensities of every country side.

There is a house on the south side of the principal street, and about the middle of it, in which Burley and Russell, and others of their companions, after putting Archbishop Sharpe to death on Magus Muir, lodged all the night. Probably they thought that by seeking shelter near to the abode of the Duke of Rothes, who was High Sheriff of Fife, their hiding-place might escape suspicion. The present house bears the date of 1681, having been rebuilt then in the room of the old house. It still belongs to the descendants of Thomas Webster, who in 1679 favoured and resetted the Archbishop's executioners.

The visitant of Leslie soon finds his attention

concentrated on the Manor House. In the days of its grandeur it formed a quadrangle resembling Holyrood Palace, but outrivalling it, for the picture gallery was three feet longer than that of Holyrood. It was built by the Duke of Rothes, in the hey-day of his prosperity, and was burned down in 1763. The present house is but a fragment of the former, having been repaired in 1767.

An old heritage were these woods and lands on which you look, for they were granted in 1282. But of the long line of noble proprietors let us select three. First is Norman Leslie, a cadet of the family, who sheathed his dagger in the body of Cardinal Beaton, and whose gallant bearing at the head of thirty Scottish Squires in the battle of St Quentins, placed him high in the lists of French chivalry. His charger fell beneath him, himself mortally wounded, was carried to the King of France's tent, and there died in 1554.

The one of all the line to which the Scottish Presbyterian turns with most interest is John, sixth Earl. We have before us an engraving taken from a painting by George Jamieson, the distinguished Scottish painter, bearing the date 1625, when the Earl was in his 25th year. There he stands, with his beaming eye and delicate features, on which the play of humour is seen, dressed in his peeked doublet, trunk breeches, gartered hose, and rosetted slippers. Early and stoutly did he uptake the cause of the Covenanted Church of Scotland. Ready was he in debate, and often by his sportive mirth did he conquer. He was the wit of the Covenanting nobles. "Much quick speech, especially from Rothes' mouth," writes Baillie, "past at the table" in General Arundel's tent, where King Charles met commissioners from the Scottish army. But wit alone is too light ballast for the ship in a gale. The gay Rothes was for a time tempted by Court preferment and promises. "The King, Charles I.," says Burnet, "gained the Earl of Rothes entirely, who hoped, by the King's mediation, to have married the Countess of Devonshire, a rich and magnificent lady, that lived long in the greatest state of any of that age." To effect this connection, in which he failed, he is represented as deserting his principles. This representation is not correct, for we have Mr George Hutcheson, a minister in Edinburgh, bearing this testimony to the

Earl of Rothes in 1656 : " All the lovers of Christ in Scotland do with thankfulness remember their obligations to the Right Hon. the Earl of Rothes, of precious memory, whom the Lord raised up to be a prime instrument in the late Reformation, and who spent himself, till his last breath, in that public service."

His son, John, the seventh Earl, and afterwards Duke of Rothes, attached himself to the King, and was no friend of the Presbyterian Church. He fought at the battle of Worcester, September 3, 1651, as an officer in the Scots army, on behalf of Charles II., and was there taken prisoner and cast into the Tower. At the Restoration, in 1660, Charles II. made Rothes President of the Council, and manifested every desire to shew him favour. But the favour of Charles II. was ever purchased at a price so dear that no true patriot could pay it, for his favour was the price of the country's liberties and true interests. Accordingly we find Rothes soon engaged in most discreditable employment. The Synod of Fife met in St Andrews, April 2, 1661 —Mr David Forret, minister of Kilconquhar, being the moderator. When the Synod were deliberating on an address to remind the people of the several parishes "of their oath to God in covenant, in case that Episcopacy should again be established in the land," the Earl of Rothes, accompanied by the Laird of Ardross, and Balfour Beton, appeared, and commanded them, on the pain of treason, to repair to their respective homes. Mr Forret followed Rothes to his chamber, and told him that "few or none of the Synod but had ministered the Covenant to hundreds, and for himself, he had tendered it to thousands, and if he should be silent at such a time, and speak nothing for it, but betray the people, he wist not what he deserved; hanging were too little for him."

Rothes was naturally a good tempered man. He had nothing of the gall of the persecutor in him. Had he not been goaded on by ambition he would have shunned such work. This was his first act of oppression, and all his better feelings rose against it. "He professed to this judicatory that it was sore against his will that he came to that employment." Use will familiarise him. Soon these feelings will cease to trouble him. But a few months passed away, when Rothes suppressed the national Church with less scruple than he did this provincial

Synod. " 1661, September 5, being Thursday, the Chancellor, Glencairn, and the Earl of Rothes, having come down from Court some days before the Council of State sat at Edinburgh, and the next day being Friday, they caused emit to be proclaimed over the cross, a proclamation in his Majesty's name for establishing Episcopacy again in the Church of Scotland, which was done with great solemnity, and afterwards printed. All, whether men or women, were discharged to speak against that office under the pain of treason."

For his subserviency, honours were showered down thick upon him. In 1664 he came from London as his Majesty's Commissioner for Scotland. For this he was to have £10 sterling a-day for his table. In addition, he at the same time held the offices of treasurer of the kingdom, president of the Secret Council, Lord General of all the Forces in Scotland, and Keeper of the Great Seal for the time. In 1667 he was proclaimed Chancellor of Scotland. Titles were multiplied for his special honour. Duke of Rothes, Marquis of Ballenbreich, Earl of Leslie, Viscount of Lugton, Lord Achmoutie and Coskieberry. The whole culminated in a death-bed of terror, and in a magnificent funeral in 1681.

When death came, the Duke sent for the covenanting ministers, whom he had oppressed, to pray with him. When Mr John Carstairs came, the Duke told how heavy the words of James Guthrie lay upon his conscience—" We all thought little of what that man did in ex-communicating us, but I find that sentence binding on me now, and it will bind to all eternity." The Duke of Hamilton said—" We banish these men from us, and yet when dying we call for them; this is melancholy work." Equally striking was the testimony of the Popish Duke of York. When he heard that the dying Rothes had sent for a Covenanting minister to pray with him, he said—" All Scotland is either Presbyterian through their life or at their death, profess what they would."

Hanging on the walls of Leslie House there are the painted shadows of three of the Duke's chief associates. There is Dalziel of Binns, arrayed in shining armour. However barbarous his beard and dress might be when he neglected both to remind him of his vow to avenge the death of Charles I., he appears, in this portrait, trimmed into the appearance of a veteran and orderly soldier. His long, prominent, stern features, shaded with his grey hairs, are of a piece with his iron coat of mail in which he is encased.

On the further side of the same wall is the bloated, swollen, butcher-looking Duke of Lauderdale. He who started as a sainted Covenanter, and, by a sliding scale of apostacy, died an infidel. Betwixt the two hangs Archbishop Sharpe, dressed in canonicals. He looks not unlike what one of his contemporaries and co-presbyters said of him, " The greatest knave that ever was in the Kirk of Scotland."

These three were the men who, in company with the Duke, " drove and shook the ark of God in the Philistines' cart," hurried the country into risings, and by the very excess of their cruelties and oppressions prepared the way for the glorious Revolution of 1688.

It is scarcely possible to imagine a more beautiful contrast than that which the character and conduct of the Duchess of Rothes supplied to the Duke's. Wodrow says of her, " She never had a parallel for religion and every good thing in her age." Even in the days of his unfaithfulness, the Duke's profligate heart ofttimes relented in the presence of her injured meekness. A Christian in heart, and a Presbyterian in principle, she remained immovable amid Court smiles and Court threatenings. All her influence was directed to mitigate the persecutions of the afflicted Church, and to protect its humble members and adherents. Leslie House itself ofttimes afforded an asylum to the intercommuned minister. On such occasions, when in good humour, the Duke would give her a significant hint, " My lady, I would advise you to keep your chickens in about, else I may pick up some of them." Or, " My hawks are to be out to-night, my lady, so you had better take care of your blackbirds." On one occasion forty individuals were seized attending a conventicle at Glenvale, on the Lomond Hill, and were carried before the Duke. " Put them," said he, good humouredly, " in Bailie Walker's back room." The Bailie was a good man, and in his back room private prayer meetings were often held. When asked what more was to be done to them, he answered, "Give them plenty of meat and drink, and set them about their business in the morning." One can scarcely recognise the same individual in the Duke acting in this kindly manner on his own domains, and the Duke as President of the Secret Council, exulting over the unfortunate sufferer undergoing the torture of the boot or screw, and savagely ordering one twist more, or another touch.

The two daughters walked in the ways of their mother. Lady Margaret, who inherited the title of the Countess of Rothes and the estates, and who was married to the Earl of Haddington, was a model of Christian virtue. She and her husband resolutely eschewed the political religion of the Duke, refused the test, and stedfastly supported the Presbyterian interest under its persecutions.

Her son became the eighth Earl of Rothes. He died young. An interesting memorial of his death has been preserved to us by Lieutenant-Colonel Blackadder, son of Mr Blackadder, the outed Presbyterian minister, who in the days of persecution, had sometimes been sheltered in Leslie House. The following is the Colonel's account :—

"May 6th, 1722.—Took a sudden resolution again to go to Leslie, hearing my Lord is very ill. Riding alone all the day ; serene, serious temper. Came to Leslie at night, and was much affected, and I hope edified, seeing my Lord's carriage. He called all his family together, and took leave of them solemnly; recommended them to the serious study of religion and holiness, as the one thing needful—as that alone which would make them happy in time and to eternity, and that when they came to be in the condition he was in (death looking them in the face), they would see it to be so. Then he prayed most fervently; this was very affecting to us all He shewed the greatest submission and resignation; and though he was in much pain, yet the greatest patience, never uttering the least fretting expression; shewing a desire to be gone, yet submitting to the will of God as to the time. About eleven at night he caused his son, Lord Leslie, read Psalm xxxiv. to him, and as he went along, he repeated the emphatical expressions, such as, *I sought the Lord, he heard me and delivered me, &c. This poor man cried, and the Lord heard him. O taste and see that God is good, &c.* I left him about twelve, being so much fatigued and affected that I fainted away.

"I waited on my Lord next day, and it was

well spent time. He shewed a lively faith, trusting in God, relying upon his promises and his faithfulness, and gave solid reasons of his hope; declaring his full satisfaction with the Gospel method of salvation; and besought a minister that was present and me to deal plainly with him, and tell him if we thought he was wrong, or if we thought his faith was true, and right founded; or if we thought it was presumption. For my part I could not refuse to give testimony to the Spirit of God, and to the truth and reality of that gracious work of the Spirit, which by all the skill and experience I had in religion, I thought I saw in him. So we encouraged him to go on believing, trusting, relying. He spoke to excellent purpose during the day; was very pertinent and ready in the Scriptures; prayed once I think publicly, and often privately, with his eyes so fixed and intent towards heaven, as if he were looking into it, and reminded me of Stephen, Acts vii. 55.

" He desired the physician, and he himself frequently felt his pulse, not for the prolonging of life, but to observe how fast he spent and weakened; and was not pleased when they promised him long time to live; telling us he had no more to do here, and was well content to go out of a vain, sinful world, *and to be with Christ which is far better* This humility and good nature he carried with him to the last; and even his brisk, cheerful temper, and pleasant way of speaking. When they told him that one of his physicians was gone, he said, smiling, 'The doctor thinks I will not die to-night, but perhaps I shall beguile him.' I sat up with him till about one in the morning, and then I left him; for he pressed me to go, and said he would send for me when he grew weak.

"May 9.—Called in the morning, my Lord being weak. This day he prayed once in public with his family with great earnestness, recommending them to God; and prayed secretly, often with fixed fervent looks towards heaven. As he weakened, he began to be delirious, but whenever spiritual discourse was begun to him, he immediately came to himself again, and joined in it with the greatest seriousness, and he bade us that were about him check him when we found him wavering, which we took the freedom to do, and which he took most kindly. About three hours before his death, his thoughts began much to waver, and the fever seized his head, and he became uneasy, but suddenly his spirit fled, and he went away calmly with little struggle. In a word, I never saw any man die more as a Christian hero, with so much natural fortitude, and such lively faith. He was pleasant in his life, and pleasant in his death. O keep the impression strong upon my heart for ever, of what I have seen and heard here!"

The names of Ebenezer and Ralph Erskine, two of the Fathers of the Secession in 1733, come in our way as incidentally connected with Leslie. Ebenezer, about the time he was licensed, acted as tutor to the Rothes family. A stouter asserter and defender of Reformation faith and Reformation principles Scotland has not produced, in any age, than Ebenezer Erskine.

In the Leslie Churchyard, this epitaph on the tombstone, of John Archer, and Agnes Walker, his spouse, both of whom died in 1711, is said to have been written by Ralph Erskine—

> " Here lies within this earthen ark,
> An Archer grave and wise;
> Faith was his arrow, Christ the mark,
> And glory was the prize.

> His bow is now a harp, his song
> Doth Halleluiahs 'dite;
> His consort, Walker, went along
> To walk with Christ in white."

These lines have the genuine ring of "The Gospel Sonnets," and "The Believer's Riddle." But within the enclosures of the grave-yard criticism is inclined to silence. The solemn mystery of life is felt. All that bare heraldry, or poetry, or sculpture can do seems insignificant compared with the spiritual hope, honestly expressed by the humble Secession minister, whose whole mind and affections were in close and constant sympathy with the mind and heart of God.

These historical notices are given as illustrative of the piety and principle of Scotland. The piety of a land is like the corn crops and the grass, which grow up in a year, and are used up in a year, for the sustenance of man and of cattle. The principles of a land are like the tall and spreading trees which adorn the valley, or shelter the mountain side, and out of which timber is got to build churches, schools, and houses, the halls of commerce, and the courts of justice.

Every one that loves his country with an intelligent love will desire that the memory of her contendings, and the knowledge of her principles, may never die out of the land.

END OF PART III.

PART IV.

St Andrews.

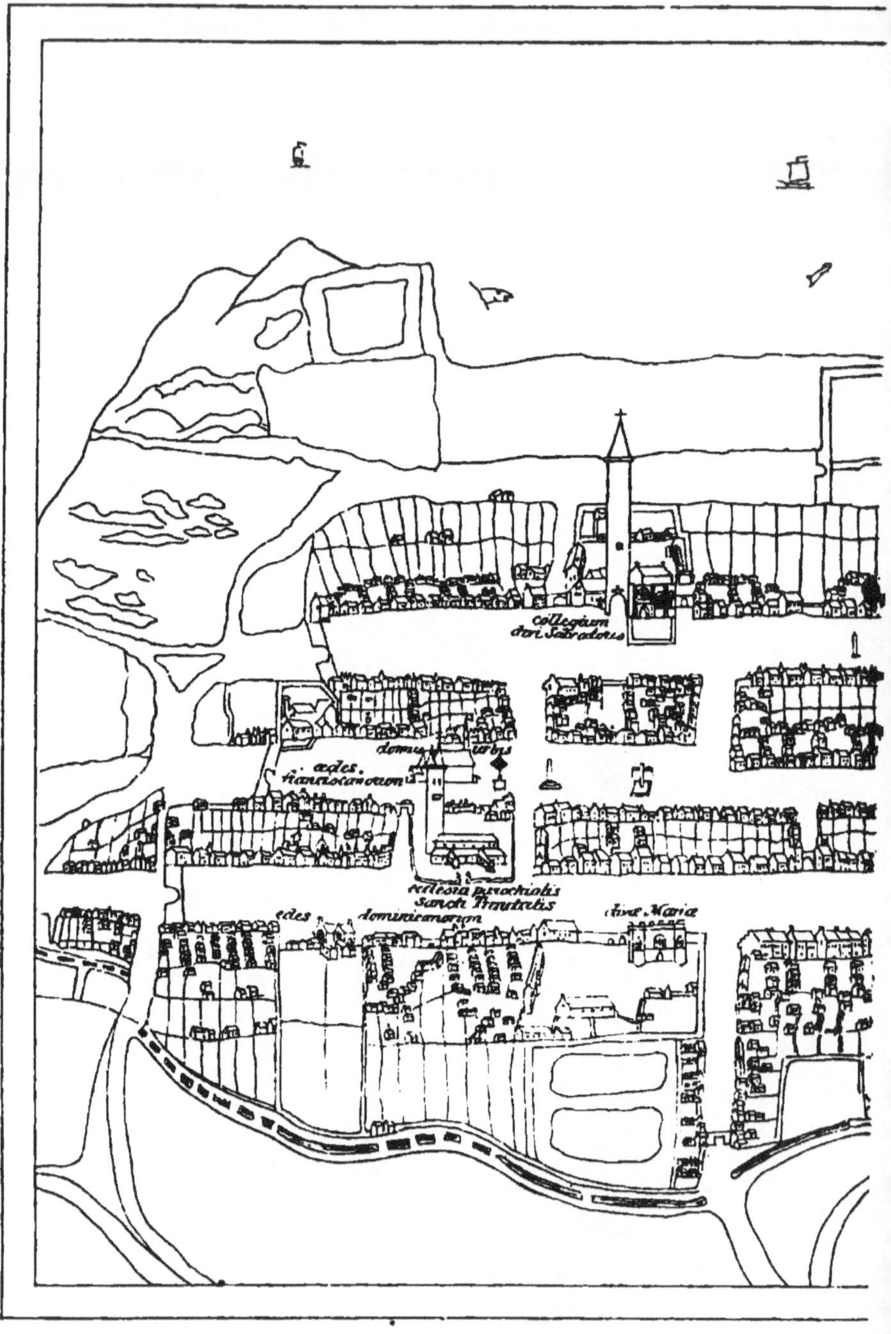

collegium dni Salvatoris
aedes franciscanorum
domus urbis
aedes dominicanorum
ecclesia parochialis sancti Trinitatis
divae Mariae

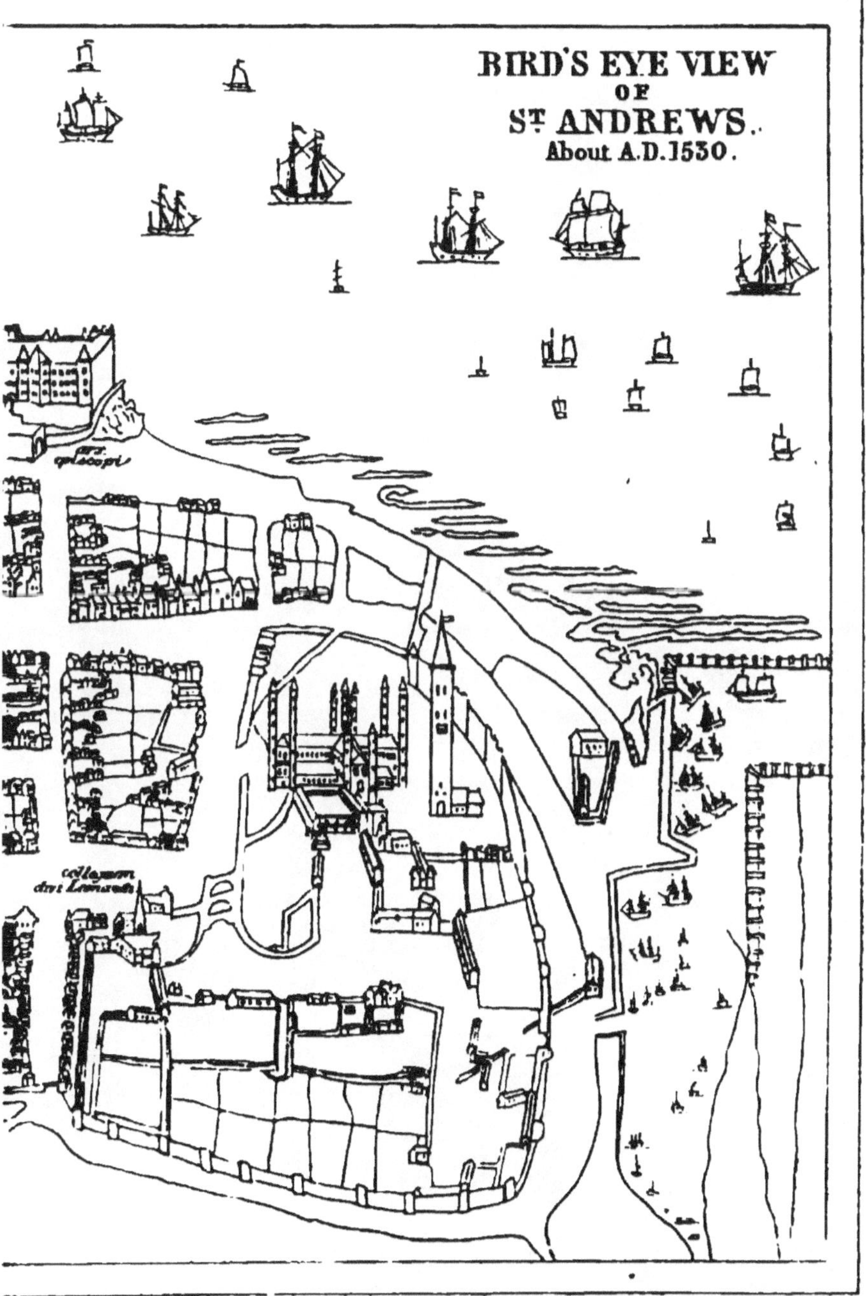

BIRD'S EYE VIEW
OF
ST ANDREWS.
About A.D. 1530.

St Andrews,

CHAPTER I.

PROBABLY no city in Scotland is more vividly
and distinctly photographed on many minds than
this old city of St Andrews.   Hundreds of educated men in all parts of the world, and of every
profession, well remember when first they heard
the long roll of the waves on the western sands,
and saw the old town standing on its rocky promontory, with its steeples and ruined towers relieved against the evening sky.   The remembrance is indelible; for it is connected with the
first separation from home, and with the first
realised conviction that life must be a work of
self-reliance and of labour.

This St Andrews is the Oxford of Scotland.

As of Oxford, so of St Andrews, it may be said, it is a town in a University. The academic here prevails. The air and aspect of the city are of Halls and Colleges. Not inappropriately did Professor Tennant, the author of " Anster Fair," say, " the very place provokes to study." Much more so was this the case a few years ago than now, for then St Andrews had not the jaunty gaity of a frequented watering place, but the sober and severe gravity of a studious retreat.

It is not easy to tell where first outgoings may conduct. It was on a country walk that we first set out to visit a few old castles, and ruined abbeys, and to connect their grey walls with the events which in olden times they had witnessed. And now in the same historical search, we find ourselves treading, in our country hobnails, the streets of the once ecclesiastical metropolis of Scotland. It is not to admire the symmetry of arch or column, or to attempt to revive from their ruins the architectural achievements of the past ; it is not on an excursion of artistic gratification that we have come. Our humble wish is to stand on spots where heart has triumphed, to allow the associations which arise unbidden to envelope us, and there to meditate for a little upon the faith and patriotism of the high-souled witness - bearing which ennobled martyrs, and which is still blessing their country. In the harvest season no songster entertains us with melody, few wild flowers smile on our pathway, because there is a larger song of praise and a wider expanse of beauty ; the hills and valleys wave with plenty, they also sing and shout to God, for He has made them glad. Even so must the æsthetic and artistic give place to the great and the heroic.

And what appearance had this old city in those days, when these scattered ruins stood in finished beauty ? Even an unimaginative mind asks this question, and forms its own picture.

Then rose the Cathedral, a completed structure—with apse, naves, and aisle, with its Gothic windows, its heavy buttresses, its niches and their saintly statues, and its copper-covered roof, shining under the sun-beams, a mark to ships far out at sea. A wall, with round towers, gave protection to the city ; and ports, with St Andrew and his cross sculptured over their wide gates, admitted carriages; while the foot traveller went in and out by the narrow postern. The College of St Salvator, with its stately steeples, surveyed the city, which is chiefly composed of narrow houses, with crow-stepped gables, covered with reed. The Castle stood in its strength, looking toward the sea, and guarded by fosse and portcullis. Three Colleges and three Monasteries were scattered throughout the town, each standing within its own inclosure ; and six Churches opened their doors for mass and confession.

The every-day aspect of St Andrews was then picturesque enough, for it was made up of variety and contrast. Shaven monks and hooded Friars, the Cardinal flaunting in scarlet, and great dignitaries of the Church in every variety of garb, armoured knights and broad-frilled courtiers, a student now and then, or a gowned regent, were seen on its streets. Bells tolled at canonical hours, and honest burghers dropped on their knees in the presence of priestly processions bearing the Host.

A more unusual commotion was awakened when Royalty arrived, or when some political combination brought together a band of nobles and their armed retainers, or when the Senzie Fair came round, and crowded the town with peaceful merchants, intent on trafficking.

Such was the notable town of Sanct Androis,

as it stood in the pomp of ecclesiastical grandeur. The Pope then ruled the Church, and the Church in turn ruled the nation.

We purpose a more minute and leisurely survey, and we begin with the times nearing the Reformation, which may be regarded as the epoch of Scotland's real history.

Let us take our stand in presence of St Salvator's College.

About the year 1450, the talk of the day throughout Scotland was busied in discussing the three great undertakings which the munificent James Kennedy, Archbishop of St Andrews, was engaged with. The first was what Lindsay of Pitscottie calls " the triumphant College" of St Salvator. The second was "his lair," or burying-place,. including under that term the present College Church, and the tomb which Kennedy erected in it to receive his own mortal remains. The third was the famous ship which he was building, and which was called the Bishop's Barge: " He knew not which of the three was costliest ; for it was reckoned at the time by honest men of consideration, that the least of the three cost him ten thousand pounds sterling."

Under the eulogising pen of Lindsay, Bishop

Kennedy rises, as he well deserves, to the dimensions of a great scholar, a great patriot, and a great Christian : " He was wondrous godly and wise, and was well learned in divine sciences, and practised the same to the glory of God." He acted as councillor to James II., and as preceptor to James III., and died in 1466.

In front of this College of St Salvator the martyr pile of Patrick Hamilton blazed, September 1525. On the morning of the day of his martyrdom, Hamilton was conducted from his prison-cell in the Castle, across to the Cathedral Church. There, in the presence of James, Archbishop Beaton, and of Bishops, Abbots, Clerks, Grey Friars and Black, he was accused of heresy by " ane black frier, callit Campbell." Most nobly did Hamilton close his testimony by these memorable words : " Nor yet believe I that there is anything can save the soul of man save only the blood of Christ, which ransom stands not in earthly things, neither mass, matins, nor dirges, but by repentance of our sins, and faith in Jesus Christ." " What need we any farther witness ?" say the Bishops and Kirkmen; " we ourselves have heard from his own mouth. He denies the institution of the Holy Kirk, and the

authority of the Holy Father the Pope." And so
they condemn him. The same day which heard
the sentence prononnced, witnessed the execution of it. The time was short, and the sentence
sharp, as another Scottish martyr afterwards
said. " Fornent this old College there was ane
great fire, and ane stake, and ane scaffold set,
whereon they put this innocent man, in presence
of the whole people." He speaks his last words
to the spectators, and offers up his last prayer to
God. The crackling flames do their work, and
in this fiery chariot his spirit ascends to heaven.
Thus fell Scotland's protomartyr. By birth he
was related to the first families of the land. In
age he was a youth, for he had scarcely completed his twenty-fourth year. In scholarship
he excelled all his countrymen. This was the
first of a long series of martyr fires, in the light
of which alone you can read Scotland's history
aright.

From the College our steps conduct us to the
Castle. Bare and cold it stands on its headland,
showing the weather taints of many centuries,
listening alternately to the waves of ocean breaking at its base, and to the rude winds blustering
round its battlements. Its date goes back as far

as to the year 1200, when Bishop Rogers built it as his Episcopal Palace. Recent excavations have exposed the fosse by which it was secured as a place of strength in turbulent times. Within its walls James I. was educated, and James III. was born. But our present object is to recall it as the scene of the captivity of that "maist godlie, learned, and noble Scots martyr, Mr George Wishart."

> " This prison is an holy place,
> And this sad floor an altar."

It was into the eastern, or sea tower, that George Wishart was thrown, in January 1546; and there he lay, straitly bound in irons, until the following March. His crime was that he preached the Word of God to be the only rule of faith, and faith in Christ the only way of salvation. He belonged to the Wisharts of Pittarrow, in Forfarshire, and is thus minutely and affectionately described by one who was his pupil in Cambridge:—"Maister George Wischart was a man of tall stature, polde-headed, and on the same a round French cap of the best. Judged of melancholy complexion by his physiognomy, black-haired, long-bearded, comely of personage, well spoken after his country of Scotland, courteous, lowly, lovely, glad to teach, desirous to learn, and was well travelled, having on him for his habit or clothing, never but a mantle frieze gown to the shoes, a black Milan fustian drubbit, and plain black hosiery, coarse new canvass for his shirts, and white falling bands and cuffs at the hands." There is an engraving taken from the original painting by Holbein, which gives an impression in some particulars different from the above description. Great gentleness and amiableness is the prevailing expression in the countenance which it pourtrays.

The trial of this witness to the truth was invested with much pomp and circumstance, so as to strike all beholders with awe. The Lord-Cardinal had caused his servants "to address themselves in their most warlike array, with jack, spear, and splint, and in warlike order to convey the Bishops to the Abbey Church." Mr George was conveyed by the Captain of the Castle, "lyke to ane lamb going to be sacrificed." As he entered the Church, a poor, lame beggar lying at the door asked alms, to whom he gave his purse.

Wynram, Dean of the Monastery, preached.

Sermon being ended, according to the order followed in the trial of heresy, they caused George Wishart to ascend a pulpit to listen to the articles of his accusation. The old chroniclers speak of the blustering threats and lying menaces of his accusers, and contrast them with his meek answers. The published reports of the trial more than warrant their statements: "Runnagate," " a heretic," " traitor," " thief," are some of the epithets applied to the gentle martyr. The reader will find in Foxe's Martyrology, or in Knox's History, his godly oration, and the pathetic prayer in which he gives expression to the wonder which exercises the souls under the altar—" How long wilt Thou suffer the rage and great cruelty of the ungodly to exercise their fury upon Thy servants, who do further Thy Word in this world?" But nothing will move the hearts of those who are resolutely set against the cause of Christ. The trial is concluded with the sentence that he be burned as " ane heretic."

Again is Mr George conducted back from the Abbey Kirk to the Castle.   A night intervenes betwixt the passing and the execution of the sentence ; and during that interval many moving things occnr. An offer is made that a priest will wait upon him for confession: "Send me," said Wishart, " the honest and godly man that made sermon yesterday." Wynram is sent for, and comes; and after an affecting interview, asks Mr George if he will have the sacrament. "Gladly," said he "if I can have it as Christ's institute." Wynram repairs to the Bishops, and bearing witness to his innocence, asks if the sacrament- might be given him. The Bishops consulted, and concluded that no benefit of the Church conld be given to an heretic. Bnt the sacrament he did get, and that, too, as Christ's ordinance, for thus it happened :—

" At the hour of noon, when the table was covered for dinner in the captain's chamber, Mr George was asked if he would partake : ' With ane gnde will,' said he, ' for that meat is my last meat.' And when they sat down and pnt silence in the house ane while, he declared unto them Christ's latter snpper, death, and passion, and exhorted them for the space of half-an-hour. This being done, he took bread and wine, and ate and drank himself, and gave it to the captain and the rest, blessing it in the name of the Father, the Sun, and the Holy Ghost."

Thus was celebrated in Scotland the first Protestant communion.

Meanwhile, in another part of the Castle, the Cardinal is entertaining his Bishops at dinner, and making merry with them ; outside the people are collecting in crowds, and the workmen are finishing the preparations of the stake, which was placed " before the Castle yett, on the west side, fornent the west blokehouse." At length all is ready. There is the stake heaped up for the martyr. There were cushions and carpeting spread on the battlements, that the Cardinal and his Bishops might at their ease survey the spectacle. The guns of the Castle are pointed towards the stake, and the men - at - arms are directed to surround it, lest a rescue should be attempted.

And now the godly martyr, clothed in coarse linen, and hung round with bags of powder, is led forth and tied to the stake. The fire is applied, and amid its crackling and enwrapping flames the martyr looks to where the Cardinal lies in pomp, and utters his doom in these prophetic words : " He that lies so glorious on yon wall-head, shall lye as shameful as he lyes glorious now."

Thus died George Wishart for the Word of God, and for the testimony of Jesus, 1st March, 1546.

Twenty-one years have passed away since Patrick Hamilton suffered a similar fate. Separated by time, Wishart and Hamilton are yet intimately associated. Both suffered at the stake as witnesses for Christ's blessed evangel; both were of high birth, of distinguished scholarship, and of eminent piety.

When there is heard the going of a sound on the top of the mulberry trees, the leaves and branches that are highest are the first to acknowledge the moving of the breeze.

It was scarcely three months until the forewarning which George Wishart uttered, regarding Cardinal Beaton, was fulfilled. The Cardinal was adding to the defences of the Castle, called by Pitscottie, "his Strength." The work was in progress on the morning of Saturday, 29th May, 1546. Masons and wrights were going out and in, and the drawbridge was lowered to receive the stones and lime, when Kirkaldy of Grange, with a few companions, approached and engaged the warder in converse. Norman Leslie, and those with him, came next and were admitted.

It was not until the rudeness of John Leslie of Parkhill, near Newburgh, Beaton's declared foe, alarmed the warder, that any attempt was made to let down the drawbridge. The resisting warder was in a moment despatched, the keys were taken from him, and his body cast into the fosse.

Kirkaldy of Grange now plants himself at the private postern. Norman Leslie busied himself in getting the workmen and retainers removed beyond the walls. Meanwhile, the Cardinal is awoke by the shouts and the clamour. He inquires from a window what the noise meant, and is answered that his castle is taken. He attempts escape by the postern, but finding it secured from without, he retires again to his chamber, and barricades the door. Leslie of Parkhill, Peter Carmichael of Balmeadow, and James Melville of Carnbee, demand admittance, and assail the door in vain, until they call for fire to burn it, when the Cardinal opens it. Both Leslie and Carmichael rudely attack and strike him, but James Melville, the friend of Wishart, and "a man of nature most gentle," interposes, and withholding them, addresses the Cardinal: "Repent thee of thy former wicked life, but especially of the shedding of the blood of that notable instrument of God, Mr George Wishart, which cries in vengeance upon thee, and we are sent to revenge it." A sword-stroke or two did the rest, and he whose name but yesterday was a name of terror in Scotland, now lies before them a lifeless corpse. Thus fell the Cardinal in the 52d year of his age. Norman Leslie, and Kirkaldy, and the rest of their companions gathered around the body, and thrust their daggers into it, to identify themselves with the deed. In Leslie House the dagger which Norman Leslie used on the occasion, is preserved.

While these things are doing, rumour runs through the town. Sir James Learmouth of Dairsie, the provost, and the other authorities, and a crowd of citizens, assemble, and from the outer side of the fosse demand to see the Cardinal. Those that held the Castle conveyed the dead body to the eastern tower, and hung it over the battlements in the sight of all men.

After being thus exposed for a time to remove all doubts regarding his fate, the body, "unknelled and uncoffined," was cast into the dungeon of the sea-tower, where it lay in salt for nine months. Thence it was taken, when the Castle was given up to Hamilton the governor, and obscurely buried in the convent of the Black Friars.

It was by the gate of this old Castle that John Knox, in July 1548, was led out, along with Mr Henry Balnaves of Hathill, and Mr James Melville of Carnbee, and other true-hearted companions, to be consigned prisoners to the French galleys. But this did not take place until Knox had disputed with the Kirkmen of St Andrews, and silenced them ; and until he had preached publicly in the Town Kirk, and denounced Popery as Antichrist. The last year had wrought a great change in public opinion. As was observed by Forsyth, the then laird of Nydie, " a man fervent and uprycht in religion," who often left the home-walks of his quiet farm that he might witness what was going on in the town—" Men now have other eyes than they had then." When Knox next appears on the scene in 1559, Scotland will be prepared for him by longer years of tyranny and superstition ; and he will be prepared for Scotland by exile, and prayer, and faith, and by the stirring of his own resolute spirit.

One other scene let us contemplate. The Castle has a new occupant in Archbishop Hamilton, the natural brother of the Governor of the Kingdom, but it still retains the old spirit of the bloody Cardinal. An aged man of the name of Walter Mylne, who had been parish priest of Lunan in Forfarshire, was seized by some of the Archbishop's messengers near to Dysart. When he was seized, he was "warming himself in ane poor wife's house, and was teaching her the commandments of God, and learning her how she should instruct her bairns, and her household, and bring them up in the fear of God." He was conveyed to St Andrews, and there, despite of his great age, for he was eighty-two years old, he was condemned to be burnt. The old man's words were very brave in answer to the charges that were laid against him. At length the Archbishop interposed, and said, " Wilt thou recant and thy life shall be spared?" "That will I not," said Mylne, " to grant myself ane heretic, for I am ane poor servant of God, whiles ganging to bed without my supper, and I desire no more wealth in this world, for I hope my reward shall be in Heaven; therefore do with me as you think best, for I will abide your judgment."

When the sentence was made known one unbroken burst of indignation was heard through the town.   The Provost, Sir Patrick Learmonth, refused to take part in the execution of the sentence, and left the town.   Not a rope, nor a barrel of tar, nor a pound of powder could be got in any booth in St Andrews.   But these obstructions were got over, and on the north side of the Cathedral, on the high ground overlooking the sea, the pile was prepared.   The old man was brought out, and was lifted up on the faggots which were to consume him.   In his dying testimony there was a strange commingling of the meekness of the martyr, and of the prophetic power of the seer: "As for me, it makes not meikle of my death, for I am four score and two years bygane, therefore by nature I have not long to live.   But if I be burnt at this time there shall ane hundred better than I rise off the ashes of my bones, and shall scatter the horrid pack of you hypocrites that perturb the servants of God. I trust to God that I shall be the last in Scotland that shall suffer for this cause."   And so it was, he was the last who suffered death for witnessing against Popery in Scotland.

A heap of stones was raised by the townspeople over the spot where he suffered, as a cairn of testimony against this deed of wickedness and cruelty. This gave deadly offence to the Archbishop and the kirkmen. Once and again was the heap demolished by them, and the Church's anathema denounced against those who should build it up again. But as often was the heap renewed, until, by night, all the stones were removed.

It was on the 25th of April 1558 that the aged Walter Mylne suffered, and over his grave it was afterwards truly inscribed that the faith of Jesus, revealed in holy Scripture, while it was to others the cause of life, was the occasion of death to him :—

Sola fides Christii sacris signata libellis,
Quæ vitæ causa est, est mihi causa necis.

A befitting close to this record of violent deaths, endured for the Word of God and the testimony of Jesus, is supplied by the words of Lord Bacon —" Martyrdoms I reckon among miracles, for they exceed the strength of human nature."

From the Castle we cross to the Cathedral.

The 10th of June 1559 saw the Cathedral in completed beauty. Its buttresses rested firmly on the ground, its turrets and minarets rose gracefully in the summer sky, and the setting sun was brightly reflected, as it had often been, from its copper-covered roof and from its glass-stained windows. This was the last day of its magnificence. On the 11th its glory was laid in ruins.

Knox, feeling that Scotland's crisis had arrived, ascended the pulpit of the Town Church in defiance of the threats of Archbishop Hamilton, and preached a fervid sermon on Christ's casting out the buyers and sellers from the Temple. His appeals fell on ears and hearts prepared to receive them. With expedition the work of demolition was begun. The provost and magistrates agreed to the removal of all monuments of idolatry; the commonalty of the town cast down the altars, and carrying the images, burnt them on the spot where Walter Mylne was martyred; while some of the baser sort, rejoicing in lawless license, hurried reformation into ruin.

In the presence of the ruins of this once magnificent Cathedral, it may be difficult to mitigate the censure of those who regard the religion of a country but as one of the fine arts. We would offer to their consideration the observation of one of the greatest of modern thinkers:—"These proud piles were, in fact, raised to celebrate the conquest, and prolong thedominion of the powers of darkness over the souls of the people. They were as triumphant arches, erected in memorial of the extermination of that Truth which was given to be the life of man."

To those whose patriotism rejoices in the solid attainments of their country, these ruins will appear as an incidental mishap attendant upon a great and salutary revolution. They will regard a humble church, destitute of architectural ornament, with bare walls and deal pews, placed in the centre of a thriving village, which week after week supplies to those who occupy its crowded benches the vigorous truths of the Gospel, which invests their cottages with the hallowed quiet of a Protestant Sabbath, and which on the Monday, sends forth the scholar to the school, and the mechanic to the workshop, and the ploughman to the fields, as far preferable to stately steeples casting their shadows over deserted streets, looking forth on undrained fields, and tolling forth a frequent summons to the observance of ceremonies which leave the mind uninformed and the heart unimpressed.

A representation of St Regulus' Tower and

Chapel formed the device on the Archbishop's seal. It is very rude, yet does it convey some idea of what that venerable building was when the square tower was surmounted by a spire and cross, when the chapel extended its front on both sides of the tower, and when a small turret, a *fac simile* of the large tower, stood on one of its corners.

The year 1560 brought with it to Scotland the glorious Reformation from Popery, with all its unnumbered blessings. The appearance of the country is changed, and on no portion of it is the change more visible than St Andrews, hitherto named " the Metropolis of Darkness." The Castle, the Archbishop's residence, is now tenantless. The Cathedral stands unroofed. The friars—grey, black, and white—have disappeared. Instead of Bishops, you now meet with Lords of the Congregation. The whole town breathes more freely, and public anxiety is on tip-toe to hail every new report of the progress which Protestantism is making through the land.

In the year 1566, a company of grave divines, dressed in Geneva cloaks and caps, attracted the notice of the inhabitants. They might be seen in the early forenoon passing along in little companies of twos and threes, with a heavy volume under their arm, and again separating to their lodgings in the evening. These are the superintendents and some of the more eminent ministers of the Reformed Church of Scotland, who have met to consider the Helvetic Confession of 1566, issued by the pastors of Znrich— among the first of these confessions emitted by the Churches of the Reformation, which, by their marvellous harmony, evince that, when truth is sought for with a single eye, unity of creed is not the visionary unattainable thing which modern writers represent it to be.

We may in passing look within the precincts of the Priory, merely to call to mind that it was from this that Regent Murray took his title and derived his revenues as Lord Prior, and that royalty was oft times hospitably entertained here. Queen Mary, on many different occasions during 1561 and 1562, abode here, " remaining for ane space." After the Raid of Ruthven, in 1583, James VI. arrived here from Falkland. Meeting some of his nobles and barons in whom he could confide, at Dairsie, " His Majesty," writes Sir James Melville of Halhill, " thought himself at liberty, expressing great joy, like a bird flown out of a cage, passing his time in hawking by the way, after his meeting them, thinking himself sure enough ; albeit, I thought his estate far surer when he was in Falkland.   For when he came to St Andrews, he lodged in an old Inn (vetus hospitium), in a very open part, the yard dykes being his great strength."

St Leonards, in its quiet retirement, with its shady entrance and sunny gardens, invites our steps.   Here the vanished past readily rises up before our thoughts. It was within this academic retreat that the doctrines of the Reformation found an unacknowledged refuge.   Hence it was a saying in years preceding the Reformation, "He hath drunk of St Leonard's Well," the meaning of which was, that the person was in his heart favourable to the Reformed doctrine. "Our hail college," writes James Melville in 1571, "masters, and schollars, were sound and zealous for the good cause.   The other twa colleges (St Salvator's and St Mary's), were nocht sae." James Melville studied here.   His autobiography will continue to fascinate with its many charms while books exist.   It was within this college-yard that John Knox was wont to come in 1572, when lodging in the Abbey, "and call us scholars unto him, and bless us, and exhort us to know God and his work in our country, and stand by the gude cause, to use our time weel, and learn the gude instructions and follow the gude example of our masters." It was in the halls of this college that, in 1574, a General Assembly was held, when Patrick Adamson announced the memorable distinction of my Lord Bishop (the Popish Bishop), my Lord's Bishop (the Tulchan Bishop), and the Lord's Bishop (the sincere minister of Christ).

Over this college the distinguished George Buchanan presided as Principal in 1566.

> " It sae bechanced at that hour,
>   That in Sanct Leonard's tapmast tower,
>   Don George Buchanan, douce and meek,
>   Was reading by his windock-cheek,
>   After a three hours' spell at Greek,
>   His Hebrew Bible richt."

The unfailingly uniform portrait of George Buchanan has made every reader familiar with his solid and sagacious countenance, surmounted with his skull-cap, and finished off with his venerable beard.

Among the sights which this spacious South

Street presented towards the latter part of the 16th century, none was more impressive than that of old John Knox proceeding from his lodging in the Abbey to the Town Church to preach. On week-day and on Sabbath-day he went, and thus was he seen : "I saw him every day of his doctrine go hulie and fear (warily) with a furring of martricks about his neck, a staff in the ane hand, and gude, godly Richard Bellenden, his servant, holding up the other oxter, from the Abbey to the Parish Kirk; and by the said Richard and another servant lifted up the pulpit, whar he behoved to lean at his first entry, but afore he had done with his sermon he was sae active and vigorous that he was lyke to ding that pulpit in blads, and fly out of it."   A word picture this most truly pre-Raphaelite.

CHAPTER II.

THIS chapter begins some years after the period at which the last closed.   John Knox has breathed his last, and is laid in his grave in the

Greyfriars' Churchyard of Edinburgh—a grave ever to be associated with the memorable words which the Earl of Morton uttered on the day of the funeral: "Here lies one who never feared the face of man." The conflict so victoriously closed by Knox had been waged with Popery, that spiritual wickedness in high places; still is the Church's history to continue a history of conflict, but now it is to be maintained with the powers of this world, and with the Church's own apostate sons.

Most notable the fact is, and worthy of being pondered, that while Hooper, Latimer, Cranmer, Jewel, and all the most eminent of the Reformation divines of England, desired that the Church of England should be modelled according to the pattern of the Scottish and other Reformed Churches, the secular politicians of Scotland laboured to have the government of the Church of Scotland conformed to that of England. A cross current this is which no ecclesiastical chart should omit. In England the desire of the divines evaporated in a few feeble and futile attempts. In Scotland the desire of the politicians ripened into a struggle long and ardent, wherein the Church and country were arrayed against King and Court, and "spiritual wisdom" was set against "black policy." No town in Scotland knew more of this contest than St Andrews.

The two Melvilles—James Melville the nephew, and Mr Andrew the uncle—inaugurated a new era in the literature and philosophy of Scotland. James Melville, when regent under his uncle in Glasgow College, was the first in Scotland who taught Aristotle's logic in Greek. Mr Andrew, as Principal, "taught things nocht heard of in this country before," for he employed the whole course of philosophy as known in the schools, and this over and above "his own ordinary profession, the holy tongues and theology." He was the first who gave instruction in Hebrew, Chaldee, and Syriac, and made the sacred Scriptures his text-book.

The fame of St Mary's College as a school of divinity dates from the coming of these two men in December 1580. This seminary was founded by Archbishop James Beaton in 1538, but it had never risen much above the importance of a Pedagogy. Now, however, its obscurity was exchanged for eminence. It became as a city set on a hill. Andrew Melville's desire was,

that as a Protestant College it should counteract the Jesuit seminaries abroad. To this he
was moved by his intercourse with Mr Thomas
Smeaton, who, having been himself a seminary
priest, was well acquainted with the devices and
plots of the Jesuits, and who ceased not to warn
ministers to study the Popish controversy.

A more engaging sight St Andrews did not
present than the tender affection which united
these two Melvilles. Often together, James
always showed the most marked respect to his
uncle, while Mr Andrew returned it with an almost fraternal kindness. Nor was it a great
difference of age which separated them. James
was in his 25th year when he became Professor
in St Mary's, and Mr Andrew was only ten years
older. James was taller than his uncle, and had
a winning gentleness of expression in his countenance. Mr Andrew was light and wiry, short
in stature, and walked with an elastic gait. His
keen eye and compressed lip shewed the heroic
stoutness which dwelt in the man.

He had travelled through much of the Conti-
nent on foot, had studied at Paris, had taught in
Poictiers, and afterwards was associated with
Theodore Beza for five years, as Professor in

Geneva. He bore the character of one of the first scholars in Europe.

Most willingly would he have spent his days in the academic quiet of St Mary's, paying court to the muses during his hours of relaxation in the lays of classic Rome, prelecting in the class-room, and with the easy familiarity of table-talk, entertaining and instructing both students and professors after dinner and supper. But "lettered ease" he had none. All his labours were conducted amid the clash and din of opposition. At the outset he had to encounter the wrath of the regents of philosophy in St Leonard's College. He had oppugned, in his public lessons of theology, Aristotle as one of "the patriarchs of heresy." Immediately the outcry was raised that "their great Diana, their bread-winner, their honour, their estimation, was assailed." But this contest had a meet ending. After "meikle fighting and fashirie," his chief opponents yielded to the truth, "became baith philosophers and theologians, and served as honest, upright pastors in the kirk." His next struggle was with the Provost and magistrates of the town, who, taking advantage of the generous and gratuitous services of James and Andrew Melville as preachers, would have held the ministry vacant, and spent the kirk rents in " goff, archerie, and gude cheer," against " the weil, baith of the town and university."

But his life-long struggle was with the King and his evil counsellors, in defence of the Church's government. That government he had seen completed by the labours of the ministers and elders of the Church, and ratified by the estates of Parliament in 1581. By that government a fence was set around the Church's doctrine. It was self-government mutually enforced by equals on each other. Its leading provision was that "bishops should be called by their ain names, or by the name of Breither iu all time coming, and that lordly authority and name be banished from the Kirk of God, which has but one Lord Jesus Christ, and that all bishops should act as pastors of particular congregations." No great difficulty was there to find Christ's authority for such a principle ; but the difficulty was to maintain it against

" The minions of a minion king,"

who would not allow that it could stand with free monarchy.

When opposed by the King and his courtiers in establishing this principle, the Scottish Reformers were led to contend for another great principle—the Headship of Christ, whereby they protested against "placing a vanishing shadow, a breath going and not returning again, with absolute power and authority in the room and seat of the Most Migh God." There is the vitality of God's truth in these principles. They have blessed Scotland, and they will bless her still.

It would be long to tell the particulars of that intrepid stand which Andrew Melville made for these great principles, and the sufferings which he endured in their defence. He was the first to decline the jurisdiction of King and Council when he was accused of no civil crime or misdemeanour, and to maintain that in matters of conscience and of doctrine he was not subject to them, but to Christ and to the Church. Thus did he lay the foundations of that liberty in which the nation now rejoices ; for it cannot be denied, and may Scotland never ungratefully forget, that it was in contending for the rights of Christ's Church that the civil freedom of this country was achieved. This formed the grand testimony of Andrew Melville. In the palace, at the council board, and in his own class-room, he maintained that there was another King, even Jesus, whose kingdom was a spiritual kingdom. For this he was banished and imprisoned, and at last died an exile in Sedan.

Nephew and uncle, as they were lovely in their lives, so in the manner of their death, they were not divided; for James, after fulfilling a short but blessed pastorate in East Anstruther, died in banishment at Berwick, 1614, aged 59.

There is one circumstance very visible in the Melvilles, and which familiarity with the personal history of the Scottish worthies would discover as characteristic of the whole class; it is the combination of every tender feeling, with the firm and robust in character. There is in the Scottish worthy unbending firmness in all that concerns the truth of God, associated with the most affecting sensibility. It is the same strange, yet fascinating combination of contraries which Nature, by one of its inimitable contrasts, presents in the flowing of soft and pliant water over hard and rugged rock.

The reader will willingly receive in illustration of this the following artless account of the feelings of James Melville, when his uncle was forced to flee to escape the wrath of the King :—

"As for myself, to confess the truth, I was almaist exanimate with heaviness of heart, the which, if it had not resolved in abundance of tears, my life had been suffocate; for the which cause I took me to a chalmer, and closing the door, let my affections break out and go loose at random, which a special loving friend of mine, waiting on me, suffered for the space of an hour; but after knocked sae and spake to me, that baith for love and reverence it behoved me to open ; who not only used all the comforts he could, but waited on me, and conveyed me hame to St Andrews ; this was Andrew Wood of Strathvithie.

" At my coming to St Andrews, my wound, scarcely stemmed, began to bleed apace, finding naething, wherever I cast my eyes, but matter of melancholy. His books were in danger, he being put to the horn, and therefore I addressed me with diligence to pack them up, and put them aside, and scarce was there ane which I had known in his common use that rankled not my wounds again, sae that that labour was very painful and heavy to me. But above all it was a daily heart-break to me to see that notable wark sae weil begun, yielding in the first spring-time of it sic appearance of plentiful fruits, with sic a calamity, cut off from all hope of harvest. I thought I felt continually a cauld heavy lump lying on my heart, lyking for to choak me ; and sure I am it had cost me my life, if the mighty hand of my God had not cured baith body and soul ; and after the curing thereof, fur-nished beyond all conscience of ability and expectation some measure of strength and gifts to take a piece of courage, and hauld on the spunk of life in the wark, until God should have mercy and return for the restoration thereof."

In every great movement, there is the reflux as well as the flow ; there is the periodical waning before the full development is reached. The fear and favour of the Court prevailed against the gallant struggles of Presbyterianism, and the old city saw the archiepiscopality re-stored, in name at least, but in greatly di-minished lustre. The first who wore the title of Archbishop of St Andrews, after the Refor-mation, was the unhappy Patrick Adamson, who, to enjoy it, turned traitor to his own pro-fessions.

The second was Mr George Gladstanes, who died in 1615.

Mr John Spottiswoode was next in succession. With him the title became extinct, in 1639, until it was revived in the person of Sharpe.

In every thing the spirit of these men was opposed to that of the Presbyterian ministers. Bishop Burnet thus speaks of them :—"As the Bishops were the creatures of King James, so they were obliged to a great dependence on him, and were thought guilty of gross and abject flattery towards him." "Some few that were stricter and more learned did lean so grossly to Popery, that the heat and violence of the Reformation became the main subject of their sermons and discourses."

The first, or post-reformation period of Scottish Episcopacy is comprehended in the lives of the three Bishops named above, so that here we may attempt to trace its characteristics. In its government it was very wily, for in its forms it tried to accommodate itself as much as possible to the forms of Presbytery, contenting itself with securing the supremacy of the Bishops. In its public worship it was non-liturgical, until a special liturgy was provided for it by Archbishop

Laud. Its psalter bore the right royal title, " The psalms of King David, translated by King James"—a poetical version of no mean merit. Its preachers in their public discourses enforced the divine right of kings, and the passive obedience of the subjects in all matters. It distracted, by its ambitions pretensions, a church which would otherwise have been nnited; and by depending for its existence upon the inquisitorial powers of the High Commission and the Star Chamber, it destroyed the civil liberties of the conntry.

In crossing from St Mary's and surveying the weather wasted steeple of the Town Chnrch, the mind is soon lost in recalling the crowding scenes of interest, which this venerable tower must have witnessed. It had seen from its calm elevation, cardinal, priest, and monk following in procession the uplifted Host. It had heard from within the walls of the old three-aisled Church dedicated to the Trinity, which stood at its base, the accents of Knox's rude eloquence, and Christopher Goodman's soberer teaching. It had listened to the didactic and expostulatory voice of Mr Andrew, and to the calmer tones of James Melville. It had seen Presbyterian Ministers, and Episcopalian Bishop or Dean alternating the service, as the influence of the crown, or the faith of the country obtained the temporary ascendancy.

In August 1639 there came to St Andrews as minister of that Church, Mr Robert Blair, being "esteemed the meetest man to fill the vacant place, where there were three Colleges, very corrupt, and the body of the townspeople addicted to prelacy and the ceremonies, it being the See of the Arch-prelate."   He had as his colleague Mr Samuel Rutherford, who consented to come to St Andrews as Principal of St Mary's College, on condition that he should have the privilege of preaching regularly every Sabbath.   The anecdote of the English merchant shortly and graphically presents the characteristic excellencies of the preaching of these two eminent ministers : "I went to St Andrews," said the merchant, "where I heard a sweet, majestic looking man (Mr Blair), and he showed me the majesty of God.   After him I heard a little fair man (Mr Rutherford), and he showed me the loveliness of Christ."

Local circumstances connect Mr Blair's name with the neighbourhood of St Andrews, for he became proprietor of Clermont, and through his exertions it was that Cameron was erected into a separate parish.

The space which he occupied in the eye of the Church and country .was large. His ministry was greatly owned of God in different parts of the land. His services were widely employed by the Church, the nobility, and the King. We meet with him as Chaplain in the Army, as Moderator in the General Assembly, as Commissioner to Westminster, and as Chaplain to the King. It was at the desire of King Charles himself that Mr Blair accepted the situation of chaplain, when Alexander Henderson died in 1646; and the terms which the King employed indicated his high estimation of Mr Blair:—" I think," said the King, " he is pious, prudent, learned, and of a meek and moderate calm temper."

Two things may be here noted in connection with Mr Blair, more especially as they characterised all Scottish Presbyterians. The one was his extreme distrust of Cromwell. When Mr David Dickson and he retired from an interview with Cromwell, Dickson remarked—" I am very glad to hear this man speak as he does." Mr Blair replied—" And do you believe him? If you knew him as well as I do, you would not believe

T

one word he says. He is an egregious dissembler, and a great liar. Away with him, he is a greeting devil." The other was his attachment to the unhappy Charles, and his strongly expressed condemnation of the King's execution. Charles had earnestly desired that Mr Blair might be permitted to be with him at his death, but this was refused. Mr Blair's feelings and purpose are thus described by his son-in-law :—" Mr Blair regretted that he could not obtain liberty, nay, not so much as to speak to the King; but thereafter did often profess, that if he had been permitted to have gone to the King, and to have been with him at his death, he would never have advised him so far to submit to that most illegal and wicked sentence of death, as to go upon his own feet to the scaffold, and that he (Mr Blair) was resolved so to speak and carry, on the scaffold, testifying against that horrid murder; that he laid his account to die with the King, and that he would as willingly have laid down his head to the hatchet as ever he laid his head to the pillow."

All this loyal attachment to the first Charles profited him nothing afterwards; for no sooner had the Restoration placed the second Charles on

the throne, than, through the intrigues of Sharpe,
Mr Robert Blair was banished from St Andrews
in 1661, and died at Couston, in the parish of
Aberdour, in 1666. His ornamented tomb-stone,
with its fading Latin inscription, may be seen in
front of the south wall of the ruined church of
Aberdour.

Stirring sights St Andrews saw during Mr
Blair's ministry.

In 1645 the Laird of Cambo marched through
the town at the head of a newly raised regiment,
with displayed banners and martial music, on
their way to Kilsyth, to oppose the progress of
the perfidious Montrose. In this battle, in which
Montrose conquered, many of these men of Fife
fell, and among them was Cambo, their captain.
But victory and defeat were not far apart. Only
a few months later, and the prisoners of Philiphaugh, where Montrose was defeated by General
David Leslie, were brought to St Andrews, and
afterwards executed. Among them was one, not
unknown in the city—Sir Robert Spottiswoode,
President of the Court of Session, and son of the
late Archbishop Spottiswoode.

In 1647 the town was alarmed by the appearance of the plague. During the alarm an affect-

ing and vigilant separation was observed betwixt the whole and the sick. Those who were whole met for public worship in the Market Street, in the Square, while the infected and suspected met in the field. Betwixt the living and the dying Mr Blair went, preaching to them both.

Occasionally some of Cromwell's troopers, with their short cropped hair and long swords, having come from their encampment at Struthers, might be seen sauntering in the streets, reminding the inhabitants by their presence of Oliver's supremacy. Lamont tells us that they sometimes intruded when their presence was not desired : " 1653, September 27. The Provincial Assembly of Fife sat at St Andrews, when Mr Robert Blair was moderator. About the close of this meeting two English officers came into the place where they satt; the judicatory inquired if they had come in with a purpose to sitt and voice with them; they answered not, but only they were commanded to come to hear and see that they acted nothing in prejudice to the Commonwealth. They answered that they had not so much as once nominated the Commonwealth since they sat down, and that they (meaning the English officers), were the first that spoke of the Commonwealth, and not the Assembly."

When we mentioned Samuel Rntherford as Principal of St Mary's College, and colleague with Mr Blair in the ministry of the Town Church, we named one of the most remarkable men of his day. He began his ministry in the secluded parish of Anwoth, in Galloway, having been settled there in 1627. It is no common person, and no common life, that leaves traces behind, which the passage of two centnries does not obliterate. There is a quiet nook which is still called " Rutherford's Walk." Two stones stand on the farm of Mossrobin, which bear the name of the Witnessing Stones of Rutherford; and one of the most iuteresting sights to the wanderer in Galloway is the old walls of the little church of Anwoth in which Rutherford preached. An earnest ministry was his at Anwoth. " Woods, trees, meadows, and hills," he wrote, " are my witnesses that I drew on a fair match betwixt Christ and Anwoth." A laborious student was he, as his study in Bushy-Bield witnessed, when with the morning light he rose to write his " Treatise on Grace," to check the rising flood of legalism, and to store his mind with that varied learning which gave him rank with the ripest scholars of his day.

Rutherford did not want tribulation, which Luther places among the three things which constitute a well-equipped minister of Christ. In December 1634, he writes to Lady Kenmure: "It has pleased the Lord to let me see from all appearances that my labours in God's work are at an end, and I must now learn to suffer, in the which I am a dull scholar. I desire not to go on the lee-side or sunny side of religion, or to put truth betwixt me and a storm, my Saviour did not do so for me, who in his suffering took the windy side of the hill." For his faithful adherence to Christ's persecuted cause he was warded in Aberdeen in 1636. In the streets of that city he used to be pointed out as the banished minister. Here he contended with the doctors of Aberdeen, and wrote those famous letters, regarding which there is no medium of opinion, for they are either the subject of highest appreciaiton, or of censure and contempt. They can afford to bear much, when Richard Baxter wrote of them: "Hold off the Bible, such a book the world never saw;" and when Richard Cecil, speaking of them, said, "They are one of my classics."

Rutherford was thirty-nine years of age when he came to St Andrews, in 1639, as Professor of Divinity in St Mary's. When the visitor enters the court of St Mary's he may observe, built into the walls, stones initialled D. R. H., M. R. H. These letters indicate the name of Mr or Dr Robert Howie, Rutherford's predecessor as Principal, and they were placed there when in his time the College was enlarged and repaired. Diligently and efficiently within this College enclosure did Rutherford ply his work as Professor, until, as Macward, one of his students, records, "God did so singularly second his indefatigable pains both in teaching and in preaching, that the University forthwith became a Lebanon, out of which were taken cedars for building the house of the Lord throughout the whole land."

Rutherford attended the meeting of the Westminister Assembly from 1643 to 1647, having been sent there as Commissioner; and when he returned to Scotland, it was with this attestation from that venerable Synod: "We cannot but restore him with ample testimony of his learning, godliness, faithfulness, and diligence, and we humbly pray the Father of Spirits to increase the number of such burning and shining lights among you."

But his very eminence marked him out for the malice and cruelty of the Prelates. Cromwell died in 1658. Charles II. was restored in 1660. Meanwhile, Sharpe, through the basest dissimulation, had betrayed the Church which sent him to London to overwatch her interests. The friends of Presbytery were now silenced and persecuted. Rutherford's name was among the first in the doomed list. His treatise, " Lex, Rex : the Law and the Prince. A discourse for the Just Prerogative of King and People," which defined with boldness and discrimination the leading principles of constitutional government, was denounced. On the 23d October 1660, a fire was lighted before the entrance of St Mary's, and that book was burnt with all the inquisitorial forms of reprobation. The author of it was suspended from his office, deprived of his income, and warded to his own house. But God's goodness prevented the remainder of man's wrath. When a messenger arrived to summon him as a traitor to appear and answer to the Parliament, which was to meet in March 1661, the messenger had to execute the summons on the sick man as he lay on his bed of death. "Tell them," was Rutherford's reply, "I have got a summons already before a Superior Judge and judicatory, and I behove to answer my first summons ; but ere your day arrive, I will be where few kings and great folks come." When this message was delivered, the Parliament, with impotent rage, decreed that he should be removed out of his house in St Mary's College, and not be allowed to die there. Lord Burleigh made this withering remark, after they had passed their resolution: "Ye have voted that honest man out of his College, but you cannot vote him out of Heaven."

On the 30th of March a funeral company assembled at St Mary's gate, and devout men carried him to his burial. They laid him in a grave under the shadow of the ruined Abbey. A stone has been placed over his tomb with the well-known inscription, in which the piety is better than the poetry—

> " What tongue, what pen, or skill of men,
>   Can famous Rutherford commend ?
>   His learning justly raised his fame,
>   True goodness did adorn his name.

> He did converse with things above—
> Acquainted with Emmanuel's love,
> Most orthodox he was and sound,
> And many errors did confound.
> For Zion's King and Zion's cause,
> And Scotland's covenanted laws,
> Most constantly he did contend,
> Until his time was at an end.
> At last he wan to full fruition
> Of that which he had seen in vision."

This epitaph had originally the date of October 9, 1735, and the initials of W. W. appended to it. Years after, the same spot received the mortal remains of Halyburton, and traditional veneration has named it *Sacred Ground*. It is gratifying to see that respect for Rutherford still lingers around his tomb, and has induced some admirer of his piety and principles of late to uplift the decaying stone, to letter it anew, and by placing it erect save it from the tread of the frequent visitors, and from the action of the weather.

Rutherford's last will and testament shows how little of this world's goods satisfied him. It is an humble inventory, in which his library, the student's wealth, bulks very large. " His books were estimat to 1800 lib. Item, the uten-

cills and domicills of his house, with the abulie-
ments of his body, all estimat to 200 lib.

" Summa of the inventori, 2000 lib."

We recur to an incident which caused no
small stir in St Andrews during Rutherford's
lifetime—it was the public entry of Charles II.
After leaving Holland, and landing at Dundee,
his Majesty came to St Andrews, 4th July 1650.
Every mark of loyal respect was paid him. The
keys of the city were presented to him at the
port, where Mr Andrew Honeyman, the minister,
made an address to him in English; and when
he came onwards in procession to St Mary's
College, Mr Samuel Rutherford made a speech
to him in Latin. The King lodged in the house
of Hugh Scrymgeour, near to the Abbey.

And here we may take occasion to allude to
the charge of disloyalty brought against the
Presbyterians of Scotland, as exhibiting one of
those historical untruths which party rage has
propagated, and thoughtlessness has received in
the face of the most flagrant evidence to the
contrary. During that long and arduous
struggle which England and Scotland maintained
for their freedom against the petulant despotism
of James VI., and the pertinacious despotism of

Charles I., the aim and desires of Scottish Presbyterians were summed up in that impressive declaration of the Earl of Loudoun : " Our desires are only the enjoying of our religion and liberties, according to the ecclesiastical and civil law of his Majesty's kingdom, and we humbly offer all civil and temporal obedience to your Majesty, which will be required or expected of loyal subjects." The Scottish Presbyterians being thus truly enlightened, and constitutional in their loyalty, were alike opposed to the unpatriotic subserviency of the Cavaliers and Churchmen, and to the violent extremes of Cromwell and the Sectarians. They stoutly protested against the execution of Charles I. They chivalrously espoused the cause of Charles II. In January 1649, Charles I. was beheaded ; on February 4th, Presbyterian Scotland proclaimed Charles II. King. In the face of Cromwell and his invading armies, they crowned Charles II. at Scone, in January 1651. During the whole of Cromwell's Protectorate, Scotland was treated as a conquered country, and was held in check by the presence of soldiers. Many were the fines levied upon Scottish gentlemen, and upon none more than those of Fife, for not yielding acknowledgment and submission to Cromwell's government.

We have made this induction of facts to show that instead of disloyalty there was a prodigal expenditure of loyalty on the part of Scotland, in behalf of the House of Stuart. In return for this, all that Scottish Presbyterians reaped after Charles II.'s restoration in 1660, was twenty-eight years of persecution and cruelty, such as no other nation had ever endured.

During these dismal twenty-eight years James Sharpe, Archbishop of St Andrews, stands out as one of the most prominent actors. To form a correct estimate of his character, the reader must view him in connexion with Leighton, Archbishop of Glasgow, author of the Commentary on Peter, which every one knows.

Both Leighton and Sharpe had been ordained, and had officiated as Presbyterian ministers— Sharpe at Crail, Leighton at Newbattle.

Both conformed to Episcopacy. Leighton did so from the fancy view he entertained of primitive Episcopacy, and from the flattering persuasion, that if rightly exhibited, it would be seen to be little different from Presbyterianism, and thus a union might be formed, and the contests of the time ended.   Sharpe conformed with the ambitious desire of aggrandising himself.

Leighton was pious; Sharpe was political. Both were re-ordained and consecrated at Westminster, 12th December 1661.   Both instinctively felt the uncongeniality of disposition and the contradiction of views by which they were respectively characterised.   The one distrusted and disliked the other.

Leighton's conscience took the alarm, as his memorable lamentation Burnet relates : " He said in a letter to Burnet 'that in the whole progress of that affair there appeared such gross characters of an angry Providence, that however he was satisfied in his own mind as to Episcopacy itself, yet it seemed that God was against them, and they were not like to be the men that should build up his Church, so that the struggling about it seemed to him like a fighting against God.' " Sharpe persevered with an ominous infatuation.

Leighton used all his influence to repress the persecuting measures which were employed to support Episcopacy.   Sharpe advocated them.   When Leighton remonstrated with Charles, the King laid the blame of these measures on Sharpe.

Leighton, after struggling for a time, withdrew from a Church from which he felt that Heaven's influences were withheld, and died in retirement, of a broken heart. Sharpe, with the bitterness of an apostate and the fury of a persecutor, continued to breathe out threatenings and slaughter against those of this way, until a violent death overtook him in 1679 on Magus Moor.

After Leighton and Sharpe were re-ordained and invested with their Episcopal dignities, Leighton refused to join in the pomp of a public entry, and quietly retired to his residence in Dunblane. The grandeur of a procession was quite a thing after Sharpe's mind, and thus are the particulars noted by our zealous diarist, Lamont:

" As for Mr Sharpe, he came to Fife April 15, 1662, and dyned that day at Abctsau (Abbotshall), Sir Andrew Ramsay's, formerly provost of Edinbro', his house, and that night came to Lesly, being attended by divers, both of the nobilitie and gentrie. The next day, being Wednesday, the 16th of April, he went to St Andrews from Lesly, attended from the Earl of Rothes, his house, with about 60 horse; but, by the way divers persons and corporations (being

written for in particular by the said E. of Rothes
a day or two before,) mett him, some at ane
place, and some at ane other, viz., some from
Faukland, Achtermoughtie, Cupar, Craill, and
about 120 horsemen from St Andrews and elsewhere, so that once they were estimate to be
about 700 or 800 horse. The nobilitie ther were
E. of Rothes, E. of Kelly, Earle of Leven, and
the Lord Newwarkes; of gentrie, Ardrosse,
Lundy, Rires, Dury, Skaddoway, Doctor Mairtin,
of Strandry, and divers others. All the way
the said Archbishop rode thus, viz., betwixt two
noblemen, namely, Rothes on his right, and
Kelly on his left hand. No ministers were present ther, safe Mr William Barclay, formerly
deposed out of Faukland, and Mr Walter Comry,
minister of St Leonard's College, that came forth
with the Bishop, his son, out of St Andrews to
meet his father. (He dwells in the Abbey in
Mr George Wemyss' house, that formerly belonged to B. Spottiswoode, Archb. of St Andrews). That night there supped with the said
Bishop the E. of Rothes, Kelly, Newwarke,
Ardrosse, Lundy, Strandry, and divers others;
and divers of them dined with him the next day.
As for Rothes and Ardrosse, they lodged with

him all night. On the Sabbath after he preached
in the Town Church in the forenoone, and a
velvet cushion in the pulpit before him ; his text,
1 Cor. ii. 2, ' For I determined to know nothing
amonge you save Jesus Christ, and him crucified.'
His sermon did not run mutch on the words, but
in a discourse of, vindicating himself, and of
pressing of Episcopacie and the utilitie of it,
showing, since it was wanting, that ther hath
beine nothing but troubels and disturbancies
both in Church and State."

In Wodrow's correspondence we have a similar accouut of Archbishop Sharpe's first sermon by
one who heard it. Wodrow's informant adds,
that the Archbishop closed his discourse by telling, " that if these arguments he had offered were
not convincing, he had more painful ones in re-
serve." This same informant, by bribing the
door-keepers, got admission into the first Synod
which the Archbishop held, and hiding beneath
the seats heard what was done : " He said there
were very many absent, at which the Bishop
stormed not a little. And further, when a minister, whom he thinks was the minister of Leuchars,
complained of the growth of Popery in their
bounds, and entreated that some means might be

U

fallen on to suppress it, the Bishop, with heat and violence said : " Let alone of that, sir; let us take care to bear down the fanatics, our greatest enemies."

For seventeen years did Sharpe enjoy his Archi - episcopal elevation ; if enjoyment it could be, to live as the primate of subservient curates, as the companion of profligate aud apostate nobles, such as Lauderdale and Middleton, as the destroyer of his country's liberties, and the oppressor of his country's Church, as a councillor of the High Commission and Star Chamber, in constant fear alike of the prayers of the godly and of the sword of the assassin. Probably no man could be named in the whole of Scotland's chequered history, whose career is more chargeable with the blood of the quiet livers of a land than Sharpe.

The executiouers of the bloody counsels, which Sharpe advocated iu the Star Chamber, were Claverhouse, Dalzell of Binns, Grierson of Lagg, and Bruce of Earlshall ; men whose soldierhood consisted in hunting and shooting down poor peasants, and whose bravery was manifested in blasphemously outragiug the forbearauce of a long-suffering God.

Popery has written her errors on flowers. Many of the names which wild flowers bear show their Popish origin. Mariolatry is inscribed on very many of them, such as Lady's Mantle, which means our Lady's, the Virgin Mary's Mantle ; Lady Grass, Lady's Bedstraw, &c. &c. Presbyterianism has associated her antipathies with weeds. There is a weed which every worker of a garden knows, a weed with a smooth leaf and spreading root, which grows in shady places, and which is most difficult to get rid of when once it has got into the soil. This weed is known in England by the name of *Goutweed*. In Scotland it is called *Bishopry*. One sunny day in June, Sharpe was sauntering in his garden within the Abbey enclosures, and was amusing himself by observing the gardener at his work. This weed came frequently in the man's way. " What do you call that troublesome weed ?" asked the Archbishop. " Aye," said the man, " it is a bitter bad weed, they ca' it *Bishopry*, my Lord, and when its ance got in, it's no easily got out." This answer cost the man his place, and two or three twists of the thumb screw, and much ill usage, for Sharpe suspected, and on inquiry found that the man was a favourer of the Presbyteria n cause.

Sharpe had only two successors in the Archbishopric. The one was Alexander Burnet, who died in 1684; the other was Arthur Ross, who was unseated in place and power by the glorious Revolution of 1688.

We are thus brought forward to the second, or Ante-Revolution period of Scottish Episcopacy, and may pause in passing to survey its characteristics. We wont be long detained, for it has but the one prevailing feature of cruelt y and persecution. It appears red with the blood of slaughtered saints. God only knows the amount of suffering and of sorrow which, by cruel deaths, by torture, by imprisonment, by fires, by banishments, poor Scotland endured at the hand of Scottish Episcopacy betwix t the years 1660 and 1688. To the last it exerted its envenomed and deadly influence against that which has made Britain great; for, while in England the Bishops were co-operating with the Nonconformists in effecting, on behalf of their common Protestantism, the blessed Revolution; and, while in Ireland Episcopalians and Presbyterians fought as fellows in the siege of Derry and Enniskillen, Scottish Episcopacy, feeling that their interests were inseparable, firmly adhered to the House of Stuart, to Popery, and to absolutism.

~~~~~~~~~

CHAPTER III.

THE seventeen years of Sharpe's primacy had given St Andrews a most undesirable distinction. While he lived a certain measure of briskness might have been imparted to the town by the expending of his Archiepiscopal revenues, and by the resort of place-seeking clergy ; but every thing that ennobleth and exalteth a place perished.   In dens and caves, in moss and moorland, where God-fearing men lay hid ; in cottages, which mourned the absence of father and brother out on the hills, with a price set on their heads ; in the flats of Holland, where noblemen and gentlemen lived in exile, the name of St Andrews was a name of ill omen.   It was the seat of that Black Prelacy which broke God's folk in pieces, and which oppressed God's heri-
~~~~~~~~~

tage.   These seventeen years have more to do with the subsequent ecclesiastical history of the town than most suppose.

The professors and ministers had acted so often the part of what was known in the phrase of these times as "Jack on both sides," that all sense of public principle had disappeared, and although the Vicar of Bray had not appeared, his resolution was uniformly acted upon, that come what might, they would hold their places, where they might eat and drink, might dose and die.   In vain after this you look for any appearance on behalf of Christ's cause.   Hereafter all Christian memories of the Scottish Worthies' kind, disappear from St Andrews and its neighbourhood.

There are two of that class which we might have introduced earlier.   Two miles from St Andrews, on the Crail road, you come on Kinkell.   It has to the passer-by only the appearance of a commonplace farm.   A wall of rock, bright with flowering whins stretches down to the farm-town, and a row of ocean-blasted ash trees surround two sides of what has once formed a court. In those days of trouble a Scottish manor-house stood here, and the proprietors wore the name of the place as their patrimonial title. They attached themselves to the cause of Christ. At their own peril they harboured outed ministers, and opened their house to the preaching of the Gospel. On one occasion, Mr John Welsh, the younger, preached at Kinkell. A profligate youth being at the University of St Andrews attended sermon, and in his spite and mockery threw somewhat at the preacher, and hit him. Mr Welsh stopped, and said he did not know who had put that public affront on a servant of Christ, but be he who he would, he was persuaded there would be more present at his death, than were hearing him preach that day, and the multitude was not small. This turned out to be Philip Standfield, son to Sir James Standfield of Newmilns, by Haddington. This unhappy youth was tried, and condemned and executed for the murder of his father. Mr Standfield acknowledged this in prison after he was condemned, and that God was about to accomplish what he had been warned of. This is told by Wodrow, as we have transcribed it. On another occasion, Mr Blackadder preached at Kinkell on a Sabbath-day to a considerable congregation. The long gallery and two chambers were full, and multitudes out of doors: "Their peaceful meeting was disturbed by the arrival of the militia to disperse them, attended by a great number of the rascality, with many of the worst got scholars from the College, and some noblemen's sons." But the stout bearing of the laird, and the kindness of his lady, quelled the militia, who retired and allowed the service to go on without further molestation.

Among the list of those who were fined for having conventicles, we meet with the name of Lady Kinkell; and among fugitives for the sake of their principles whom it was illegal to reset, we find the first in the Fife lists, John Henryson, servant in Kinkell.

When in November 1688, William of Orange unfurled the flag of liberty on the headlands of England, and when the loud acclaim was heard throughout the land, it would, we fear, be but feebly returned from this city of St Andrews. What the nation hailed as a glorious Revolution, was here regarded as a civil rebellion, for the sympathies of the leading citizens were with the dethroned Stuarts. But professors and ministers contrived to get over these feelings, and to adjust themselves to the altered state of things. King William was often heard to say, "That he won-

dered what was become of the Episcopal party."
And the author of Robinson Crusoe remarks it,
as "very observable in the Revolution, that the
people of Scotland came all into the principles of
the suffering sincere party."

But the convincing logic of events very soon
demonstrated that even the material prosperity
of a place decays with its religious interests. In
1697, we find these time-serving professors
hatching "ane proposal for transporting the
University to Perth,"—a proposal which would
have deprived St Andrews at once of its importance and its principal means of support. From
the papers which relate to this projected translation, we transcribe the following, which forms
part of a letter from Mr John Craigie: "The
victuals are dearer here than anywhere else, viz.,
fleshs, drinks of all sorts. This place is ill-
provided for all commodities and trades, which
obliges ns to send to Edinburgh and provide
ourselves with shoes, clothes, hatts, &c., and what
are here are double rate. This place is ill-pro-
vided of fresh water, the most part being served
with a stripe, where the foul clothes, herring,
fish, &c., are washed, so that it is most pairt
neasty and unwholesome. This place is a most

thin and piercing air, even to an excess, seeing that nitre grows upon the walls of chambers where fires are used, if there be a light to the north. As also why infectious diseases have been observed to begin and rage most here, as in the visitation in 1640, when Dr Bruce died. This place being now only a village, where most part farmers dwell, the whole streets are filled with dunghills, which are exceedingly noisome and ready to infect the air, especially at this season, when the herring gutts are exposed in them, or rather in all corners of the town by themselves, and the season of the year apt to breed infection, which partly may be said to have been the occasion of last year's dysenterie, which from its beginning here raged through most part of the kingdom." A truely doleful picture this! It looks as if place and people had been alike covered with the hairmould of decay.

From this we turn to a very different subject of contemplation, to

" Man's highest triumph, man's profoundest fall,
    The death-bed of the just."

In September 1712, Halyburton lay on his death-bed. His weighty dying sayings are words of life to survivors. Speaking of dying, he said:

"This is a lesson of practical divinity; this is the practice of religion to make use of it when we come to the pinch." "It is good to have Him to go to when we are turning our face to the wall." This was his estimate of the ministry: " I would rather be a contemned minister of God than the greatest prince on earth. I preached the Gospel of Christ with pleasure, and I loved it, for my own soul's salvation was upon it." Thoughts of St Andrews were much on his spirit: "That which fills me with fear is a mis-improven Gospel in St Andrews." "Sirs, I shall be a witness against St Andrews." Steadily contemplating death, and all in it that is terrible to nature, the dying believer could say: "Blessed be God, I am provided; God is a good portion. I want death to complete my happiness." Meagre truly is this passing notice, but it is enough

" To express,
If not his worth, yet our respectfulness."

We shall see from the subject now to be narrated, that events, which to no inconsiderable extent affect the present ecclesiastical condition of Scotland, took their rise in very commonplace times, and with very commonplace persons. In 1720, Mr James Hadow was Principal of St

Mary's College. Previously to this he had been minister of Cupar, and Professor of Divinity. His theology seems to be of that fussy kind which is always in dread of heresy, which, like a jointed automaton, moves with a regulated precision, which wants the freedom and humanity of Scripture, and which is apt to be " too orthodox to be evangelical." Associated with him as Professor of Ecclesiastical History was Mr Archibald Campbell, formerly minister of Larbert. Mr Campbell's views took an extremely opposite direction from Principal Hadow's. In an Essay on " Enthusiasm," he laid down principles which subverted the whole scope and character of revealed religion, and which derided as extravagance the idea of an anxious inquirer "consulting the Throne of Grace, laying their matters before the Lord, and imploring his light and direction." Principal Hadow was an Ultra-Calvinist; Professor Campbell was a Rationalist.

Betwixt these widely-differing phases of sentiment there existed a class of ministers, who feeling deeply the necessities of their own hearts, and who receiving the declarations of God's Word in the simplicity of faith, maintained that God has in the Gospel offer made a deed of gift

and grant of his Son unto mankind lost, so that
each one is warranted on the ground of that
offer to take Christ as his own to rest on, and what
Christ has done as belonging particnlarly to
himself for appropriation and participation. This
class embraced snch men as Boston of Ettrick,
Hog of Carnock, Wilson of Maxton, Webster
of Edinburgh, Wilson of Perth, and the Erskines
These men felt that the free and unconditional
and sincere offer which the Gospel makes to
every one, is the only foundation of the sinner's
faith and hope.

It was around this as the fonndation-doctrine
that the controversy gathered. The higher
Calvinists, snch as Principal Hadow, brought
forward their views of election so as in reality
to impede and fetter the Gospel offer. The
misty divines perplexed and puzzled themselves
and their hearers, by throwing in faith and repentance as conditions betwixt the sinner and
the Gospel offer. The Paganised divines, such
as Professor Campbell, looking down with a self-
complacent air from their philosophic height,
professed to treat the whole subject as the rub-
bish of theological jargou—the word-war of
weak-brained and narrow-minded enthusiasts.

It was only such men as Boston and his associates who saw and estimated aright the vitally important truth imperilled.

To these times and to these persons we must look, when we search for the sources of those ecclesiastical divisions which Scotland mourns. Boston names Principal Hadow as "the spring" of the movement against the truth. He encountered with much success the Principal in the Commission, and defended the doctrine which himself and his associates maintained, viz., the absolute and unconditional freedom of access to the Saviour, which the Gospel gives to every sinner. Along with his eleven brethren, Boston bore the Commission's rebuke, protested against their deliverance, and to the day of his death bewailed it. Some years later, the remembrance of what was then done, and the growing oppression of the Church Courts, forced Erskine, Moncrieff, Wilson, and Fisher, into the first great separation from the Church of Scotland.

Late in a dusky evening in the month of August, 1773, a post-chaise rattled over the rough streets of St Andrews. The travellers it contained were Dr Samuel Johnson, and Boswell his biographer. The old city was somewhat fluttered by the arrival. Next day the sun shone cheerily, and many curious eyes watched the portly form of Johnson, arrayed in his wide broad-skirted brown coat and top-boots, and steadying his rolling gait by a large English oaken stick. He walked through the streets and wynds, marked, as himself describes it, " by the silence and solitude of inactive indigence and gloomy depopulation." He surveyed the Castle. He sauntered amid the ruins of the Cathedral, with his head uncovered, speculating in sonorous phrase regarding the scenes which the crumbling walls had witnessed.

But Johnson's sympathies were most vividly affected by social intercourse It was when he supped at the " the Mitre," or drank tea in his own rooms, in company with Goldsmith, Reynolds, and Garrick, that the powers of his mind were seen in full play. The Professors " entertained Johnson and Boswell with a very good dinner," and in the intercourse which flanked it, and in his breakfastings and tea-drinkings, would the great Cham of literature be seen to advantage. Had the entertaining of Johnson and Boswell devolved on Fergusson the poet, they would not have fared so well as they did. Fergusson's Scotch pride was stung by Johnson's prejudices against Scotland, and in a poem " to the Principal and Professors of the University of St Andrews, on their superb treat to Dr Samuel Johnson," he thus addresses them:—

> St Andrews town may look right gawsy,
> Nae grass will grow upon her causey;
> Nor wa'flower of a yellow dye
> Glour dowy o'er her ruins high;
> Sin Samy's head, weel bang'd in lear,
> Has seen the Alma Mater there.
> Regents, my winsome billy boys,
> 'Bout him you've made an unco noise.
> * * * * *
> But hear me, lads, 'gin I'd been there,
> How I wad trimm'd the bill o' fare!
> For ne'er sic surly wight as he
> Had met wi' sic respect frae me.
> Mind ye what Sam, the lying loun,
> Has in his dictionar laid down?
> That aits in England are a feast
> To cow, an' horse, and sic like beast;
> While in Scots ground this growth was common
> To feast the gab o' man and woman.
> Tak tent, ye Regents! then an' hear
> My list o' gudely hameil gear.

The poet's bill of fare consists of " A Haggis fat," " A gude sheep's head," " O gude fat brose, a dainty dose,"

And white and bloody puddin's routh,
To gar the Doctor skirl o' drouth.
Then let his wisdom girn and snarl
O'er a weel toastit girdle farl ;
An' learn, that maugre o' his wame,
Ill bairns are aye best heard at hame.

From 1780 to 1819 St Andrews was familiar
with the grave aspect of Dr George Hill, Principal of St Mary's College, and successor to Principal Robertson, in guiding the counsels of the
Church when Moderatism was in the ascendant.
His life has been written by one who was related
to him, and who succeeded him in ecclesiastical
influence—the late Dr George Cook.

The Americaus, when they speak of the liberality of their institutions, not unfrequently crown
their argument with the boast that the humblest
citizen may fire his ambition with the hope of
one day sitting in the President's chair. Britain,
in a quieter way, has also her own stories to tell
of the open door to honour, and of the advance-
ment which merit may secure to the humblest.
In 1795 there was among the theological students of St Mary's a big-boned student, who
passed among his fellows as by no means remarkable for talent or attainment, who wore his black

coat until it was rusty, and who eked out his slender income by private teaching. That obscure student sat on the Woolsack as the Right Hon. Lord Campbell, Lord Chancellor of Great Britain.

Contemporary with Lord Campbell as a student in St Andrews, was the celebrated Dr John Leyden, poet, philologist, aud " the most marvellous of Orientalists." He was prematurely cut off in 1811, by fever, in India, where he held the situation of judge.

But we hasten to close these details by a passing notice of the greatest of modern Scotchmen, as St Andrews knew him thirty years ago. That dreamy-looking man, whose shaggy hair is tinged with grey, clad in an olive-coloured great-coat, with a white neckcloth loosely twisted round his neck, walking with an absorbed air, and bearing a roll of manuscript and books huddled up to his chin, is Dr Chalmers. He is on his way to his class. Chalmer's students need no porter's bell to summon them. Already are they clustered on the outer stairs that lead to the lecture-room. The censor who calls the roll has no absentee to mark. No student here adopts the equivoque for his being away, "I was indisposed, sir," for every student is disposed to attend. And well are they rewarded for their attendance. Chalmers is no ingenious constructor of systems. He is but an interpreter of the nature and wants of man. *Philosophy discovers man's wants, Christianity supplies them.* Such the ethics Chalmers taught; himself taught by the searching experience he had passed through.

If it was said of Samuel Johnson that he *Johnsonized* the public taste by his writings, it might be said of Thomas Chalmers that he *Chalmerianized* the mind of young Scotland, betwixt the years 1823 and 1829, in the low-roofed crowded class-room which looked out with two dim windows in to the Butts Wynd. He had exalted the pulpit by the noble fervour of a restored and vindicated Evangelism. Now he is in the second stage of his great mission, and is rescuing the class-room from the old and mischievous metaphysics of false philosophy, and is making ethical science instead of the perverter the handmaid of the Gospel of Christ. A great work this, and such as only a mind great in genius and devotion could undertake and accomplish. It was part of the fulfilling of the great proposition which Chalmers' life so brilliantly establishes — VERITATEM PHILOSOPHIA QUÆRIT, THEOLOGIA INVENIT, RELIGIO POSSIDET.

No sketch of Dr Chalmers in St Andrews would be complete without an allusion to two of the most distinguished of his students. That tall figure, crossing the street and looking thoughtfully to the ground, stooped somewhat in shoulders, and his hand awkwardly grasping the lappet of his coat, is Alexander Duff, the pride of both Colleges, whose mind has received the impress of Chalmers' big thoughts, and the form of his phraseology. Under Chalmers he was the institutor of Sabbath Schools, and the originator of Students' Missionary Societies. Now he labours on the bank of the Ganges, an acknowledged chief among missionaries. The companion that attends Duff *non passibus equis*, younger and smaller, with a pale countenance, and bright eye and springy gait, is John Urquhart, whom the grave prematurely claimed.

Let us try and recall the appearance of that old College Court of St Salvator, as it looked thirty years ago. Dingy and decaying and old-world-like it seemed, but it was full of interest. On its east and south sides were the ruins of the houses in which the College bread was baked, and the

College beer brewed. Along the north side extended a range of barrack-like building, supplying in its upper stories rooms for the collegians, and from which the last occupant was driven by the nightly invasion of a ghost; and affording, under the piazzas, class-rooms for Greek and logic. The west side was occupied by the long, bare, and cold-looking common halls, where the students were wont to dine, where the laws of the College were yearly read in the presence of Principal, professors, and students, and in the corner of which, drawing the curiosity of all eyes, stood the old pulpit from which John Knox's voice had roused Scotland to the Reformation.

This area is associated with forms which the student's mind never forgets. There is the accomplished Latinist, Dr John Hunter; age has bent his venerable figure and whitened his streaming hair. That is Dr Thomas Gillespie, stout and stiff in person, his chin buried in his neckcloth, and his spectacles spread upon his breast; beloved of his students for his kindliness of heart, his fine taste, and his laughter-moving wit. There is Professor Thomas Duncan, in his unfailing drabs, his black coat rubbed with the chalk off *the board*, his hand in his pocket, his shoulder forming an obtuse angle, and his gold-linked watch chain with its complement of seals, dangling at full length; even the biggest dunce in his class respected him for his mathematical enthusiasm and learning, and the most staid student was often forced into a smile by his innocent peculiarities; he will ever be known as the life-long friend of Dr Chalmers. That is the philosophic Jackson; and this Dr George Cook; many metaphysicians have every sense except common sense—Dr Cook's strong common sense, undimmed by the mist of metaphysics, was to him *et decus et tutamen*. There is Dr James Hunter, marching to his class-room with the military air of a colonel of grenadiers; and he who walks with an elastic step through the court is Professor Alexander, who always felt an honest anxiety for the good of his students.

A whole generation of professors death has thus removed. "My last remaining tie with the College is dissolved by the death of Professor Alexander," writes one who, engaged in life's business, is yet a good way off from life's middle stage.

"Vitæ summa brevis spem nos vetat inchoare longam."

We would but deepen the pathos of this reflection, as well as widen its scope, by going to St
Mary's College and recalling other two, whom
the city but lately knew and now knows no
more. We miss the busy Principal Haldane,
who in his day occupied many situations, and
displayed a singular aptitude for each, whether
as the country minister, the professor of mathe-
mathics, the teacher of divinity, the moderator
of the General Assembly, or the city preacher.
There is also Professor Tennant, a son of mirth-
ful song, whom literature claims for herself, a
true Phil-Hebraist, with whom the love of Hebrew
was a passion before it procured for him a chair.
You hear the sharp stroke of stilts, and on looking round, you see the Professor swinging on his
crutches, for he was lame in both his feet; his
hat is tied by a ribbon under his chin, and his
happy face is rosy with buffeting against the
wind. Why is it that the public have been deprived so long of those lectures on Hebrew
literature and the Holy Land, which he so carefully elaborated in the seclusion of Devon Grove,
writing them first on a slate before he trans-
ferred them to paper, and which when delivered
electrified every one who listened to them?

On Friday evenings a feeble light uniformly glimmered from one or two of these old class-rooms. This was the product of a few thin tallow candles placed in wide wooden blocks, and intimated that this was the night for the meeting of the Debating Societies. The Literary and the Classical Societies were there in their strength. But the most celebrated, both for its age and position, is the Theological Society which meets in St Mary's. This Society can count up its two and a-half centuries, for it dates from the days of Andrew Melville, who instituted it. When the Duke of Wellington saw the Eton scholars at cricket and foot-ball, he said to the friend who attended him : " It is in places like this that Waterloo was gained." This remark may be appropriately applied to these debating societies. They exercise a fontal influence on the student, oftentimes calling forth powers of which the possessor was unconscious, and giving shape and course to his after life. Were some student to gather together the salient facts connected with these societies, and the subjects of their discussion, the work would not be without its interest and use.

Here these notices close, for they connect

themselves with the past, leaving living men and present things to fulfil their day and work.

Like the shell which lies on the shore, is this old city. Apply the shell to the ear, and you hear within its windings the sound of the sea in its varying moods. Sometimes it is the swelling surge of the great billows, lifting up their voice, and making a mighty noise; and sometimes it is the dirge-like song, the mournful monotone, when in the language of the Prophet, "There is sorrow on the sea, and it cannot be quiet." Even it is thus with St Andrews. The thoughtful mind looks on the city, and reads in it an epitome of these eventful doings, which for weal or for woe have swept over Scotland.

END OF PART IV.

CONJECTURAL DERIVATION

FROM THE

GAELIC OF SOME NAMES OF PLACES

CHIEFLY IN THE

NORTH OF FIFE.

Ayton, a manor or gentleman's seat, from *ait* a place.

Airdit, a height, from *airde,* a high place.

Auchtermuchty, from *uchdard,* the ascent of a hill, and *much* or *muchg,* a sow. The hill on the face of which Auchtermuchty stands is one of the long shapeless hills which are called " sow-back." It means the town on the face of the sow-back hill.

Ballanbreich, trout-town, *bal* town and *breac* a trout ; or deriving it from *braich* barley, it may signify barley-town.

Balmerino, the sea-town, *bal* town, and mara, gen. of *muir* the sea.

Balmullo, the town on the hill, *bal* town and *mallach,* a summit or hill.

Balmeadow, the wooded town, *bal* town and *maide* wood.

Balintagart, the priest town, *bal* town, *sagart*, pronounced *tsagart*, priest.

Balhelvie, the town of St John's work. *Bal*, town, and *ealbhuidh*, pronounced *eal-a-vhue*, St John's work. This yellow wild-flower had grown luxuriantly here.

Balgove, the town of the blacksmith. *Bal*, town, and *gobha*, a blacksmith.

Blebo, from *bleagh*, milk, and *bo*, a cow. The place may have been celebrated for its breed of milk cows, like crummie in the song,

> My crummie is a usefu' cow,
> And she is come of a good kin',

or its dairy pasture may have been of a superior quality.

Cairnie, from *carn* a heap of stones loosely thrown together. Cairnie, Murdoch-Cairnie, Myre-Cairnie, Lord's-Cairnie, Hill-Cairnie, all take their names from the conical, cairn-like hills in the neighbourhood.

Carphin, from *caer*, a fort, and *Finn*, a North-man, the fort of the Northmen, in allusion to Norman, or Northman's Law, which forms the back-ground of Carphin.

Clachart, the high rock, from *clach*, a rock, and *ard* high.

Colluthie, the back of the morass, from *cul*, the back of any thing, and *lith*, a pool or morass. Colluthie is close by Luthrie or Lithrie, the pool or morass. A few cottages in the neighbour-hood are known by the name of Myrehead, which is just the English rendering of Col-luthie.

Collairnie, the back of the field, from *cul*, the back, and *lair* a field.

Coultra, behind the sea-shore, from *cul*, the back, and *traigh*, the sea-shore.

Craigfoodie, under the hill or crag, from *cruach*, a hill, and *fodhe* under, beneath.

Craigrothie, encircled with hills, from *cruach* a hill, and *roth* a wheel.

Craigsanquhar, the old fort on the hill, from *cruach* hill, *seann* old, and *caer* fort.

Creich, hilly, from *cruach*, a hill or heap.

Cruvie, from *crubh*, *cruibh*, a horse shoe, in allusion to the curve which the hills form behind the farm-town.

Cunnoquhie, the place that was well seen, or from which a good view could be had, from *chunnaic*, pret. of the irreg. verb *faic*, to see.

Cupar, the cup-like or hollow field, from *cop* or *cup*, a bowl or cup, and *ar* a field.

Clatto, from *cleit*, pronounced *Klagt*, a rocky emiuence.

Drumnod, the bare ridge, from *druim*, a ridge, and *nochd*, naked, bare.

Dunbog, from *dun* hill, and *bog* or *buig*, a marsh or fen.

Dunmuir or *Dunmore*, the big hill, deriving its name from *Norman Law*, at the foot of which it lies.

Dura, water, from *dur* water. Hence *Aberdour*, the mouth of the water, *aber*, the mouth and *dour* or *dur* water.

Drums, from *druim*, a ridge.

Drumcarro, from *druim*, a ridge, and *caer*, a fort

—a fortified-looking hill. As seen from distant views Drumcarro has much of this appearance.

Fernie, abounding in the alder tree, from *fearn* an alder, or *fearnach* abounding in alder.

Fliskmiln, Flisk-height, from *Flisk*, and *maolan*, a height or bleak eminence.

Foodie, under, below, from *fodha*, at the foot of, showing the position of the place to the adjoining hill.

Fife, from *Fiu*, (which is the Gaelic name for Fife), worth or value. It has always been considered a valuable and desirable province, alike from situation, climate, and soil.

Flisk, from *fliche*, witness, and *uisge*, a river. Often in winter when the wetting mist gathers on the hills and descends towards the Tay, scarcely anything is seen but only the river and the dagging vapour.

Glenduckie, the glen of little hillocks, from *glean* a glen, and *duc*, *ducca*, a heap or little hillock. There is a place near still called " Sandy Knowes."

Grange, a grain farm, from *grainnee* which signifies a grain farm.

Inchrye, the island of the king, or the prominent island, *innis* an island, and *righ* king.

Kinsleith, the end of the hill, from *ceann* the end or head, and *sleabh* a hill. The old name of Kinsleith is Kinsleaves.

Kinnear, above the water, from *ceann* the head, and *near* water, stream.

Kinnaird, the top of the height, from *ceann* the head, and *naird* upwards, to the height.

Kingask, the end of the slope, from *ceann* the head, and *gaisg* a slope.

Kilmaron, the cell of St Roan, from *cill* a churchyard or chapel.

Kilmany, the chapel of the monks, from *cill* a chapel and *manach* a monk. Kilmany seems to have been a place of Ecclesiastical importance, for in a report given in to the General Assembly of 1572 by a commission appointed to consider the formation of Kilmany, it is styled " vicariae de Kilmanie" the vicarage of Kilmany.

Letham, a soft morass, from *leth* a morass and *am* soft.

Lindifferon, either the stream or the meadow of the alder trees, as you derive it from *loin* a little streamlet, or *lin, loin*, a meadow, and *fearn* an alder tree.

Lindores, the ruffled or angry lake, from *linn* a lake and *dorr* rough, angry.

Lochmalonie, the loch of the meadow, from *loch* a lake or loch, and *lon, loin* a meadow.

Lomond, bare hill, from *lom* bare and *monadh* a hill.

Lucklaw, or *Lughla* hill, from *lughla* less, and *law* a hill. Lucklaw is one of the terminating points of the Ochils to the east. In height it is less than the hills which run westward.

Lumquhat, bare residence, from *lom* bare and *cuchailte* a residence.

Luthrie or *Lithrie*, from *leth* a port or morass and probably *righ* a king, a principal or prominent morass.

Moonzie, the mount or hill, from *monadh*, a hill.

Mountquhanie, the hill of the view, from *monadh*, a hill, and *chunnaic*, pret. of the irreg. verb *faic* to see.

Naughton.—The old name of Naughton, as given in the Register of St Andrews, is *Hyhat-nachton*. This is evidently composed of *aite*, a place, which, when aspirated, would be written *Haite*, and *Nachton*, the name of a Pictish king, by whom Abernethy was restored. It means the dwelling place of Nachton, and very likely was one of his seats.

Nydie, from *neid* a battle. The hill of Kemback was anciently called Nydie hill, and the derivation of Kemback is by some supposed to be *Kemp-achar* the field of battle.

Parbroath, locally pronounced Parbrode, good grain crop, from *barr* a crop and *brod* the best of grain.

Pittachop, the hollow of the cup or bowl, from *pit* a hollow and *chop* cup or bowl. Many of the fields on this farm decline into hollows.

Pitblado, the smooth hollow, from *pit* a hollow, and *bladh* smooth.

Pitscottie, the little hollow, from *pit* a hollow, and *scot* little.

Pitlair, low ground, from *pit* a hollow, and *lar*, *lair* ground.

Pitcairlie, from *pit* a hollow, and *cairlcum* verb act. and neut. to tumble about, and describes a place where the surface is very irregular—heights and hollows all tumbled together.

Pitlethie, the low morass, from *pit* a hollow, and *leth* a morass.

Pitcullo, the back-lying hollow, from *pit* a hollow, and *cul* the back.

Pitormie, from *pit* a hollow and *or-mhadainn* the break of day—the hollow which looks to the east.

Pittulloch, from *pit*, a hollow, and *tulach*, a knoll. A place marked by a height and a hollow, or by heights and hollows.

Ramornie, the great road, from *rad, raid* a road, and *more* great.

Rathillet, many roads, from *rad* road, and *tullead* more, additional.

Scotscraig, little hill, from *scot* little, and *cruach* a hill.

Scottarvit, little Tarvit, from *scot* little.

Starr, the place of sedges, from the Scotch word *starr*, a sedge.

Struthers, from *sruth*, a stream.

Tarvit, a fertile place, from *tarbach* fruitful, and *ait* a place.

Tor, a hill, from *torr* a hill.

Wormit, from *urram* or *urramach*, revered, worshipful, and *ait* a place. Probably it was an hermitage or retreat, to which the Culdees of Kilmany may have retired for meditation.

The End.

JOHN CUNNINGHAM ORR, PRINTER, CUPAR.

LIST OF WORKS

PUBLISHED BY

OHNSTONE, HUNTER, & COMPANY.

PHŒNIX BUILDINGS, 4 MELBOURNE·PLACE,

EDINBURGH.

LIST OF WORKS

PUBLISHED BY

JOHNSTONE, HUNTER, & CO., EDINBURGH.

MAGAZINES—

    The Christian Treasury: A Family Miscellany.
    Edited by Dr Horatius Bonar. Super-royal 8vo.

        Weekly Numbers, Price One Penny.
        Monthly Parts, Price Sixpence.

    The Reformed Presbyterian Magazine.
        Published Monthly. Demy 8vo. Price Fourpence.

J. H. & CO.'S SABBATH SCHOOL TICKETS—

    Crown folio, printed in Colours.

Sheet No. 1.—THE ATTRIBUTES OF GOD. 120 Tickets. Price Twopence.
Sheet No. 2.—THE TITLES OF CHRIST. 120 Tickets. Price Twopence.
Sheet No. 3.—THE PROVERBS OF SOLOMON—No. 1. 60 Tickets. Price Twopence.
Sheet No. 4.—THE PROVERBS OF SOLOMON—No. 2. 60 Tickets. Price Twopence.

    Assorted Packets, Sixpence and One Shilling each.

J. H. & CO.'S PICTURE HYMN CARDS—

    Crown folio, printed in Colours, and Illustrated.

Sheet No. 1, containing 20 Cards, 4½ by 3. Price Twopence.
    Do. 2,   do.   do.   do.   do.
    Do. 3,   do.   do.   do.   do.
    Do. 4,   do.   do.   do.   do.
Packet No. 1, containing 50 Cards, 4½ by 3. Price Sixpence.
    Do. 2,   do.   do.   do.   do.
    Do. 3,   do.   do.   do.   do.
    Do. 4,   do.   do.   do.   do.

<table>
<tr><td>

THE FOURPENNY SERIES—
    Enamelled Wrapper.

</td><td>

THE SIXPENNY SERIES—
    Extra cloth gilt.

</td></tr>
</table>

Super-royal 32mo, Illustrated.

1. JEANIE HAY, THE CHEERFUL GIVER. And other Tales.
2. LILY RAMSAY; or, 'Handsome is who handsome does.' And other Tales.
3. ARCHIE DOUGLAS; or, 'Where there's a Will there's a Way.' And other Tales.
4. MINNIE AND LETTY. And other Tales.
5. NED FAIRLIE AND HIS RICH UNCLE. And other Tales.
6. MR GRANVILLE'S JOURNEY. And other Tales.
7. JAMIE WILSON'S ADVENTURES. And other Tales.
8. THE TWO FRIENDS. And other Tales.
9. THE TURNIP LANTERN. And other Tales.
10. JOHN BUTLER; or, The Blind Man's Dog. And other Tales.
11. CHRISTFRIED'S FIRST JOURNEY. And other Tales.
12. KATIE WATSON. And other Tales.
13. BIDDY, THE MAID OF ALL WORK.
14. MAGGIE MORRIS: A Tale of the Devonshire Moor.
15. THE SUFFERING SAVIOUR. By the late Rev. John Macdonald, Calcutta.
16. TIBBY, THE CHARWOMAN. By the Author of 'Biddy.'
17. OUR PETS.
18. THE TRUE CHRISTMAS. And other Tales.
19. THE BROKEN IMAGE. And other Tales.
20. FRED AND HIS FRIENDS.
21. THE STORY OF THE MICE; AND OF ROVER AND PUSS.
22. THE TREASURE DIGGER. From the German.
23. THE AYRSHIRE EMBROIDERER.
24. FRENCH BESSIE. By the Author of 'Biddy.'
25. THREE STRAY LEAVES.

THE DIAMOND SERIES—Price Ninepence—
    Demy 32mo, cloth extra, Illustrated.

1. THE DIAMOND: A Story Book for Girls.
2. THE PEARL: A Story Book for Girls.
3. THE RUBY: A Story Book for Boys.
4. THE EMERALD: A Story Book for Boys.

J. H. & CO.'S ONE SHILLING SERIES (Enlarged)—

Small 8vo, extra cloth gilt, Illustrated.

1. THE STORY OF A RED VELVET BIBLE. By M. H., Author of 'Labourers in the Vineyard,' etc.

2. ALICE LOWTHER; or, Grandmamma's Story about her Little Red Bible. By J. W. C.

3. NOTHING TO DO; or, The Influence of a Life. By M. H.

4. ALFRED AND THE LITTLE DOVE. By the Rev. F. A. Krummacher, D.D. And THE YOUNG SAVOYARD. By Ernest Hold.

5. MARY M'NEILL; or, The Word Remembered. A Tale of Humble Life. By J. W. C.

6. HENRY MORGAN; or, The Sower and the Seed. By M. H.

7. WITLESS WILLIE, THE IDIOT BOY. By the Author of 'Mary Matheson,' etc.

8. MARY MANSFIELD; or, No Time to be a Christian. By M. H., Author of the 'Story of a Red Velvet Bible,' etc.

9. FRANK FIELDING; or, Debts and Difficulties. A Story for Boys. By Agnes Veitch.

10. TALES FOR THE CHILDREN'S HOUR. By M. M. C.

11. THE LITTLE CAPTAIN: A Tale of the Sea. By Mrs George Cupples.

12. GOTTFRIED OF THE IRON HAND: A Tale of German Chivalry. By the Author of 'Little Harry's Troubles.'

13. ARTHUR FORTESCUE; or, The Schoolboy Hero. By Robert Hope Moncrieff, Author of 'Horace Hazelwood.'

14. THE SANGREAL; or, The Hidden Treasure. By M. H.

15. COCKERILL THE CONJURER; or, The Brave Boy of Hameln. By the Author of 'Little Harry's Troubles.'

16. JOTTINGS FROM THE DIARY OF THE SUN. By M. H.

17. DOWN AMONG THE WATER WEEDS; or, The Marvels of Pond Life. By Mrs Charles Brent.

18. THE SUNBEAM'S STORY; or, Sketches of Beetle Life. By Mrs Charles Brent.

19. RICHARD BLAKE, AND HIS LITTLE GREEN BIBLE. A Sequel to the 'Story of a Red Velvet Bible.' By M. H.

20. LITTLE MISS MATTY: A Tale of the Sea. By Mrs George Cupples.

21. BESSIE BROWN, AND HER FIRST SERVICE. By Jane M. Kippen.

22. MARY'S WORK. By Hetty Bowman.

23. GENTLEMAN JACK. And other Tales.

24. THREE LITTLE GIRLS IN RED. And other Tales.

J. H. & CO.'S REWARD BOOKS—In Shilling Packets—

Enamelled Covers, and Illustrated.

1. PLEASANT WORDS FOR LITTLE FOLK. By various Authors.
   24 Halfpenny Books. Illustrated.

2. SHORT TALES TO EXPLAIN HOMELY PROVERBS. By M. H.
   12 Penny Books. Illustrated.

3. SHORT STORIES TO EXPLAIN BIBLE TEXTS. By M. H.
   12 Penny Books. Illustrated.

4. WISE SAYINGS: And Stories to Explain Them. By M. H.
   12 Penny Books. Illustrated.

5. LITTLE TALES FOR LITTLE PEOPLE. By various Authors.
   6 Twopenny Books. Illustrated.

6. CHOICE STORIES. 4 Threepenny Books. Illustrated.

7. JEANIE HAY; LILY RAMSAY; ARCHIE DOUGLAS.
   3 Fourpenny Books. Illustrated.

8. MINNIE AND LETTY; NED FAIRLIE; MR GRANVILLE'S JOURNEY
   3 Fourpenny Books. Illustrated.

9. JAMIE WILSON; THE TWO FRIENDS; THE TURNIP LANTERN.
   3 Fourpenny Books. Illustrated.

10. JOHN BUTLER; CHRISTFRIED'S FIRST JOURNEY; KATIE WATSON.
    3 Fourpenny Books. Illustrated.

11. STORIES. By the Author of 'Biddy.'
    3 Fourpenny Books. Illustrated.

12. OUR PETS; THE TRUE CHRISTMAS; THE BROKEN IMAGE.
    3 Fourpenny Books. Illustrated.

13. AUNT LETTY'S STORIES. 3 Fourpenny Books. Illustrated.

14. STORIES OF HUMBLE LIFE. 3 Fourpenny Books. Illustrated.

15. HAPPY STORIES FOR BOYS. 24 Halfpenny Books.

16. HAPPY STORIES FOR GIRLS. 24 Halfpenny Books.

17. GEMS. 48 Farthing Books.

18. JEWELS. 48 Farthing Books.

J. H. & CO.'S 'CHRISTIAN CLASSICS:'—

Super-royal 32mo, cloth boards, - Per Vol., One Shilling.
  Do.   do.   gilt edges,   -   „   Eighteenpence.

1. THE PILGRIM'S PROGRESS. By John Bunyan. Complete, with 8 Illustrations.
2. COME AND WELCOME TO JESUS CHRIST. By John Bunyan.
3. THE ALMOST CHRISTIAN DISCOVERED. By Matthew Mead.

J. H. & CO.'S EIGHTEENPENCE SERIES—
Super-royal 32mo, cloth extra, gilt edges, Illustrated.

1. SHORT TALES TO EXPLAIN HOMELY PROVERBS.   By M. H.
2. SHORT STORIES TO EXPLAIN BIBLE TEXTS.   By M. H.
3. THE STORY OF THE KIRK: A Sketch of Scottish Church History.   By Robert Naismith.
4. LITTLE TALES FOR LITTLE PEOPLE.
5. WISE SAYINGS: And Stories to Explain Them.   By M. H.
6. STORIES OF HUMBLE LIFE.
7. PLEASANT WORDS FOR LITTLE FOLK.
8. AUNT LETTY'S STORIES.
9. CHOICE STORIES FOR YOUNG READERS.
10. STORIES.   By the Author of 'Biddy.'

J. H. & CO.'S TWO SHILLINGS SERIES—
Small 8vo, cloth extra, gilt edges, Illustrated.

1. ALFRED AND THE LITTLE DOVE.   By the Rev. F. A. Krummacher, D.D.   And WITLESS WILLIE, THE IDIOT BOY.   By the Author of 'Mary Matheson,' etc.
2. THE STORY OF THE BIBLES.   By M. H.
3. ARTHUR FORTESCUE; or, The Schoolboy Hero.   By Robert Hope Moncrieff. And FRANK FIELDING; or, Debts and Difficulties.   By Agnes Veitch.
4. MARY M'NEILL; or, The Word Remembered.   By J. W. C.   And other Tales.
5. ALICE LOWTHER; or, Grandmamma's Story about her Little Red Bible.   By J. W. C.   And other Tales.
6. NOTHING TO DO; or, The Influence of a Life.   And MARY MANSFIELD; or, No Time to be a Christian.   By M. H.
7. BILL MARLIN'S TALES OF THE SEA.   By Mrs George Cupples.
8. GOTTFRIED OF THE IRON HAND.   And other Tales.   By the Author of 'Little Harry's Troubles.'
9. THE HIDDEN TREASURE.   And other Tales.   By M. H.
10. WATER WEEDS AND SUNBEAMS.   By Mrs Charles Brent.
11. MARY'S WORK.   By Hetty Bowman.   And other Tales.

THE MELBOURNE SERIES—
Extra foolscap 8vo, printed on toned paper, Illustrated.

Cloth extra,   -   -   Per Vol., Eighteenpence.
Do. gilt edges,   -   Do.   Two Shillings.

1. THE COTTAGERS OF GLENCARRAN.   By Letitia M'Clintock.
2. THE ROYAL CAPTIVE; or, The Youth of Daniel.   From the French of the late Professor Gaussen.
3. THE KING'S DREAM; or, Daniel the Interpreter.   From the French of Professor Gaussen.

THE MELBOURNE SERIES—*Continued.*

4. THE IRON KINGDOM; or, The Roman Empire. From the French of Professor Gaussen.
5. THE KINGDOM OF IRON AND CLAY. From the French of Professor Gaussen.
6. AUNT MARGERY'S MAXIMS: Work, Watch, Wait. By Sophia Tandy.
7. MARY BRUNTON AND HER ONE TALENT. By E. A. D. R.
8. LINDSAY LEE, AND HIS FRIENDS. By P. E. S., Author of 'Biddy,' etc.
9. QUIET TALKS WITH MY YOUNG FRIENDS. By M. H.
10. TALES FROM THE HOLLY TREE FARM. By Mrs Charles Brent.
11. TO ROSLIN: FROM THE FAR WEST. With Local Descriptions.

THE HALF-CROWN SERIES— | THE THREE SHILLINGS SERIES—
Cloth, plain edges. | Cloth, gilt edges.

Extra foolscap 8vo, with Illustrations.

1. ROSA LINDESAY, THE LIGHT OF KILMAIN. By M. H.
2. NEWLYN HOUSE, THE HOME OF THE DAVENPORTS. By A. E. W.
3. ALICE THORNE; or, A Sister's Work.
4. LABOURERS IN THE VINEYARD. By M. H.
5. THE CHILDREN OF THE GREAT KING. By M. H.
6. LITTLE HARRY'S TROUBLES. By the Author of 'Gottfried.'
7. SUNDAY SCHOOL PHOTOGRAPHS. By Rev. Alfred Taylor, Bristol, Pennsylvania.
8. WAYMARKS FOR THE GUIDING OF LITTLE FEET. By the Rev. J. A. Wallace.
9. THE DOMESTIC CIRCLE. By the Rev. John Thomson.
10. SELECT CHRISTIAN BIOGRAPHIES. By the Rev. James Gardner, A.M., M.D.
11. JAMES NISBET: A Study for Young Men. By the Rev. J. A. Wallace.
12. NOBLE RIVERS, AND STORIES CONCERNING THEM. By Anna J. Buckland.
13. THE HARLEYS OF CHELSEA PLACE. By Sophia Tandy.
14. VIOLET AND DAISY; or, The Picture with Two Sides. By M. H.
15. THE MELVILL FAMILY, AND THEIR BIBLE READINGS. By Mrs Ellis.
16. THE COTTAGERS OF GLENBURNIE. By Elizabeth Hamilton.

THE 'CHILDREN'S HOUR' SERIES—
Cloth Elegant, cut edges,   -   Per Vol., Half-a-Crown.
Do.   gilt side and edges,   „   Three Shillings.

Complete in Twelve Volumes.

An admirable Series for the Family or for School Libraries.

1. MISS MATTY; or, Our Youngest Passenger. By Mrs George Cupples. And other Tales. Illustrated.
2. HORACE HAZELWOOD; or, Little Things. By Robert Hope Moncrieff. And other Tales. Illustrated.

THE CHILDREN'S HOUR SERIES—*Continued*.

3. FOUND AFLOAT. By Mrs George Cupples. And other Tales. Illustrated.

4. THE WHITE ROE OF GLENMERE. By Mrs Bickerstaffe. And other Tales. Illustrated.

5. JESSIE OGLETHORPE: The Story of a Daughter's Devotion. By W. H. Davenport Adams. And other Tales. Illustrated.

6. PAUL AND MARIE, THE ORPHANS OF AUVERGNE. And other Tales. Illustrated.

7. ARCHIE MASON: An Irish Story. By Letitia M'Clintock. And other Tales. Illustrated.

8. THE WOODFORDS: An Emigrant Story. By Mrs George Cupples. And other Tales. Illustrated.

9. OLD ANDY'S MONEY: An Irish Story. By Letitia M'Clintock. And other Tales. Illustrated.

10. MARIUS FLAMINIUS: A Story of the Days of Hadrian. By Anna J. Buckland. And other Tales. Illustrated.

11. THE INUNDATION OF THE RHINE. From the German. And other Tales. Illustrated.

12. THE LITTLE ORPHANS. From the German. And other Tales. Illustrated.

<table>
<tr><td>

THE THREE SHILLINGS AND SIXPENCE SERIES—

Cloth, plain edges.
</td><td>

THE FOUR SHILLINGS AND SIXPENCE SERIES.

Cloth, gilt edges.
</td></tr>
</table>

Crown 8vo, cloth, with Illustrations.

1. SKETCHES OF SCRIPTURE CHARACTERS. By the Rev. Andrew Thomson, D.D.

2. STARS OF EARTH; or, Wild Flowers of the Months. By Leigh Page.

3. ELIJAH, THE DESERT PROPHET. By the Rev. H. T. Howat.

4. CHAPTERS IN THE LIFE OF ELSIE ELLIS. By Hetty Bowman.

5. NANNETTE'S DIARY: A Story of Puritan Times. By Anna J. Buckland.

6. ETHEL LINTON; or, The Feversham Temper. By A. E. W.

7. SUZANNE DE L'ORME: A Tale of France in Huguenot Times. By H. G.

8. LILY HOPE AND HER FRIENDS. By Hetty Bowman.

J. H. & CO.'S FIVE SHILLINGS SERIES—

Extra foolscap 8vo, cloth, gilt side and edges.

1.	THE CHILDREN'S HOUR ANNUAL.	First Series.	656 pp.	60 Illustrations.	
2.	Do.	Do.	Second Series.	640 pp.	70 Illustrations.
3.	Do.	Do.	Third Series.	640 pp.	70 Illustrations.
4.	Do.	Do.	Fourth Series.	640 pp.	60 Illustrations.
5.	Do.	Do.	Fifth Series.	640 pp.	60 Illustrations.
6.	Do.	Do.	Sixth Series.	640 pp.	60 Illustrations.

7. THE STORY OF DANIEL. From the French of Professor Gaussen. By Mr and Mrs Campbell Overend. Toned paper, 450 pp. 5 Illustrations.

MISCELLANEOUS WORKS.

Authorised Standards of Free Church of Scotland: Being the Westminster Confession of Faith, and other Documents. *Published by authority of the General Assembly.* Demy 12mo, cloth limp, - £0 1 6

———————— Cloth boards, - - - - - 0 1 8

————— Superior Edition, printed on superfine paper, extra cloth, bevelled boards, antique, - - - - - - 0 3 6

———————— Full calf, lettered, antique, - - - - 0 5 0

Brodie (Rev. James, A.M.) The Antiquity and Nature of Man: A Reply to Sir Charles Lyell's Recent Work. Extra foolscap 8vo, cloth, - - - - - - - - 0 2 6

————— **The Rational Creation: An Inquiry into the Nature and** Classification of Rational Creatures, and the Government which God exercises over them. Crown 8vo, cloth, - - - - 0 5 0

————— **Our Present Position on the Chart of Time, as Revealed in** the Word of God. Enlarged Edition. Extra foolscap 8vo, - - 0 1 0

———————— Cloth, - - - - - - 0 1 6

————— **The True Text of the Old Testament, with some Remarks** on the Language of the Jews. Crown 8vo, cloth, - - - 0 3 0

Burns (Rev. Geo., D.D.) Prayers for the use of Sabbath Schools. 18mo, sewed, - - - - - - - 0 0 4

Calvin's Treatise on Relics. With an Introductory Dissertation on Image Worship and other Superstitions in the Roman Catholic and Russo-Greek Churches. By the late Count Valerian Krasinski. Extra foolscap 8vo, cloth, - - - - - 0 2 6

Catechisms—

 Catechism of the Evidences of Revealed Religion, with a few Preliminary Questions on Natural Religion. By William Ferrie, D.D., Kilconquhar. 18mo, stitched, - - - 0 0 4

 Catechism on Baptism: in which are considered its Nature, its Subjects, and the Obligations resulting from it. By the late Henry Grey, D.D., Edinburgh. 18mo, stitched, - - - 0 0 6

 The Assembly's Larger Catechism; with (*Italicised*) Proofs from Scripture at full length. Demy 12mo, sewed, - - - 0 0 6

Catechisms—*Continued.*

THE ASSEMBLY'S SHORTER CATECHISM; with (*Italicised*) Proofs from Scripture at full length; also with Additional Scripture References, selected from Boston, Fisher, M. Henry, Paterson, Vincent, and others. Demy 18mo, stitched, - - - - £0 0 1

THE ASSEMBLY'S SHORTER CATECHISM; with References to the Scripture Proofs. Demy 18mo, stitched, - - - - 0 0 0½

THE CHILD'S FIRST CATECHISM. 48mo, stitched, - - - 0 0 0½

SHORT CATECHISM FOR YOUNG CHILDREN. By the Rev. John Brown, Haddington. 32mo, stitched, - - - - 0 0 0½

PLAIN CATECHISM FOR CHILDREN. By the Rev. Matthew Henry. 18mo, stitched, - - - - - - 0 0 1

FIFTY QUESTIONS CONCERNING THE LEADING DOCTRINES AND DUTIES OF THE GOSPEL; with Scripture Answers and Parallel Texts. For the use of Sabbath Schools. 18mo, stitched, - - - 0 0 1

FORM OF EXAMINATION BEFORE THE COMMUNION. Approved by the General Assembly of the Kirk of Scotland (1592), and appointed to be read in Families and Schools; with Proofs from Scripture (commonly known as 'Craig's Catechism'). With a Recommendatory Note by the Rev. Dr Candlish, Rev. Alex. Moody Stuart, and Rev. Dr Horatius Bonar. 18mo, stitched, - - 0 0 1

THE MOTHER'S CATECHISM; being a Preparatory Help for the Young and Ignorant, to their easier understanding The Assembly's Shorter Catechism. By the Rev. John Willison, Dundee. 32mo, stitched, - - - - - - 0 0 0½

WATTS' (DR ISAAC) JUVENILE HISTORICAL CATECHISMS OF THE OLD AND NEW TESTAMENTS; with Numerous Scripture References, and a Selection of Hymns. Demy 18mo, stitched, - - - 0 0 1

A SCRIPTURE CATECHISM, Historical and Doctrinal, for the use of Schools and Families. By John Whitecross, Author of 'Anecdotes on the Shorter Catechism,' etc. 18mo, stitched, - - 0 0 1

A SUMMARY OF CHRISTIAN DOCTRINES AND DUTIES; being the Westminster Assembly's Shorter Catechism, without the Questions, with Marginal References. Foolscap 8vo, stitched, - - 0 0 1

Christian Treasury (The) Volumes 1845 to 1860.

16 Volumes. Royal 8vo. A complete Set will be forwarded to any part of the country, carriage paid, on receipt of - - - 2 2 0

—— Volumes 1861 to 1873.

Super-royal, cloth, green and gold—each - - - 0 6 6

Cloud of Witnesses (A) for the Royal Prerogatives of Jesus Christ:

Being the Last Speeches and Testimonies of those who have Suffered for the Truth in Scotland since the year 1680. A New Edition, with Explanatory and Historical Notes, by the Rev. J. H. Thomson. Printed on Toned Paper, with Full-Page Illustrations. Demy 8vo, cloth extra, - - - - - - 0 7 6

—————— Calf, antique, red edges, - - - 0 15 0

Cochrane (Rev. Thomas). Home Mission Work: Its Duties, Difficulties, and Encouragements. Super-royal 32mo, -   - £0 1 0

Confession of Faith (The), agreed upon at the Assembly of Divines at Westminster. Complete Edition, with the *Italics* of the Elegant Quarto Edition of 1658 restored. (Authorised Edition.) Demy 12mo, cloth limp, -   -   -   -   - 0 1 4

——— Cloth boards, -   -   -   -   - 0 1 6

——— Roan, sprinkled edges, -   -   -   - 0 1 9

——— Roan, gilt edges, -   -   -   -   - 0 2 0

——— Superior Edition, printed on superfine paper, extra cloth, bevelled boards, antique, -   -   -   -   - 0 3 6

——— Full calf, lettered, antique, -   -   -   - 0 5 0

——— Without the other Documents. Demy 12mo, stitched, -   - 0 0 6

Dill (Edward Marcus, A.M., M.D.) The Mystery Solved; or, Ireland's Miseries; Their Grand Cause and Cure. Foolscap 8vo, cloth, -   -   -   -   -   -   - 0 2 6

——— The Gathering Storm; or, Britain's Romeward Career: A Warning and Appeal to British Protestants. Foolscap 8vo, cloth, - 0 1 0

Family Prayers for Four Weeks. Edited by the Rev. John Hall, D.D., New York. Extra foolscap 8vo, cloth, -   -   - 0 2 0

Family Prayers for Working Men (for Two Weeks). By Ministers of various Evangelical Denominations. Edited, with a Preface, by the Rev. John Hall, D.D., New York. Extra foolscap 8vo, stiffened boards, -   -   -   -   -   - 0 0 6

——— Limp cloth, -   -   -   -   -   - 0 0 6

'Fifty-One Hour' Wages Reckoner, The: Consisting of Compu- tations per Week, and Computations per Hour, for a Working Month. With Supplementary Comparative Table, applicable to Weeks of 48, 54, 57, and 60 Hours respectively. By a Retired Banker. 256 pp., extra foolscap 8vo, cloth, -   -   -   -   - 0 2 6

Fleming (Rev. Robert). The Rise and Fall of Papacy. Reprinted from the Edition of 1701, with a Preface by the late Rev. Thomas Thomson. Extra foolscap 8vo, sewed, -   -   -   - 0 1 0

——— Cloth, -   -   -   -   -   - 0 1 6

Forbes (Rev. Robert, A.M.) Digest of Rules and Procedure in the Inferior Courts of the Free Church of Scotland. With Appendix, embracing a Ministerial Manual, and also containing Forms and Documents. Third Edition, Revised. Extra foolscap 8vo, cloth, - 0 3 6

Habit; with Special Reference to the Formation of a Virtuous
Character. An Address to Students. By Burns Thomson. With a
Recommendatory Note by the late Professor Miller. Second Edition,
Revised. 18mo, - - - - - - £0 0 2

Handbook and Index to the Principal Acts of Assembly of the
Free Church of Scotland—1843–1868. By a Minister of the Free Church
of Scotland. Extra foolscap 8vo, cloth, - - - 0 2 6

Helps at the Mercy-Seat. Selected from the Scriptures, the Old
Divines, and the Poets. By the Rev. John M. Putnam. Extra fools-
cap 8vo, cloth, - - - - - - 0 2 6
———————— Gilt edges, - - - - - - 0 3 0

Howat (Rev. H. T.) Sabbath Hours: A Series of Meditations on
Gospel Themes. Extra foolscap 8vo, cloth, - - - 0 3 6

Hunter (James J.) Historical Notices of Lady Yester's Church
and Parish, Edinburgh. Compiled from Authentic Sources. Extra
foolscap 8vo, cloth. Printed on Toned Paper, - - - 0 2 6

Hymns for the Use of Sabbath Schools and Bible Classes.
Selected by a Committee of Clergymen. Royal 32mo, sewed, - 0 0 3

Knitting Book of Counterpanes (A). With Diagrams and Direc-
tions. By Mrs George Cupples, Author of 'The Stocking-Knitter's
Manual.' Printed on Toned Paper, with Illuminated Cover. Extra
foolscap 8vo, - - - - - - 0 0 6

Meikle (Rev. Jas., D.D.) Coming Events. An Inquiry regarding
the Three Prophetical Numbers of the last Chapter of Daniel. Extra
foolscap 8vo, cloth, - - - - - - 0 2 6

Miller (Rev. James N.) Prelacy Tried by the Word of God.
With an Appendix on the Prelatic Argument from Church History.
Foolscap 8vo, limp cloth, - - - - - 0 1 0

Miller (Professor Jas.) Physiology in Harmony with the Bible,
respecting the Value and Right Observance of the Sabbath. Royal
32mo, limp cloth, - - - - - - 0 0 6

Newton (John). Cardiphonia; or, The Utterance of the Heart.
Extra foolscap 8vo, cloth, - - - - 0 3 0

Ocean Lays. Selected by the Rev. J. Longmuir, LL.D. Illustrated.
Square 16mo, cloth, - - - - - - 0 2 6

Patterson (Alex. S., D.D.) The Redeemer and the Redemption.
Extra foolscap 8vo, cloth, - - - - - 0 2 6

Philip (Rev. John, M.A.) Rays of Light: or, Church-Themes and
Life-Problems. Extra foolscap 8vo, cloth, - - - 0 3 6

Pond (Professor Enoch, D.D.) The Seals Opened; or, The Apocalypse Explained for Bible Students. Crown 8vo, cloth, - £0 3 6

Rochdale Discourses. By Clergymen connected with the Synod of the United Presbyterian Church in England. With a Preface by Professor John Cairns, D.D. Crown 8vo, cloth, - - - 0 5 0

Scots Worthies, The. By John Howie of Lochgoin. A New Edition. Edited by the Rev. W. H. Carslaw, M.A. Printed on Toned Paper, with 150 Illustrations on Wood. Demy 8vo, cloth extra, - 0 7 6
———— Calf, antique, red edges, - - - - 0 15 0

Steele (James). A Manual of the Evidences of Christianity. Chiefly intended for Young Persons. 18mo, cloth, - - 0 1 0

Stocking-Knitter's Manual (The): A Companion for the Work-Table. By Mrs George Cupples, Author of the 'Knitting Book of Counterpanes.' Extra foolscap 8vo, Illuminated cover, - - 0 0 6

Sum of Saving Knowledge, The. Extracted from the Westminster Confession of Faith. For the use of Bible Classes. Super-royal 32mo, stiffened boards, - - - - - - 0 0 4
———— Cloth limp, - - - - - - 0 0 6

Tasker (Rev. William). The Territorial Visitor's Manual: A Handbook of Home Mission Work. Small 8vo, cloth, - - 0 2 0

Thompson (Rev. John, A.M.) Life Work of Peter the Apostle. Extra foolscap 8vo, cloth, - - - - - 0 3 6

Thoughts on Intercessory Prayer. By a Lady. Royal 32mo, limp cloth, - - - - - 0 0 6

Wallace (Rev. J. A.) Communion Services, according to the Presbyterian Form. Extra foolscap 8vo, cloth, - - - 0 2 6

———— A Pastor's Legacy. Extra foolscap 8vo, cloth, - - - - - 0 2 6

Watts' (Isaac, D.D.) Divine Songs for Children; with Scripture Proofs. For the use of Families and Schools. Square 32mo, sewed, - 0 0 2

Wilberforce's Practical View of Christianity. Complete Edition. Extra foolscap 8vo, cloth, - - - - - 0 2 0

Willison (Rev. John). Sacramental Meditations and Advices for the use of Communicants. Crown 8vo, cloth, - - - 0 2 6

———— The Afflicted Man's Companion. A New Edition. Demy 18mo, - - - - - - 0 1

MUSIC.

The Treasury Hymnal. A Selection of Part Music, in the Ordinary Notation, with Instrumental Accompaniment: the Hymns selected from Dr Bonar's 'Hymns of Faith and Hope.' The Letter-Note Method of Musical Notation is added as a help to young singers. Twenty-four Numbers. (For Contents, see next page.) Super-royal 8vo—each · · · · · · · £0 0 1
——— Part I., Nos. 1 to 12, in Printed Wrapper, · · · 0 1 0
——— Part II., Nos. 13 to 24, in Printed Wrapper, · · · 0 1 0
——— The Whole Work complete. Cloth extra, gilt edges, · · 0 3 6

The Children's Harmonist. A Series of Part Songs for the Family and the School-room. Harmonised, on the Letter-Note Method, for Two Voices, with a Bass Accompaniment. By David Colville, Author of 'The Letter-Note Singing Method,' etc. Twelve Numbers. (For Contents, see J. H. & Co.'s separate 'List of Musical Publications.') Super-royal 16mo—each · · · · · 0 0 1
——— The Whole Work complete. Cloth, lettered, · · · 0 1 6

Choral Harmony. Edited by David Colville. A Selection of Music, chiefly of an easy character, in Vocal Score, for the use of Choral Societies, Classes, Schools, etc. Upwards of 130 Numbers published. (For Contents, see J. H. & Co.'s separate 'List of Musical Publications.') Royal 8vo—each · · · · · 0 0 1
——— Vol. I. (50 Numbers), cloth boards, · · · · 0 4 0
——— Vol. II. (50 Numbers), cloth boards, · · · · 0 4 0
——— Vols. III. and IV.—*In progress.*

The Letter-Note Singing Method: Elementary Division, in Twenty-three Lessons. By David Colville. Royal 8vo, sewed, · · 0 1 0
——— Cloth, · · · · · · · · 0 1 6

The Choral Guide: Being the Exercises contained in the foregoing Work. Two Parts, sold separately—each · · · 0 0 3

A Course of Elementary Practice in Vocal Music. For use in connection with any Method of Solmization. Composed and Arranged by David Colville. Two Parts—each · · · · 0 0 4

A Graduated Course of Elementary Instruction in Singing on the Letter-Note Method (*by means of which any difficulty of learning to Sing from the common Notation can be easily overcome*), in Twenty-six Lessons. By David Colville and George Bentley. Royal 8vo, in Wrapper, · · · · · · 0 1 0
——— Cloth, · · · · · · · 0 1 6

The Pupil's Handbook: Being the Exercises contained in the foregoing Work. For the use of Classes and Schools. Two Parts, sold separately—each · · · · 0 0 3

An Elementary Course of Practice in Vocal Music, with numerous Tables, Diagrams, etc., and copious Examples of all the usual Times, Keys, and Changes of Keys. For use in connection with any Method of Solmization. By David Colville. Complete in Two Parts—each · 0 0 4

Colville's Choral School: A Collection of Easy Part Songs, Anthems, etc., in Vocal Score, for the use of Schools and Singing Classes. Arranged progressively, and forming a complete Course of Practice in Vocal Music. In Twenty Parts—each · · · 0 0 4

THE TREASURY HYMNAL:

A Selection of Part Music, in the Ordinary Notation, with Instrumental Accompaniment: the Hymns selected from Dr Bonar's "Hymns of Faith and Hope." The Letter-Note Method of Musical Notation is added as a help to young singers. Twenty-four Numbers. Super-royal 8vo. One Penny each.

1. FORWARD, - - - - - - *Old Melody.*
   A BETHLEHEM HYMN, - - - - *Arranged from Mozart.*
2. THE FRIEND, - - - - - *Haydn.*
   LOST BUT FOUND, - - - - *Pleyel.*
3. A LITTLE WHILE, - - - *Adapted from Mendelssohn.*
   A STRANGER HERE, - - - *Pleyel.*
4. THE BLANK, - - - - - - *Do.*
   THE NIGHT AND THE MORNING, - - *Adapted from Rode.*
5. THE CLOUDLESS, - - - - *Haydn.*
   THE SUBSTITUTE, - - - - *Do.*
6. THY WAY, NOT MINE, - - - *Altered from Pleyel.*
   REST YONDER, - - - - *Steibelt.*
7. EVER NEAR, - - - - - *German Melody.*
   QUIS SEPARABIT, - - - - *Beethoven.*
8. ALL WELL, - - - - - *Haydn.*
   DISAPPOINTMENT, - - - - *Do.*
   CHILD'S PRAYER, - - - - *Weber.*
9. GOD'S ISRAEL, - - - - *Atterbury.*
   THE ELDER BROTHER, - - - *Beethoven.*
   DAY SPRING, - - - - - *German Melody.*
10. THE NIGHT COMETH, - - - *Venetian Melody.*
    HOW LONG, - - - - - *Mendelssohn.*
11. THE TWO ERAS, - - - - *Spohr.*
    THE SHEPHERD'S PLAIN, - - *Whitaker.*
12. BRIGHT FEET OF MAY, - - - *Do.*
    HEAVEN AT LAST, - - - - *Clementi.*
13. NO NIGHT DESCEND ON THEE, - - *Graun.*
    THE VOICE FROM GALILEE, - - *Kirmair.*
14. THE FIRST AND THE LAST, - - *Schubert.*
    ECCE HOMO, - - - - - *Mozart.*
15. A CHILD OF DAY, - - - - *Spohr.*
    THE SHADOW OF THE CROSS, - - *Haydn.*
16. THE SLEEP OF THE BELOVED, - - *Polish Melody.*
    STRENGTH BY THE WAY, - - - *Weber.*
17. THE BATTLE SONG OF THE CHURCH, - *Colville.*
    THE DAY AFTER ARMAGEDDON, - - *Hummel.*
18. SABBATH HYMN, - - - - *Dr Miller.*
    MARTYR'S HYMN, - - - - *Hindostanee Melody.*
19. HE IS COMING, - - - - *Himmel.*
    LIVE, - - - - - - *Handel.*
20. SUMMER GLADNESS, - - - *German Melody.*
    LINKS, - - - - - - *Spohr.*
21. USE ME, - - - - - *Anonymous.*
    SMOOTH EVERY WAVE, - - - *Hering.*
22. BEGIN WITH GOD, - - - *Anonymous.*
    HOMEWARDS, - - - - - *Mozart.*
23. THE DESERT JOURNEY, - - - *Hastings.*
    LAUS DEO, - - - - - *Bost.*
24. THINGS HOPED FOR, - - - - *Pleyel.*
    HE LIVETH LONG WHO LIVETH WELL, *Beethoven.*